Praise for *Em's Awful Good Fortune*

"*Em's Awful Good Fortune* takes its reader across the world and deep into the heart of its trapped, privileged, suffering, and, ultimately, invincible narrator. Equally funny and brutal, this novel breathes vivid life into a much maligned and little understood "type"—the expat wife. Maxfield poured her heart into the writing, and it shows: the pages crackle."

—Junot Diaz, Pulitzer Prize-winning author of
The Brief and Wondrous Life of Oscar Wao,
Drown and *This Is How You Lose Her*

"A fast-paced, blink-and-you'll-miss-it whirlwind of a book capturing the good, the bad, and the ugly of being a 'tagalong' expat wife. Marcie Maxfield will take you on a global ride—and personal journey—in this funny, poignant novel."

—Stephanie Suga Chen, author of The Straits Times bestseller
Travails of a Trailing Spouse and *Disunited Nations:
International School Mums at War*

"*Em's Awful Good Fortune* is ferocious and hilarious, with a writing voice so unique it will knock your socks off. This breathless story of a woman's attempt at balancing love with self-love as she navigates the few joys and many pitfalls of the tagalong life will keep you reading until the wee hours, and might even change the way you view marriage, travel, and feminism."

—Corine Gantz, author of *Hidden in Paris* and
the tril⸺ ⸺ *f Broken Things*.

"Maxfield calls Em⸺ ⸺ privilege,' but the novel isn't just ⸺ re that's more universal, which wo⸺ ⸺ are sure to find familiar: the notion ⸺ ⸺ing the care of one's own health and happiness in the name of love of family and marriage."

—*Kirkus Reviews*

EM'S AWFUL GOOD FORTUNE

A NOVEL

MARCIE MAXFIELD

SHE WRITES PRESS

Published 2021
Printed in the United States of America
Print ISBN: 978-1-64742-142-7
E-ISBN: 978-1-64742-143-4
Library of Congress Control Number: 2021902924

For information, address:
She Writes Press
1569 Solano Ave #546
Berkeley, CA 94707

She Writes Press is a division of SparkPoint Studio, LLC.

For Richard, Jade, and Jordan

MAAAYYYBEEE

Sometimes I wish he would hit me. Not that I would ever let anyone hit me upside the head. I'm just saying—it would be easier to make a decision if he were an abusive husband, clear-cut. My girlfriends would say, "That guy is no good; you're better off without him." But my girls are all drooling over Gee, and not just because his pretty-boy baby face is becoming mannishly handsome. No, they're solidly in Camp Gee because he delivers the fantasy. "Em," they say, "you get to quit your job and live a jet-set lifestyle."

What's the problem? They wanna know.

It's just that it wasn't my dream, that's all. I had a different fantasy: best friends, equal partners. You cook; I do the dishes. Then we curl up on the couch with our books (mine new, his noir), both of us exhausted from work. Maybe I get a foot rub. That's why lately I've been thinking it would be a whole lot easier if he just hit me, instead of stomping on my dreams. Okay, maybe "stomping" is too violent a word. He doesn't stomp; he steps over my life in the pursuit of his career.

We're on a look-see for an expat assignment in China. Mind you, Gee already accepted the post. This trip is all about me. The only question on the table is, will my husband move to Shanghai alone, or will I tag along? Hence the term "tagalong wife," also known as "trailing spouse," which always makes me think of a snail carrying its home on its back. Not literally, not lugging around pots and pans—more

1

like the sense of home. Because that's my tagalong job: to provide a sense memory of home. Gee insists that I can say no. That I can stay in Los Angeles. Although that doesn't feel like an option. It feels like the plane has taken off and there's no turning back.

We clink champagne flutes in business class, and Gee toasts to another adventure. Then he puts on noise-canceling headphones, leaving me to peruse the menu, inspect my goody bag, and pick out a movie. I can't help but wonder if this will be a metaphor for the next three years of our lives. Once again, I'm weighing the pros and cons: no interest in moving to China versus not wanting to lose my husband.

My husband. As if I own him, which couldn't be further from the truth. The company owns him. France. Japan. Korea. It's hard to keep our story straight. Here's a cheat sheet: If it's Daejeon, Ruby and Rio were toddlers. If it's Tokyo, the kids were teens. If it's Paris, me and Gee were fighting. In between posts, I live with the kids in Los Angeles. With or without him. If it's without him, odds are we're still fighting.

"Em," he always promises, "it'll be an adventure."

But this—this is China, and it's three years, and even Gee's employer knows it isn't an adventure; it's a hardship post. That's why they're bankrolling this jam-packed look-see weekend in Shanghai. They want to make sure I can wrap my head around living there.

The flight attendant hands me a wet washcloth to clean my hands before meal service. It's warm too. My cuticles are ragged from where I've been picking at them. Gee's been talking about moving to China for months, and I've been tuning it out, picking my cuticles until they bleed. But business class on the company dime, that's something you don't want to tune out. That's how Gee's company reels you in— with cloth place mats and real silverware. The sleeper pod is like a flying cocoon, mad comfy. You get good swag on international flights, not just throwaway socks and eye masks. They give you samples of

Philosophy's Hope in a Jar skin cream and Hope in a Stick lip moisturizer. I smear some hope on my mouth and try to engage Gee in conversation, but he's deep in his own private pod. Gee has this travel thing down to a science: what to pack in his carry-on, when to sleep, how to shut out noise and avoid jet lag.

Me, I drink too much wine and not enough water. I stay up the whole time watching movies—and ruminating. Worrying about how this is all gonna play out. What am I going to do all day? Three years is a long time to kill. Maybe I should become a yoga teacher. You can teach yoga anywhere. Even in China. Mina says Beijing has the bad air and Shanghai has the culture, and she's head of Global Mobility for Gee's company. So she should know. Will the kids be okay without us? Gee says they'll be fine; technically they're adults. That's Gee—he thinks everything is always going to turn out better than you can possibly imagine. It never does. Not really. But by the time we figure out what went wrong, it's too late. Done. Spilled that milk.

On a good day, I know Gee is doing his best to support our family and he's my life partner; you don't get more than one of those. There are lots of guys out there, but there's only one father to my kids. Even though sometimes, like *right now*, him shutting me out with noise-canceling headphones, I worry there isn't enough love between us to make this work.

Stop! Push that thought out of your head, Em.

I remind myself that "embrace change" is my new mantra; it came to me in yoga class, washed over me like a tsunami when I was in child's pose, forehead to the mat.

Gee emerges from his pod, hair all Flock of Seagulls, and I catch a glimpse of the guy I married. It makes me smile. I pop a breath mint and try to make myself presentable. They say expat assignments are more successful when the family stays together. No early departures, no breakups or burnouts. No screwing around. Absolutely no KTV girls! My role is to be the grounding force; the person my husband comes home to at the end of a long fucking day in a foreign country. And it helps if that person—me—is wearing a smile. Maintaining that smile, that's what concerns me. I want this to be a good thing for us, but relocations can be tricky; they're especially hard on the tag-along wife. We're forced to create a whole new life from scratch. No office water cooler. No social network. No posse, no crew. No reason to get out of bed in the morning. Especially now that it's just the two of us. This will be our first relo without the kids. It's also the first time we've been required to take an advance trip merely to decide if we are *willing* to live somewhere. People call Shanghai the Last Frontier. It's the Wild Wild West, they say. Except that it's in the Far East, and instead of bandannas, everyone wears face masks. And this is before the pandemic.

∎ ∎

We breeze through customs and are met by a driver holding a plac-ard with our name. It's April; the air is a hazy shade of particulate gray. The ride from Pudong airport to our hotel is flanked by miles and miles of dismal, same-same new construction; laundry climbing apartment buildings like textile scaffolding, red underwear waving from windows. There's no *whoosh* of cars as we crawl through traffic, only the occasional hack and spit of our driver clearing his throat.

I've read that Shanghai is expat friendly, so my first thought is that it must be a mistake when the driver drops us at a hotel that is so Chinese, it doesn't even have a Western name. Here's what it does have: massive amounts of marble, excessively high ceilings, and ornate chandeliers. Train station cold. Every sound amplified. Hotel staff in shit-brown polyester, their voices echo and bounce in an acoustic assault of guttural sounds. There's a huge open bar with tons of empty seating in garish red velvet. Not a single Westerner in sight.

"It's all so Chinese-y," I say.

I expected bright lights, big city. Internationally generic would have been okay. This hotel has a People's Republic of China vibe that scares me. If the whole city feels like this place, I'm not sure I can do this. Back home, my clients are architects and designers, people who obsess over natural lighting, organic materials, and LEED certification; their design snobbery has rubbed off on me. Or maybe I'm just trying to hold on to some sense of me in the whole Gee-ness of yet another move.

As we check in, Gee asks for my travel papers. I shake my head no.

"Check your bag," he insists, his jaw clenching. It does that when he's aggravated.

"No way," I mutter under my breath. I'm sure he's thinking his careless wife has misplaced her passport. Her keys. Her phone. *If her head wasn't screwed on . . .*

His passport is tucked securely in a zipper flap in his carry-on. When we get to the room, he'll put it in the safe. He's meticulous that way. Handing him my documents, I shake my head no again, trying to make it clear that I'm not talking about the passport. He turns away from me to give our papers to the clerk at the front desk; I sidle up to him and whisper into his ear, "No. Fucking. Way."

No way am I going to live here.

A few minutes later, he turns back and grins knowingly. "I've upgraded our accommodations," he says, handing me a key to our "best-quality" corner room.

My first lesson in basic China survival: Throw money at unhappiness.

While I shower, Gee searches *Time Out Shanghai* and makes reservations at a Spanish restaurant on the Bund. He's much savvier than I am; I might have gone to the hotel bar, sat in the crushed red velvet chairs, and complained about the decor all night. We taxi to the restaurant, crossing the river from Pudong to Puxi. We might as well have flown to Barcelona for the evening: El Willy is filled with beautiful people, global expats, everyone speaking in a mishmash of foreign accents, Chinese women so slinky thin and stunning, you can't not stare. The people-watching; the vibrancy; the view of the Huangpu River; that glorious, iconic skyline all lit up in cobalt blue, screaming green, and hot-pink-neon hearts.

So this is it—this is Shanghai. *She pretty,* I think. She flashy, like the Vegas strip, minus tacky tourists walking around in shorts, drinking rum and Cokes out of plastic Big Gulps. Shanghai has a night pulse that surges full force; it's as if someone fed NewYorkParisTokyoMadrid into a blender, sifted it through an electric socket, and poured it into a martini glass.

We order squid and cocktails.

"Okay," I say, sipping my mojito. *Maaayyybeee.*

And for a moment, I forget to worry.

LOOK-SEE

The look-see is a blur of sensory overload: apartments, hospitals, pollution, construction. China has used more cement in the past three years than the United States did in the entire twentieth century, Gee says.

He finds this statistic particularly interesting: the astonishing growth, the commitment to modernization, like it's a twenty-first-century accomplishment and not the sign of a country careening toward a world health crisis. Jackhammers blasting *rat-a-tat*, like machine guns in a high school gym. Although that particular scary monster, gun violence, is totally American. Stuff like that doesn't happen in China, or pretty much anywhere else we've ever lived outside the United States. It's the upside of being an expat—not just kid safety, but also the ability to see America from the outside in, to get a global perspective. It's the real carrot in the whole "it'll be an adventure" proposition. You learn as much about your own country as you do about the world when you move overseas.

Gee and I take it all in, watching Shanghai unfold from the back of a van. Jake is up front in the passenger seat. Jake is our relocation consultant, hired by Gee's company.

My eyes already sting from the pollution.

"Why can't we go back to Paris?" I whisper to Gee. *Or, better yet,*

I'm thinking, *someplace tropical, like Belize. I could totally embrace change in Belize.*

But of course we don't end up in Belize. We end up at the expat health center, where the clinic manager greets us in the waiting area. She's very professional, hair bobbed just above her shoulders, straight skirt just below the knee, British accent—the picture of international chic. It's drizzling outside, and my hair is a frizzy mop on top of my head. My clothes are all wrong. I feel like a mess, and I'm not sure Shanghai is going to be a good look for me.

"Don't just pack yoga pants," Gee reminded me before we came.

So I packed jeans. Now I realize he meant that Shanghai is more stylish than Los Angeles. I forgot about that—how LA laid-back looks sloppy overseas.

While Brit Lady launches into her sales pitch, her staff scuttle a table, chairs, and medical equipment out the front door, scooting around us, carrying blood pressure pumps and thermometers, setting up what looks to be a makeshift exam area outside the entrance.

"It's a checkpoint for bird flu," Brit Lady explains matter-of-factly.

Jake and Gee nod their heads in understanding, as if this makes total sense. They're like the Bobbsey Twins, in pressed jeans and button-down shirts, pale blue for Gee, white for Jake. No tie. Business casual. Blinders on. Good corporate soldiers. Whatever happens, no one do anything to stop the flow of money.

What? I'm thinking. *Have you not seen* Contagion! Gwyneth Paltrow hosts a dinner party at a restaurant in Hong Kong to celebrate some business deal. She shakes hands with the chef, who forgot to wash his hands before leaving the kitchen, hands that only moments before were deep inside the cavity of a raw chicken that ate some bat shit on the pig farm. Then Gwyneth gets on a plane, flies back to the States, and hooks up with an old boyfriend on a layover in Chicago, and the next thing you know, everybody dies. China is ground zero for apocalyptic, end-of-the-world CDC superbugs. *This is batshit crazy!* I want to scream. My anxiety is on high alert, but all I can manage is an astonished whimper.

"Bird flu checkpoint?"

Brit Lady dismisses my concern. "It's a precautionary measure," she insists.

Jake smiles and nods, glancing at his watch to signal that the meeting is over. And we're back in the van before any of us can process the health risk we just passed through. Jake's name isn't really Jake, of course. Everyone in China takes a Western name when dealing with *lǎowài* (slang for foreigners), because, the thinking goes, it would be chaos if they didn't, since most of us are so linguistically challenged that we can't even pronounce, let alone remember, someone's Chinese name. This would be insulting if it weren't so true. I ask Jake what his real name is, and I've forgotten it by the time we get to our next stop: Shanghai Hospital in Pudong.

Can I just say that if you're trying to make someone feel comfortable about moving someplace, it might not be such a great idea to schedule back-to-back visits to a health clinic and a hospital as the first two stops on the win-them-over tour? It's not making me feel safe. It's like trying to prove you're not crazy: The more you deny it, the crazier you sound.

Gee insists that living in China for three years won't kill us. He bases this assurance on the fact that there are billions of Chinese people walking around, very much alive, and lots of them are old. He points to them out the car window.

"See, Em?" he says. "Old people."

It's true. You see them dancing or doing tai chi in Fuxing Park, babysitting the little emperors and empresses, playing mah-jongg on the sidewalk. Old guys strolling in makeshift mankinis, T-shirts rolled up, bare bellies exposed. You see the elderly everywhere. But also, you can't help but notice how many people are hunched, stooped, limping, toothless, hacking, and spitting in the gutter. So, it's a crapshoot. That right there is Gee and me in a nutshell: I'm always waiting for the other shoe to drop, while Gee's a glass-half-full guy. He doesn't see shit coming until it hits him in the face. And sometimes, even then, he still doesn't see it.

The walk to the hospital is lined with sick people, from the parking lot straight on through to the lobby. Jake whisks us into the elevator and up to the calm bubble of the VIP suite, for expats only, where we are greeted by the marketing director, who is from Seattle. He's an American version of Jake, who was born in Taiwan and educated in the States. They both have essentially the same job: to make us feel comfortable about moving to China.

I'm not particularly interested in this hospital tour, because I am never coming back here, or entering any hospital in China, for that matter. I'm sure of that. But Marketing Guy is more buff than Jake, so I grill him about exercise and air quality.

"I run every morning," he says. "Along the Huangpu River."

This guy looks like he works out—lean and healthy, so toned he could be a spokesperson for sneakers. Just do it. Only, to be on the safe side, *don't* do it if the air quality index (AQI) is over one hundred.

"So, it's safe to practice yoga?"

"Sure," he says. "The air is usually okay before six a.m. and after ten p.m."

Now I'm the one nodding my head in understanding. Like the boys. We're bobbleheads, eyes glazed over as we ignore the obvious risks of moving here: Gee ignores the environment to pursue his career; I ignore my own needs to make the marriage work.

I hear the numbers but fail to translate these time parameters into real life, that they mean I would have to practice yoga before I wake up in the morning, or after I'm home for the evening, in my jammies, getting ready for bed. All I hear is that it's doable; that's my takeaway. His one solid piece of health care advice: The magic number is AQI 100. That's the line between okay and risky. Between sane and crazy.

"Plus, there's an app for that," Marketing Guy tells me.

Right away, the pieces start to fall into place. He makes it sound totally manageable, like you can beat the whole smog thing if you just follow a few rules, treat pollution like an inconvenience attached to rush-hour traffic and factory schedules. And if you're smart, you can avoid it altogether by practicing yoga early in the morning or late at night. Make good decisions, like I tell my kids.

I buy into it hook, line, and sinker and immediately relax, breathe deep like a yogi, thinking, *This could work.* I'm good when someone gives me a how-to plan, like no carbs after 4:00 p.m., or always wear sunscreen, or never let your husband move overseas without you. That sort of thing.

I figure, how bad can it be? It's not like living in Daejeon was such a picnic.

"Your spirit was dying," the therapist said when I came home from South Korea and told her how one day, my left arm went limp out of nowhere. Couldn't fasten my own bra. Dr. B. Queensly said it was a panic attack, as well as a physical manifestation of my subconscious loss. My spirit was dying. Like Tinker Bell. I just needed someone to clap for me.

Don't get me wrong, Gee always brags about my teaching English to kids when we live overseas. He's so impressed that his wife doesn't just eat and shop with the tagalong crowd. But really, c'mon, I used to make more money than he did. I was the rainmaker.

"So, why did you agree to move?" B. Queensly asked me one day during our session. Saying, "If my husband asked me to close my practice and move overseas for *his* job, I'd be like, 'No way!'" Then she dug her heels into the carpet as if she were stepping on the brakes, her arms outstretched, wrists flexed, palms pushing away from her. It was a full-body *oh, hell no.*

What strikes me as strange about the whole thing, looking back, is that I didn't even freak out when my left arm stopped working. I was just super glad to be right-handed. As it happens, I am incredibly adaptable, although I'm not sure whether that's a strength or a weakness. And I'm not sure whether my husband has my best interests at heart or whether he's exploiting my adaptability to his own advantage.

■ ■

The next day, before the driver drops me off at the airport, Jake takes us to the Fake Market in the basement of the science center; this is where designer goods that fall off the back of the truck end up. Cartier LOVE bracelets and Burberry scarves. I peel away from the boys, choosing to window-shop on my own. I'm standing in a purse stall, eyeing a wall of bags, when a salesperson comes up to me and asks if I like Prada; she's got more colors. Maybe I like Chanel; she's got Chanel bags, too, in the back.

"You want see?"

It's overwhelming. I don't even know if I prefer Prada to Chanel; realistically, it's never been a choice I've had to make. I tell her politely that I'm just looking, but she doesn't leave. Instead, she hovers off to the side, commenting on everything I touch. "This one very good." "That one come in red too." It makes me so uncomfortable that I stop touching anything.

"*Bu yao!*" the woman next to me says, and the saleslady walks away.

"Are you new here or visiting?" she asks me in English. I can't quite place the accent—most likely Australian.

"I'm not sure," I reply.

"Well, just in case you stay, this is a good phrase to know: *bu yao*. It means 'don't want.' But you can't just say it *nicely*; you have to say it like you mean it, use your big-girl voice. You have to throw it down like it's in all caps. *BU YAO*."

The boys look at me like I've failed Shopping when I return empty-handed. Apparently this is part of the tour, the look-see wrap-up activity: The tagalong wife leaves Shanghai with a designer purse, like a gift bag at the end of a kid's birthday party. Their disappointment pressures me to buy something—and fast, because I've got a plane to catch. Jake knows a guy with a secret door in the back of his stall, where I spot a Dolce & Gabbana leather bag, black-and-white checks with pink floral appliqués, something utterly couture and totally impractical. Something I don't particularly need or want but wouldn't mind having. A consolation prize for being a good sport.

"Is it real leather?" I ask.

"This real leather," the guy says, and to prove his point, he does this trick with a lighter where he puts the flame to the bottom of the bag and we all gather in close to watch it *not* burn.

"See," he says, "plastic burn. This no burn. This real leather, not plastic."

We haggle a little, just because it seems expected, and then we buy it. My first fake designer bag.

The drive to the airport is butt ugly, like I said, but so is the drive from the Valley to LAX. Tacky billboards, endless mini-malls, urban sprawl—you just tune it out when you live in Los Angeles. I remind myself of this fact while trying to keep an open mind about moving to China, sitting quietly in the back seat of the van, my forehead pressed to the glass. State of mind: mild excitement laced with dread. I thought this trip would never come, thought it would remain somewhere out there on the horizon, a dangling relocation. The strap on my new purse starts to crack and peel even before I board the plane. Not a good sign.

THIS IS HOW IT STARTED

Gee walked in the door and announced, "We're going to Osaka." Just like that, like it was nothing, like he was saying, *Hey, babe, I'm home, let's grab some sushi.* Only the sushi bar was halfway around the world.

I was standing in the living room, baby on my hip, pasta on the stove, thinking I must have misunderstood him. But no, that's what he said. Walked in the door with this shit-eating grin plastered across his face and told me that he went out to lunch with his college buddy, had a few beers, and took a gig in Japan.

"You do know you're married," I said, shifting Ruby from one hip to the other.

"It'll be an adventure, Em."

Then he grabbed the baby and pretend-threw her in the air, chanting, "*Konichiwa*, Osaka, we're going to Japan!"

"What do you mean, *we*?" I asked.

I had finally landed a decent job in LA, not the epicenter of the business but on the fringe, more like music-industry adjacent, working for a headbanger magazine, local newsprint, turned your fingers black just flipping the pages, but still . . . in the biz.

"What about my job, Gee?"

"You'll get another job. You're fucking good at what you do, Em; you always land on your feet."

It's Gee who always lands on his feet. There's always another auto show or expo or Vegas attraction to be wired for sound. The record business is like musical chairs: There are never enough jobs, and every time there's a reshuffle or restructure, the music stops, everyone hustles to land a desk, and someone always ends up without a backstage pass. Next thing you know, boom, you're in sales at a factory that presses CDs for record labels.

"Japan, baby! It'll be so cool. C'mon, Em, you love sushi." As if loving spicy tuna rolls meant wanting to live in the birthplace of sushi. He was practically jumping out of his skin with anticipation.

"No, thanks," I said, taking the baby back. "I'm good where I am."

Plus, I'd been to Japan. Before we got married, before I moved to Los Angeles to marry Gee, I chaperoned a Valentine's Day promotion to see the Romantics in Tokyo. Detroit homeboys. Red leather suits and one big hit: "What I Like About You." Right at that moment, I was wondering what I liked about *him*, my husband, and coming up empty. He had just made a life-changing decision over beer without even consulting me. Wasn't this something couples were supposed to discuss, chew on, mull over, dissect inside and out, sit at the kitchen table with a yellow legal pad and make lists of pros and cons about, before coming to a decision? And by "decision," I mean *no effing way.*

"You need to call Jared and tell him no," I insisted.

"Did you just stamp your foot?" Gee asked, laughing.

Yep. Stamped my foot like a wild pony.

This is why women are so often compared to horses—headstrong; bucking and neighing; necks straining left and right, backward and forward, in a violent shake, trying to break free of bridal constraint.

"Em." His tone was casually resolved. "It's only eleven months."

And that's when he dropped the real bomb and admitted that he had already quit his job. That's right, he went out to lunch, high on hops, signed on to a gig in Japan, stumbled into his office, overserved and happy-man, and quit his job, all without even talking to me. And now he wanted me to quit my job and tag along.

"It's like you think I'm some sort of concubine."

"Wrong country, Em. In Japan, you'd be a geisha."

"Well, I am not a geisha. And I'm not moving to Japan, either."

It finally felt like I was settled in Los Angeles. Married, with a baby and a job at a music magazine, everything—the perfectly happy pieces of my life—coming together. I was thinking he might be the most selfish asshole on the planet, but I swear I didn't say that, although the look on my face may have been transmitting poison darts.

"Goddamn, there's no pleasing you," he said. "You complain when there's not enough money, and you complain even more when I get work. I tell you I get a gig in Japan, and you're pissed. I'm just following the money; seems like that's all that matters to you these days, ever since the baby. Money. And, fuck, it's never enough. As soon as you got pregnant, we had to move out of Koreatown—wasn't good enough for you. You couldn't see yourself with a baby stroller on Vermont and Kenmore, so, okay, we moved to Los Feliz. Hipster heaven and overpriced French pastry shops. You could see yourself there, my princess bride. That made you happy for, like, a millisecond, but as soon as the baby came, wham, when are we gonna buy a place of our own, you wanna know. What happened to the rocker chick I married, the one with the fine ass and easy smile? That's what I want to know. The girl who'd go down on me in the front seat of my car while I was pulling into the garage, because she couldn't wait to get into the house. Where'd *that* girl go?"

I wanted to say that girl worked all day, picked up the baby from daycare, and was now making dinner. But I'm not sure it would have supported my case; he would just have said it was all the more reason for me to quit my job and follow him, again, like I did when I moved to Los Angeles to get married. He was perched on the couch my mother bought me from Englanders in Detroit, back when I got my first radio gig: assistant director, advertising and promotion. The couch was covered in black parachute material, delicate and modern—perfect when it was just me, but now, with him and the baby, the two of them drinking and crawling all over it, it was starting to fray. It was completely threadbare in some spots, but we couldn't afford a new sofa.

"Are they at least paying you a lot of money?" I asked. And when he said yes, I said, "Good," staring past him to the hole in the couch.

"We'll get a new couch, Em," he promised, giving Ruby and me a hug.

I felt a twinge of guilt, mixed with awkwardly misplaced new-mother understanding, as if he were my son, not my husband. He seemed so jazzed about going to Japan that I didn't want to rob him of the experience. The excitement in his voice, his energy pumping—I recognized this feeling. Only this time it was *his*.

"It's a great opportunity," he said.

"For you, maybe."

"For us, Em. We're a team."

Here's the thing: I never played team sports. I grew up swimming in the Great Lakes, canoed the Manistee River, biked, hiked, took ballet and jazz, but I never joined a team.

"A year is a long time to be apart," I said quietly, already missing him.

"It's only eleven months, Em."

In eleven months, Ruby would be a walking, talking little person. There was no *only* eleven months. It was eleven *effing* months!

Usually, when one of us got a new job or promotion, I'd throw a bed picnic for two: finger foods, cheese and crackers, olives and nuts. And champagne. But this time, I didn't feel like celebrating. A week later, he was gone, leaving me alone with the baby and a full-time job. It wasn't like being divorced, because I didn't date. It wasn't like being married, because I slept by myself. It was some sexless, in-between marital status, where I had all the responsibilities of a family and none of the benefits of being single.

• •

My boss at the magazine loved to tell the story of why he hired me. How when he called me for a phone interview, he could hear the baby cry in the background, and then the crying stopped. That's because I put Ruby in the playpen and locked myself in the bathroom to drown out the noise. After I told him that, all he heard was that being a mother would not get in the way of this woman's career. And it wouldn't. Nor would my marriage. That was how I sealed the deal, how I snagged the job—my ability to compartmentalize.

Everyone had an opinion about my decision not to go to Japan with my husband. Andra, who had followed me to California, like a tagalong, thought I was nuts.

"They offered you a per diem just to go with Gee? They were going to pay you *not* to work, and you said no? Maid service and breakfast buffet every day? Ruby could grow up like Eloise at the Plaza!"

My mom called to tell me that her manicurist told her to warn me about Japanese girls. That's a mouthful, I know. She must have been bragging about her son-in-law with the big overseas job.

"Lady," the manicurist told my mom, "you tell your daughter Japanese girls are like catnip for American men. Those girls got one thing on their mind, and it isn't what you think—it's a plane ticket out. Asian girls see an American man alone, they don't care if he got a wife and baby back home—their black eyes light up green card. They know how to get what they want. You know what I'm saying? You like the pink or the coral today, lady? Modern marriage? Bah! No such thing. You tell your daughter: Sheila says she best be keeping an eye on her man."

"Oh, Mom!" I laughed when she told me what Sheila had said. "That's so retro. It isn't like that anymore."

"Emma, your husband is a man, isn't he?"

No, I thought, *he's a boy*. He had a ponytail. Dyed blue.

Gee's mom wasn't worried about our marriage; she was too full up on the fabulousness of Gee's international assignment. Always blowing sugar up my ass, saying stuff like, "You must have a terribly important job, dear, not to go with your husband to Japan." There was this unspoken undercurrent that a good wife would have accompanied her husband to Osaka. But I was not a good wife; I was an *awfully* good wife.

Milly was a master at inserting her truth between the lines. Full disclosure: Milly and I did not get along. It went deep and way back. Something about my being fun to have at a party but not the kind of girl one marries. Maybe it was the black miniskirt and ripped stockings I was wearing the first time we met. In my mother-in-law's worldview, this whole single-mom hell I was living through while Gee was in Japan was all my own doing, my choice, as if my career was nothing but paper towel, disposable, though I should point out that my income was not so disposable in those days.

At work they teased me that Gee didn't exist, joking that I'd made up a baby daddy. On Valentine's Day when flowers were delivered to my office, I waved the tiny envelope, saying, "See! Flowers from the hubby!" As if a bouquet of flowers was indisputable proof that my husband existed. After I read the card, I quickly hid it in my purse. The flowers weren't even from Gee; they were from Milly, covering for Gee, like she had somehow known her son would be too busy to remember to send his wife flowers on Valentine's Day.

∎   ∎

One morning I was in the kitchen, warming a bottle for Ruby, when Gee's mom called. Wet hair, half-dressed, wishing I had not picked up the phone and let in Gee's family drama.

"Grandpère is in hospital," she said. That's how she talked, dropping articles and peppering her speech with French like she was posh. And she always used Gee's full name. "Can you please have Gregory call me," Milly asked, "if it's not too much trouble, dear?"

"Yes, of course," I said, not even sure how to do it. This was before cell phones, before the Internet. Plus, there was the whole time-difference thing. I didn't want to admit that I'd never called him. Usually I waited for Gee to call me so that it would be on the company dime. In the beginning, he called every day. Then every other day. Then, as our phone conversations went from "I miss you" to "This is so hard" to "When are you coming home?" to "I'm so fucking exhausted I could scream," their frequency decreased until pretty much, he only checked in once a week. Like how some people always call their parents on Sunday, I had become an obligation. The less he called, the angrier I got, or maybe it was the other way around.

The number for Gee's hotel was stuck to the back of a takeout menu on the fridge and took me a few panicky minutes to find. They barely spoke English at the Hotel Osaka, but it sounded like there was no answer in Gee's room.

"Please have him call his wife," I told the desk clerk. It was Friday morning. I still had to blow-dry my hair, put on my makeup, dress Ruby, and now we were running late. Ruby clutched her toy phone, babbling "Dada" contentedly. "Yes, baby," I cooed, "you can take Dada to daycare." To Ruby, Daddy was a plastic telephone from Toys "R" Us.

I was so swamped, it was midmorning before I realized I hadn't heard from Gee. That's when I called his office in LA and asked the project assistant to get in touch with him.

"It's three a.m. in Osaka," Mina said. "Can it wait until morning in Japan?"

For his birthday, I gave Gee a watch that kept track of two time zones. I should have gotten one for myself. It's confusing to me how you can lose or gain a day, like you're traveling backward or forward in time. Crossing the international date line seemed like such an abstract concept until that moment. Thank you, Mina, for clarifying the time difference, for putting it in concrete terms: It was 3:00 a.m. on Saturday in Osaka, and I had no idea how to reach my husband.

I got another call from Milly, this time clearly agitated. "I know you are so very busy at your publishing job, dear," she said, dripping with honey, "and I would never dream of bothering you at work, but Gregory's grandfather is gravely ill."

"Of course," I said. "I understand. It's just that it's the middle of the night in Osaka and Gee's probably asleep."

"Can't you wake him up, dear?"

This time, the "dear" was curt.

"I'm doing my best," I told her.

The next time I called Mina, the receptionist said she was in a meeting. So I ran downstairs to the cafeteria, grabbed a sandwich to eat at my desk, and returned to a stack of messages, pink "while you were out" notes impaled on a spindle: one from Andra, two from Tower Records, and another from Milly, marked "urgent." Nothing from Mina. By midafternoon, everyone was dodging everyone's calls. I knew how this game worked. I never took a call if the client wanted to confirm the back cover and I didn't know if it was available, the client didn't pick up if I was trying to confirm space and they didn't have the budget, and Mina would not return my call if she couldn't find my husband. As for Milly, I was not inclined to return her call, because she always found a way to blame me for anything having to do with Gee.

•   •

When we were first married, Milly wanted to throw Gee a party for his birthday, not trusting that I would mark the occasion sufficiently. She made arrangements to ship lobs—that's what she calls lobsters—from Maine to Los Angeles.

"All you have to do, sweetie"—this was before I was promoted to "dear"—"is invite the guests and provide the fixings: coleslaw, corn on the cob, a baguette (make sure it's crusty). Oh, and some blueberry pie."

As if the apartment would clean itself while I was at work, but sure, I'd throw Gee a party for her, I promised.

Us, she corrected me.

Yeah. Us.

On the day of the party, when the lobsters didn't arrive by noon, like Milly said they would, I went to the office.

"If you had stayed home and waited for them," she quipped, in her most unveiled accusatory tone to date, dropping the sugar, no "sweetie" or "dear," "this wouldn't have happened. Of course someone stole the lobs off your front porch! You can't just leave a box marked 'Seafood' out in the open. It's too much temptation." Her party was ruined, and it was all my fault.

Only it wasn't ruined. At the last minute, I ran out and got a bucket of fried chicken, and our guests dined on greasy food and crazy mother-in-law stories. Milly never apologized, not even after Gee tracked the package and discovered that those lobsters never made it past Chicago. She was right about one thing, though: the temptation factor. No way was I going to tell her that I had lost her son in Japan.

Just before five, Mina called to say that the crew in Japan had pulled an all-nighter. Up against deadlines, she explained. It crossed my mind to drop the baby off at HQ with her Toys "R" Us telephone and a note pinned to her bib that said, "Call my daddy" and keep right on going to LAX, then grab the next flight home to Detroit. Instead, I picked up Ruby and stopped at the market on the way home, like I always did. The phone was ringing off the hook when we walked in the door to our apartment: first Milly, then Gee. And he was testy.

"We've been pulling all-nighters," he said. "This show is such a fucking mess, you would not believe. I'm dead tired; that's why I put 'do not disturb' on my hotel-room phone."

That was the story. It was totally conceivable. It might even have been true. If you loved your husband, if you'd had a test run at being a single mom and didn't want your life to be an endless stream of diapers and deadlines, rushing to daycare so you could get to work by nine, eating at your desk so you could skip out early enough to pick up the baby before six, dragging her with you everywhere because your coparent was never around—and if you didn't want to be this bone-tired mad all the time—this was a story you could cling to.

"I got five messages from Mina, Em. What's so damn important?"

"Your grandfather died. Call your mother."

LIGHTBULBS

I must have been around ten years old when I walked into my mom's bedroom and found her sewing up the crotch of my dad's cotton underwear, the old-fashioned kind, white like sheeting. Packing his suitcase and sewing his boxers shut. I'd never seen my mother sew before. It wasn't the type of thing she did. She wasn't crafty or kitchen-y; she had a master's degree in social work, although she didn't practice anymore. She was more of a professional volunteer. My dad traveled a lot on business. Milwaukee, Cleveland, Pittsburgh. Pit stops, really. When my husband travels, it's usually France or Japan. Sounds so much more glamorous. I mentioned this story to my mother near the end of her life, the sewing of the boxers.

"You remember that?" she responded, her voice weak, eyes distant, like she had already left the world. She was sitting on the fake Eames chair; next to her on the table was a shot of vodka and an egg timer to remind her to get up and move every twenty minutes.

"Why did you sew Daddy's boxers shut?"

"That was so long ago, dear."

And that was it—the whole conversation. She had nothing to add. This was a story she would take to the grave. It's like women of her generation took a vow of secrecy. She was always covering for my dad. He'd been dead for years, and she was still covering for him.

• ∎

I thought it was time to visit Gee in Japan, so I took a week off work and flew all the way to Osaka for a conjugal visit. That's how I thought of it. That's how I negotiated extra vacation time when my husband moved to Japan. "I'm going to need conjugal visits," I told my boss. And he gave them to me—plus flexible hours and a raise too. I was becoming a superstar at the magazine. And they didn't want to lose me.

We were in Gee's office, if you could call it that; it was really a trailer on a construction site. There was this Hello Kitty card tacked to the bulletin board above his desk. A black-and-white outline of a kitten head adorned with a big pink bow. The kind of card a young girl would send her BFF or high school crush. We were talking about where Ruby and I should go for lunch. Never mind that I had just burned up my own vacation time, flown twenty-five hours halfway across the world, cramped in economy, holding a fussy baby on my lap, just to see him; he was too busy to eat with us. He drew a map to show me where I could find a bowl of ramen.

It's hard to read signs in Japan, so directions are all in landmarks: go two blocks; turn left at the gas station; walk one block past the supermarket; it'll be on your right, next to the massage parlor. "It looks more confusing than it is," he said, handing me the map. I was thinking, *Who does this?* Who takes a job in a foreign country and leaves his wife at home with a full-time job and the baby for a whole year?

"It's only eleven months," Gee said, as if he could read my mind.

What if I dumped the baby on him and moved to Spain? Living in Spain is my alternate-universe fantasy; I did a summer abroad at the Universidad de Salamanca and fell in love with the city—the food, the people, strolling the Plaza Mayor. I could brush up on my

Spanish and get a job there. Maybe. But I wouldn't. Women don't do things like that. We turn down jobs that don't fit into the whole work-life-balance thing. I would never take a job that has more than a half-hour commute. And not just because of a what-if scenario: What if there's an emergency and I have to fetch the baby in a hurry? It's also that time spent in traffic is a black hole; it's time lost. Commuting eats into parenting, and when you're a working mother, every minute counts.

By this point, Ruby was crying and Gee dropped his pencil on the floor. She with the jet-black bangs, the girl he was banging, the green card–grabbing J-girl in a polka-dot dress, size 0, bent over to pick it up, caught that pencil almost before it even touched the ground. She was that fast.

"Here's your pencil, Mr. Gee-san."

To be honest, I didn't know for sure if he was banging this girl or not; I was just taking notes. I'm good at that.

Freshman year in college, I took this class called Alternate Reality; we had to simulate a Miskito Indian diet and keep a journal about it. For two whole weeks, all I was allowed to consume was black coffee, white rice, canned tuna, and hard-boiled eggs. Friends tried to tempt me with a late-night run to the Halfway Café. No, thanks, I'd say, grabbing my journal and writing two more pages about how eating is connected to community, observing also that dietary restrictions can cause isolation, noting that temptation lurked everywhere and that this project was making me simultaneously hungry, lonely, and filled with desire. My entire journal was about food, how it smelled and what I missed most: the whipped-creamy texture of cafeteria soft-serve; the greasy smell of melted cheese on a slice of pepperoni pizza; french fries dipped in mayo; milk in my coffee. When you can't have something, that's all you can think about. That's how much I missed my husband—two weeks of starvation multiplied by all the weeks we'd been apart.

Gee had picked me up at the airport two days earlier. I had baby spit all over my top and was sweaty and smelly from traveling halfway around the world; he was clean and pressed, sitting next to me in the taxi, Ruby heavy on my lap. I was also loaded with stuff, things he'd asked me to bring him from home: his favorite toothpaste and pretzels, brands he couldn't get in Japan, the things he couldn't live without. Not like Ruby and me—us, he could live without.

I set the diaper bag on the floor by his feet next to his briefcase, and he moved it to my side of the car, complaining that it bothered his legs, like we were cramping his style with all our baggage. And it's not like he's tall, either. Not that long legs would have been any kind of excuse for his complaining about being uncomfortable while I was doing everything, holding up both our ends as parents. All Gee had to do was go to work. Every other Friday night, I had to take Ruby to work *with* me. After Gee moved to Osaka, during deadlines I'd pick up Ruby from daycare and take her back to the office with me to hang out. Sometimes deadlining the magazine lasted past midnight. Ruby was a trouper. And a responsibility.

"Can you please hold the baby?" I asked. "She's been on my lap for two days." I was pretty sure there'd be a permanent imprint of her bum on my thighs after this trip.

"It's not two days, Em. It just seems that way because you crossed the date line."

I was still just taking notes. I missed him so much, it was like I was starved for that man. That night, I had this dream that I was at a sushi bar. There was a ton of sushi on display—salmon roll; yellowtail sashimi; and *toro*, the good stuff, the belly of the fish—and I was staring at it all, salivating, but they wouldn't serve me, not one piece of sushi, until Gee arrived. *Where's Gee?* I wondered, getting impatient. Then, all of a sudden, I was in a hotel room and there was Gee, with his shirt off, and the place was filled with Japanese girls, all young and thin, hair perfectly straight, bangs like fringe on a flapper dress, like curtains drawn across the forehead, peekaboo eyes, each girl more delicate, more beautiful than the last, and I was standing there, all baby fat and messy wild hair, ancient female rage seeping from my pores, and I lunged at him, clawing at him, pounding my fists into his chest. I woke up and shook it off like it was just a bad dream.

■ ■

A year is a long time. It's his birthday and mine; it's Valentine's Day and our anniversary. Or, if you measure it in lights gone out, it's about five bulbs. When Gee came home for Christmas, loaded with gifts for Ruby and me, that's when I knew. I took the porcelain geisha doll in the silk kimono he brought for Ruby, ripped her head off, and hung her decapitated body upside down from the mantel like a stocking. Merry Christmas, Mr. Gee-san. My mother woulda just sewn up his boxers and been done with it.

You wanna know how I knew?

When he walked in the door and didn't hug me first thing, saying it had been a long flight and he needed a shower, and then passed out in bed. Nope, I was still just taking notes.

The next morning, we were making love, the sun coming in through the window slats. I was scratching at him, trying to reintroduce myself to every part of his body, rubbing my cheek, catlike, across his stubble; he was changing positions, like he couldn't get comfortable, moving through the *Kama Sutra*, pressing my knee into my armpit, flipping me over.

He was taking too much time—that's what he was doing.

That's when I knew. His lack of urgency stabbed me, like a body blow, and I knew that he was not hungry, had not spent his time in Osaka journaling about what he missed in Los Angeles. And me dumb enough to ask. Sometimes a guy should lie. Some lies are okay, and this is one of them. But Gee was all George Washington, when he should have been Bill Clinton. And now I was Hillary. Hateful, haggard, pants-wearing Hillary, the first First Lady not to pretend to love baking. I threw on a pair of jeans and a T-shirt, grabbed the car keys, and drove aimlessly up Los Feliz Boulevard, into Griffith Park, past the pony rides and the cowboy museum, past the zoo and the choo-choo train, listening to Sinead O'Connor's "Nothing Compares 2 U" on repeat, tears flooding my eyes, so wet I had to turn on the windshield wipers. *It's been eleven months and ten days since he took his love away. Since he's been gone, I do most everything. I pay the bills and kiss the boo-boos, I work all day and sleep alone, spend Saturday nights at a restaurant, me and the baby, put Ruby in a booster with a sippy cup and crackers, order pasta and a single glass of chardonnay. Since he's been gone, my love has been on hold, waiting for him to come home.*

Only he didn't come home. Another version of him did.

The one thing—the only thing—that I did not do was change the lightbulbs. It started with the ceiling light in the kitchen, and I figured I'd just use the one over the stove instead. As months went by and more lights went out, I switched to candles. Vanilla grapefruit. Lavender. There were candles in the bathroom, in the bedroom, candles on the dining room table. I thought it was a romantic gesture. Marking time.

Gee came home, opened the front door, flipped the light switch in the hall, and the first thing out of his mouth was, "Jesus, Em, can't you even change a fucking lightbulb?"

He did not think it was romantic. He took it like a dig, like I was throwing it in his face that he hadn't been around to do household chores. Like I was pointing out how long he had been gone. What he didn't understand was that I was holding space for him. Because yeah, sure, I could change a lightbulb—I could do everything, all of it: take care of the baby, hold down a job, touch myself before I fell asleep—but if I went to Home Depot, came back with a bag of bulbs, got the ladder out of the garage, carried it into the apartment, and changed the lightbulbs, too, how would I know I was still married?

• •

Somehow I wound up in the hot tub with Andra, who was house-sitting in the hills. She was wearing oversize shades, hair pulled up and falling around her face, twisting every which way, olive skin glistening. She looked Hollywood Regency. Like a hip Grecian goddess. Andra the Great. Which makes sense—her full name is Alexandra. Everything about Andra's appearance was polished except for her hair, which could be coarse and unruly. Good thing, too—it gave her character; otherwise, she'd be way too perfect. We smoked a joint. I didn't even like pot, but Andra said to think of it as medicine. We'd been best friends since our Detroit radio days. A year after I quit my job and moved to California to marry Gee, she divorced the doctor and followed me out here. Chain migration.

"Do you ever regret splitting with Sam?" I asked her.

"Sometimes," she said. "But if it weren't for my marriage breaking up, I would never have moved to LA. Now look at us: We're in the canyons; we're sitting in a fucking hot tub in the hills with a view of the Hollywood sign. In the middle of December. I'm never going back, Em." Then she launched into a few bars from our favorite bad music video, "It's So Cold in the D." So bad it made us howl. Normally I would have joined in, but I was lost in thought. Andra stopped singing.

"Earth to Em," she said, splashing water at me.

I'm not going home, I was thinking, weightless and floating, the backs of my calves resting on the edge of the hot tub. *Let him be the dad for a while. Let him not dawdle for one minute, not go out for drinks with the guys, not have a moment to himself. Let him be a hamster on a treadmill for a whole year. Correction: eleven months. You exaggerate, Gee always says, as if the linguistic jump from months to years, the calendar callout, is the issue. Or perhaps if he can catch me on a technicality, he can discredit my perception of this past year, the year of our living apart. He can paint me as the hyperbolic bitch.*

"Can I move in with you, An?" I asked. There were magazines and takeout containers, wet towels and dirty ashtrays strewn around the Jacuzzi. The place was a total mess, and small, but there had to be a guest room somewhere.

"Em, I'm house-sitting for my boss! He's coming home in two days. And he's going to go ballistic if I don't clean this place up." She laughed.

I'm going to go ballistic as soon as I stop being weepy, I thought. *But I'm not ready to stop crying.*

"Maybe I'll take the baby and move back home with my mom."

"Nobody loves you like your mother," Andra said.

It's one of our universal truths. Unconditionally. But also without boundaries, so that's kind of a double-edged sword. *Why would I want anyone to love me like my mother does, always judging me, telling me to fix my face—and "Emma, can't you do anything with your hair?" Like my hair is from outer space or something, like I'm the only person in the world to have curly hair. But, come to think of it, I am the only one in my family with this hair. Maybe the mailman had curls. And that's why Mom has always loved me best.*

"Nobody loves you like your mother," I replied.

"That's why you gotta go home," Andra said. "For Ruby."

When I walked in the door, there was Gee, on a ladder, in the middle of the living room, changing the damn lightbulbs.

■ ■

Everyone said it didn't mean anything—and I told a lot of people. I wasn't keeping this thing a secret, holding it close, or sweeping it under a rug, like my mother-in-law wished I had the common decency to do. It was out there, bleeding and belching and vomiting all over anyone who would listen. Here's what everyone said: It doesn't mean he doesn't love you.

Have you ever noticed how people speak in double negatives when they want to obscure some obvious truth? What they meant was, it didn't mean anything *to him*. The whole episode was refracted through the prism of male perspective. What mattered most to everyone was how *Gee* felt when he was screwing the girl who was not me. Turns out it mattered more how I felt.

It was a sea change, a seismic betrayal. It was the end of the beginning, my married-lady fantasy where everything bad was good because we were in it together. Just scraping by was okay because we were scrimping together; renting was okay because we were sharing a bedroom; not having a new couch was okay as long as our legs were in a cozy jumble on the old one; being the one who dropped off and picked up the baby from daycare was okay because we didn't add it up or break it down like that, who did what or how much. The part of me that was willing to overlook all that shit just shut down, not because Gee had dipped into someone else's honey, but because he left me alone to do everything while he was living large in a hotel with laundry and maid service, blowing his per diem at karaoke bars while back home his wife had become the family workhorse, a burro, a nagging bitch with a full-time job and a baby.

Things were not okay with us for a very long time—so long I gave it a name, called it the Decade of Hate. Maybe I should have taken the baby and made a run for it, though not because he's a bad guy. He's a good guy. I know that now. But I know me better too. I'm not a person who forgives—I'm a person who keeps score, who makes lists, who hits replay in her head and ruminates for months, sometimes years. I'm a person who remembers details and holds a grudge. This is perhaps not the greatest quality to have in a marriage.

■   ●

"It was a mistake," Gee told the marriage counselor, adding, "It didn't mean anything." He said he felt terrible and it would never happen again. Said it like there was nothing else to discuss, like my feelings were *my* problem and not *his* bother, and he never came to another session. The next week, I went by myself.

"Where's your husband?" Wayne asked.

"In London, on business," I told him. Which was true. But the next time, the third visit, when Gee was a no-show and Wayne asked where he was, I said, "He's not coming back." Then I asked, "Can't we do this marriage-counseling thing without him?"

Wayne was a no-bullshit kind of therapist. "Emma," he said, "My practice is filled with couples like you and your husband. I'm going to save you a lot of money. I'm going to tell you exactly what I'd tell you after a year of counseling: This is who you married, and he's not going to change. He's a road guy. This is Hollywood—half of this town is some variation on Gee: location scouts, directors, actors, musicians, people whose lives are defined by their careers and whose careers are defined by travel. You have two choices," he said. "Either you accept this lifestyle or you get a divorce."

And then Wayne broke up with me.

"I only work with couples," he said.

● ■

Wayne was wrong, though. There was a third option: real estate. Gee and I bought a house in Glassell Park, a downscale piece of LA that we just barely squeaked into. It was on a hill (not *in the hills*), a tree-shrouded hideaway with concrete floors before that style became popular as an industrial-chic design statement. It was a cabin, really. This was the house that Osaka bought. Not just Gee's bonus for completing the gig—that wasn't nearly enough cash for a down payment. No, Gee's family kicked in for that house. I told him—after he came home stinking of "Whatever Her Name Was"—that we needed to buy a house. It was my brother who gave me the idea; he's a personal injury lawyer. And if your husband screwing Japanese girls isn't a personal injury, what is? So I called my brother and asked what I'd get in a divorce.

"What do you have, Em?" he asked. Meaning investments and real estate.

We were renting a duplex on Tica Drive at the time; we had a toddler and some credit card debt.

"You'll get half of that," he joked.

Only it wasn't funny. "I've been thinking maybe I should take the baby and come home to Detroit," I said.

That's when my brother got all lawyerly and started talking about crossing state lines, kidnapping, courts, and visitation rights. Just having that conversation hurt my head, so I decided to give Gee another chance, but this time with a real estate insurance policy. I know this might sound cold and calculating, but I made Gee call up his dad, tell him what a shit excuse for a husband he was, and ask for the money.

"Don't call your mom," I said. "She's never liked me."

I remember Gee's aunt, the one with the red hair, once telling me that Gee's mom cried when she heard we were getting married. She blubbered on about how Gee was not going to marry "that woman." Like I was poor white trash, only worse—Midwestern and middle class, from a family of suits—when Gee's family were all artists. Reverse snobs. Making me feel soiled because my family had some sense of a spreadsheet. I always got the feeling his mother would rather Gee be gay than marry me; being gay had more cachet than a girl from Detroit. That's how much I didn't fit into Gee's family. Or maybe that's how much Gee loved me, depending on how you look at it, him being willing to defy his mom and all.

My side of the family loved Gee from the start. "He's a keeper," they said, and not because he had financial potential. He showed up for our wedding with a blue ponytail and no steady employment, not exactly the picture of marriage material, but he charmed them. My dad thought Gee was a straight-up guy underneath the blue hair, and my mom, well, she was just happy that her baby was getting married. *And* she liked how I let Gee get close to me, let him drape his arm around my shoulder or rest his hand on my thigh. That I smiled at him like he lit up my world.

Ortheia Barnes sang "You Are My Friend" at our wedding. Ortheia was Detroit soul royalty, big and bluesy. Andra and I used to hang out at a nightclub where she worked, sit in the powder room with her on breaks between sets and gab. "If I ever find the right guy," I'd tell her, "that's the song I'm gonna play at my wedding."

"Girl, if you ever find that guy, I'll come and sing it at your wedding."

And she did. Belted out "You Are My Friend" a capella in my parents' living room like Patti Labelle was in the house. The in-laws were standing there, all East Coast, pretentious classical connois-seurs, Pachelbel's Canon in D, so pale I thought they were gonna pass the fuck out. And this was before they saw the outrageous tower of fruit my mother ordered from the caterer. The fruit sculpture was her response to Gee's and my request that she keep things simple—just a small wedding at home, fresh berries for dessert, nothing fancy.

Gotta wonder why the redhead told me that story in the first place, about my mother-in-law bawling and calling me "that woman." That hurt more than I let on. I never trusted her after that, either of them, Milly or the redhead. Anyway, Gee's parents sent us a bundle. It was a save-the-marriage loan. His aunt chipped in too; all of a sudden, everyone was trying to make this marriage work. Andra called that house the love shack, and it was a shack, but it was never about love—this was the "hell hath no fury" house. The neighbors had a Doberman pinscher that growled and stalked the chain-link fence. An angry, territorial bitch. I was afraid of that dog almost as much as I was afraid of becoming her. I did not want to live there alone.

My mother always told me being alone was the worst thing in the world. Unsurvivable. Worse than being broke, which can be temporary. "Fortunes change," she said, "but love lasts forever. Being alone . . ." she said, her voice tapering off, and then she just shook her head like there were no words to describe it. What she didn't tell me was that it was possible to be alone in a marriage, that marriage can actually feed loneliness.

All I knew was that working full-time and being a mom without a partner can turn a person mean and angry fast. I felt like I had my back up against competing hells. Maybe I took the easy way out, or maybe I threw in with love, but my job—although it was in the music industry and I had negotiated a pretty sweet work-from-home deal, with flexible hours and an expense account—was just a job. And even though I was comped on guest lists for live shows up and down Sunset Strip and got paid to do what I loved, even though I was passionate about music and made as much money as Gee, still, like my mama told me, fortunes come and go. I figured it would be easier to replace that job than find a new husband. And I knew our marriage wouldn't survive another overseas separation. So when Gee was offered a gig in Korea, this time, me and Ruby—and the baby—all tagged along.

MONSOON SEASON

The first thing I noticed when we landed at Gimpo airport was the smell of garlic. Not fresh garlic, but garlic regurgitated through sweat and seeping from pores. After a while, it didn't bother me, probably because that's how I smelled too. It's definitely how Gee smelled. He sweated a lot at work and came home stinky. And still I was happy to see him. A person can adapt to just about anything, I mused, smiling to myself, stirring glass noodles. Even living in Daejeon, South Korea.

Every morning, I took the kids to the park. They'd swing and slide and play contentedly in the sandbox. That would last for about half an hour before they tugged at my sleeve, complaining, "Mommy, I'm bored." *Me, too,* I'd think, glancing at my watch. *Ten o'clock, and I have nothing planned for the rest of the day. This was it, our big outing, a trip to the park.* My mommy bag of tricks was empty.

Somehow I got my hands on an English-language book called *Korean Cookery,* by Lee Wade, and learned to make *chap chae* from scratch. It took forever. You have to julienne all the vegetables—carrots, onions, scallions, four different kinds of mushrooms (*p'yogo, mogi, nutari,* and *sogi*)—stir-fry each one separately, sauté the spinach and garlic, boil the noodles, and cook the meat. Last thing is the dressing: soy sauce, sesame oil, rice vinegar, sugar; then you combine it all in one big pot. So many ingredients, two trips to the market, carting food on my back—it took hours; it took all afternoon with the kids in tow. *Who has the time to do this*, I wondered?

I did, obviously.

I was a stay-at-home mom making *chap chae* from scratch. Before moving to Korea, I was the number one salesperson at a rock magazine, I had an expense account, and took record execs to fancy restaurants. Now I smelled like garlic and my hair was sticky with sesame oil. I didn't even like to cook—or, rather, I liked to cook *with* Gee, not *for* him. This made me want to scream. This feeling, this shriek that wanted to explode all over my life, it sat there in my throat, burning a hole, because I didn't want to wake Ruby and Rio. Never wake sleeping children. Instead, I took a nap. I was sleeping night and day. Gee was working around the clock.

After dinner, I fed and bathed the kids, read them a book about wild things, and told them a bedtime story about Rubina and Rioli, a princess and prince who found themselves alone in a strange land. Their mother, the queen, who was not without powers, had been taken hostage by a great and mighty force.

"What's it look like, Mommy?"

"It looks like love, sweetie."

Gee came home from work and found me in bed, not even dozed off on the couch with a book; couldn't even pretend to have just nodded off for a minute. I had nap-all-day foggy brain.

"What did you do today?" he grilled me.

"What time is it?" I replied, wiping my eyes, rubbing my tongue along my teeth. *Better brush them*, I thought. My mouth tasted bitter. Kimchee. I liked Korean food, but it made my breath smell like a fire-breathing dragon. I wanted to say, "I didn't sign up for this," but I sort of did when I quit my job and agreed to follow Gee to Korea— like a bad 1950s pop song, "I Will Follow Him." Still, no one told me that we'd be the only English-speaking family in town. No Mommy and Me, no chardonnay playdates. It was precisely because there was nothing in Daejeon—just farmland, marshes, and cranes flying low, with elegant necks and wingspans—that they could build an expo and employ Gee in this backwoods part of South Korea.

"Why can't you find something interesting to do here?" Gee wanted to know. He sounded disappointed in me, not as a wife and mother, but as a person. As if I lacked the adventure gene.

"I made *chap chae*," I told him.

"Wow," he said. "Really, that's so cool."

He had no idea how angry I was that he had brought us here. Brought *me* here and tried to pass it off as an adventure. It was monsoon season. The clothesline on our balcony no longer seemed so charmingly Third World–y as dark spots spread across the baby's onesies and my damp-for-days jeans grew rank with mildew, the air so muggy my hair looked like it belonged on a cartoon character with her finger stuck in a wall socket. A sea of almond eyes framed by inky black, stick-straight hair stared at me: this frazzled and frizzy Western woman with two kids in tow. Sometimes they giggled and tried to pet Ruby's hair. I said, *"Aniyo!"* and politely shooed away their hands.

• •

Daejeon was a town in transition, on the verge of becoming a science center, a government hub, but back then, there was no expat community. No tagalongs. There was only one supermarket, located in the community center, along with a bowling alley and a movie theater that showed American films dubbed into Korean. In the basement was a brand-new food court, bright and clean, where they sold fifty different types of tofu, freshly sliced—try pitching that to a pair of American toddlers.

Look, kids, the tofu lady!

That's where I first met the Christian missionary. I was having a bowl of rice at the food counter; she had stringy hair and a herd of messy kids, white and pasty, with runny noses. She was the only other Western woman I had ever seen in this city.

"Do you need an oven?" she asked.

"I could use a dryer," I told her.

"Oh, golly. Dryers are hard to find. Come to Bible study," she suggested, pressing her card into my hand. I didn't need religion; what I needed was clean, dry sheets.

But I took her card anyway, thinking never in a million years would I call this woman. After that, every time I ran into her and her kids, five of them, she dangled an oven in front of me like a carrot and I described how my kids' clothes were crawling with mildew. It became a sort of comedy routine, her offering me something I didn't want, me needing something she couldn't give me. It would have been funnier if it hadn't been such a spot-on mirror of my marriage: Gee offering me an overseas adventure. When what I needed was to be home, networking, moving my career forward in Los Angeles.

Sometimes I fantasized about Gee dying in a fluke work-related accident. It could happen. He wore a hard hat. He had a collection of hard hats with his name on them, from every job site he'd ever worked on. Gee. Mr. Gee. Gee-san. There was this one incident he told me about when he came home from work late, pissed off. He had been standing in a fountain that was drained for repairs, working on faulty electrical wires or something, when someone in the control booth turned the water on and Gee got soaked. Gee doesn't get mad often, but when he does, watch out—telephones fly. He stormed into the control booth, dripping wet, and did a strip show in front of all of the Korean workers. Took off every stitch of clothing, even his choners—that's his word—item by item, wringing them out on the floor, slapping the desk with them, like his shirt was a locker-room towel. Then he stood there, a dripping wet, buck naked, big dick, angry American man.

"They'll never do that again." Gee laughed, slamming his beer on the table.

All I could think was, *Holy shit, he could have been electrocuted!* It never occurred to me until that moment that Gee was sort of a construction worker. Accidents happen all the time. This became my forbidden fantasy. One day the phone would ring and it would be Gee's boss calling. *There's been an accident,* he'd say softly, breaking the bad news gently, by telephone, not even in person. Because Gee worked for a production company, not the military. *Your husband has been electrocuted,* his boss would say. *Anything you need, don't hesitate to ask.*

I would have to pack up my things and move back the States right away. And then I'd get the insurance, plus probably more, on account of its being a work-related accident—maybe even a company settlement. I'd get the insurance money *and* I'd get to go home. *Double Indemnity,* baby! That was Gee's favorite movie. I'd miss him, but I'd get over it; it wasn't that I didn't love my husband, but he wasn't around all that much anyway.

Meanwhile, I was more likely to die in Korea than Gee was. One day, my left arm stopped working, which was inconvenient, to say the least. *Good thing I'm right-handed,* I thought, or I wouldn't have been able to get dressed in the morning. Then, a month later, my arm back to normal, I felt a lump in my right breast. And then, because I felt a lump, I couldn't stop feeling it. And pretty soon my breast was really tender. It hurt just to touch it. Anxious thoughts were piling up in my head. Maybe because I didn't have anyone to talk to.

These are all the words I knew in Korean: *ne, aniyo, eopseo.* Yes, no, forget about it. *Yeogi, chigum.* Here and now. That was useful in taxis. Three ways to say hello: *annyeong, annyeong-haseyo, yoboseyo.* There are many ways to say goodbye. *Annyeonghi gyeseyo* means "goodbye, *I'm* leaving." There's another way to say goodbye if the other person is going. Or you could just say *anyong,* but then you risk sounding

like a child, or as if you were talking to a child. At first it seemed
an unnecessarily complicated linguistic distinction to make. Who's
staying? Who's going? What does it even matter?

I didn't know how to say I was lonely, but here's what I did out
of desperation: I called up the Christian missionary, the one who
tried to bribe me with an oven if I would just come to Bible study,
and I said I *might* consider it if she could come up with a clothes
dryer instead. And I made a playdate. On my way to her house, the
sky cracked open and rain pounded the taxi in a flash downpour of
biblical proportions. She fed my children Jesus and American food
that she bought at the military base in Seoul. The kids were seduced
by the comforts of home.

"Grilled cheese!" they exclaimed. Like it was an ice cream sundae.

I will never hear the end of this, I thought. *Why don't we have
cheese? They will ask. Because, my darlings, they don't sell cheese at the
market, I will say. Or bread, for that matter.* And then they will want
to go back to the Christian missionary's house for another playdate
with her five kids, their noses running green and snotty because she
doesn't believe in antibiotics, and I will say okay because they are the
only other American family I have ever seen in Daejeon.

That night, first Rio, then Ruby puked up the processed cheese,
frozen french fries, and stale Cheetos the missionary brought back
from the military base. I tried to calculate how long the drive from
Seoul to Daejeon was, in swamplike heat, her groceries turning
rancid and her frozen food thawing. Didn't anyone ever tell that
woman you're not supposed to refreeze? Chunks of half-digested
Wonder Bread covered the floor, stuck in my hair, and soaked the
sheets. The sheets could be washed, but they would never dry. Not
on a clothesline. Not in monsoon season. The rain was unrelenting.

I wiped the bedding as best I could and rotated the mattress so
the wet spot would be on Gee's side. *He'll never know*, I thought. The
idea that he wouldn't know he was sleeping on puke-stained sheets

made me laugh out loud. It was the first time I had laughed, really belly-laughed, in months. That's when I decided to go home. Not home to Los Angeles—there were renters in the love shack. Home to Mommy. I'm bringing the kiddies for a visit, I told her over the telephone. Just for a couple of weeks, I said. Adding that I needed a mammogram. I figured I'd hold off on telling her I wanted to stay longer. Like forever, maybe. Or, at least until Gee's gig in Korea was over.

This is what I took: the kids and our passports. Nothing else mattered. Everything else could be replaced. Even Gee. Well, maybe even Gee. This is what I left: my wedding ring. It may sound spoiled to call your wedding ring cheap, but what else do you call a fourteen-karat gold band that cost less than a hundred bucks? I thought of it as a placeholder, something to be upgraded when me and Gee were flush, but flush never came and a load of crap came instead, and now I flung it on the bathroom counter. This was a temporary move, a half-move; if I had flushed it down the toilet, that would have been permanent, not just a grand gesture. That would have been a real decision. Maybe I should've married the Paper Bag Man, like my mama told me to do back when I was a catch, but I pooh-poohed her advice then, and now the Paper Bag Man drove a Bentley and my husband drove a Ford pickup and dragged me around the world in service of his career, if you believe building expo pavilions in Korea is a career move. I wasn't sure how much more of this I could handle, but this much I knew: I couldn't go back in time. The Paper Bag Man was married, his wife had her claws in deep, and I had two kids and stretch marks. And healthy breasts, I reminded myself. It turns out there was nothing wrong with my boob, no suspicious bump. "Just muscle," the doctor said.

• •

"Oh, honey!" My mom laughed when I asked if I could move in with her, just for a little while longer, just until I got back on my feet. Then she put on her world-weary, truth-telling, this-is-how-it-is face and said, "Divorce is for the very rich or the very poor. The rich can afford it and the poor have nothing to lose, but you, Emma, are not rich. And you have two children to think about." We were trapped. Me and the kids. We were going to have to suck it up and go back to Korea. But not until it stopped raining.

When monsoon season ended, I returned to Daejeon, boxed up the apartment, and moved the family to Seoul. That was the deal I struck with Gee, after the string of phone calls my mother insisted I take, handing me the phone while covering the receiver, whispering, "He's your husband."

It's your bed, missy. . . .

I listened to his sorrys and promises to spend more time with us, not to work six days a week and leave me alone with the kids in a foreign country, from breakfast to bedtime, with no friends and no relatives and a day planner filled with blank pages. I knew we had to go back to Korea, but I was milking this time away for all it was worth; I went to movies and ate hamburgers with real cheese and hung out with friends. I missed my job, even the suckiest parts of my job, like impossible sales quotas and insane deadlines and the way my left eye would sometimes twitch from the pressure. Well, I didn't miss that. Or him. I didn't miss his touch. I didn't miss the way he slurped noodles and sweated garlic like he was born there. And I didn't miss how he made me feel flawed for being unhappy, as if it was my fault, as if his glass being full wasn't the reason mine was almost empty.

■　■

Maybe you're thinking, *Why'd she stay with this asshole if she didn't love him? Why'd this girl quit her job and follow this guy all around the world?*

The problem was, I did love him—I just didn't trust him after the whole Japanese thing happened and everyone said it was no big deal.

After Andra said it didn't matter, as if there was some sort of alternate DMZ, demarried zone, and it didn't count if your man cheated on you when he was on the road. It wasn't like *her* husband, she said, the one she divorced because he was sleeping with a nurse at the hospital where he worked. That was actionable. It doesn't count if you're not living on the same continent, she said; it just means he's a guy. And guys have needs.

So do I. That's what I was thinking. *I have needs too.*

But I didn't fuck the editor of the magazine where I worked, the guy with the soft voice who liked to phone-talk me for hours about alternative bands the whole time Gee was living in Osaka. Okay, maybe I *almost* did, but that was *after* I found out about the J-girl. And no one knows about this, not Gee, not even Andra, so it's not making it into this memoir, that's for sure. But maybe it should, because that's really why I ended up staying with Gee.

That date with the editor was so awkward, the chicken under-cooked, the rice burned. Gee's a good cook; he's got this one dish, "marry me" pasta: *aglio e olio*—that's my favorite. He's also a good dancer. He does this full-body mosh-pit thing, even to this day. I always joke that it should have been a deal breaker, the way he jumps up and down like it's still the '80s, but that's me acting like maybe I made a mistake marrying him, when in truth I dig his willingness to let loose. If someone saw the two of us dancing, they'd think we were totally mismatched—him doing this punk-rock pogo; me doing a swivel-hips, super-oozy, *I'm from the D* thing—but they'd be dead wrong. What makes us work is the trancelike, total abandon we each bring to the dance floor. Sure, we've got different styles, but we both commit to the beat 100 percent.

Anyway, we were lying on the hardwood floor of his apartment, which wasn't in Los Angeles (because if I learned anything from the Osaka Affair, it's that sex in a different city doesn't count)—no shag rug; no cozy, oversize throw pillows; not super conducive to romance—and we were listening to the Replacements. All music editors jones for the Replacements, like they're some sort of best-kept secret. *Don't Tell a Soul.* One thing led to another, and we started kissing. I can't remember the last time me and Gee sat on the floor, listening to music and making out. Married people don't do that shit. Andra says when the kissing goes, the relationship is over. But Andra wasn't married very long, so she's not exactly an authority.

We were making out, and it felt sort of foreign, like being in Asia and you're not sure what to do when they serve you grasshoppers squirming in oil, trying to pass it off as a delicacy. Gee would so get that reference. I think if I had been single and not pissed at my husband for cheating on me, I would have just laughed and said, "Let's be friends." And then it would have been a perfect night hanging out and listening to records, not CDs, because editors still collect vinyl. But I was on a mission to get laid by someone other than my husband, and I'd put a lot of effort into this flirtation—hours on the phone talking hip-hop versus hard rock—and I was determined to see it through. Even the score. So I kept at it a bit. How to describe this particular version of bad sex? The whole time we were fooling around, fumbling around was more like it, cottonmouth, dry skin, and elbows jabbing, lacking heat like the undercooked chicken he made for dinner, I was thinking, *This is not my guy.* It made me feel so alone, weepy-hearted. How could Gee get it up for that girl in Japan and I couldn't go through with this, couldn't even screw this one guy I kinda-sorta liked? But kind of liking is not the same thing as belonging to each other, not at all. And we didn't fit, me and the editor who liked the Replacements but wasn't one. We didn't have rhythm.

"It'll get better," he said. "Next time."

"No next time for us," I said, kissing him sweetly on the cheek. After all, it wasn't his fault; he just got caught in the crossfire of our marriage.

I left him there wanting what Gee didn't have the good sense to hold precious, went back to my hotel room and wept for the love of Gee, and how broken he had made us. My flesh was bound to him, but I was unable to trust him anymore. I filed this incident away and never told anyone on account of this one little detail: I might have been pregnant at the time. So that's why this story is really not making it into the book. But maybe it should. Because that's when I decided to go all in and stay with Gee. I wanted that second baby so bad. Only children are always fucked-up little emperors, and my daughter was gonna have a sibling, come hell or whatever, a sister or brother, and not be spoiled or have broken-home syndrome. Gee and I were gonna make it work. And that's really why I followed him to Korea.

■ ■

Things went better in Seoul. For one thing, it's a big city with an international community. I put Ruby in daycare, and Gee's company found us a babysitter for Rio so I could go to the market without dragging him along. Mi Chung was a lifesaver. She had this childlike spirit; I could tell she loved being on the merry-go-round as much as the kids did. And the way I knew this was that I often accompanied her to the park. I didn't need a babysitter so much as a friend, and Mi Chung, a college student, spoke pretty good English. For her part, she probably would have taken care of the kids for free, just to perfect her language skills—she was hoping to move to America—but we paid her anyway. For his part, Gee made good on his promise not to work all the time. On weekends, our family went on picnics or shopping in Itaewon, where we bought an antique Korean wedding chest for good luck, then ducked into Nashville, an expat club that served the military base. "This Is America": the Far East version. It was a portal, a Hollywood set where they played Motown, screened classic movies, served burgers in baskets with ketchup and fries. It even had an English-language lending library. It was almost like being home. And—another improvement—Gee's company loaned me Mr. Kim, a Korean surfer with a beat-up van, to drive the kids and me around town.

Most of my pictures from Korea are of my helpers: Mi Chung playing dolls with Ruby; Mr. Kim carrying Rio up a flight of steps to a temple; Mr. Kim and me on a ferry crossing the Han River, my hair windswept, he in his driver's uniform, a thin burgundy-and-black cotton vest. I hung out with Mi Chung when she "babysat" the kids, and insisted that Mr. Kim act as my tour guide when he drove me to museums or the hardware store. Not just because I was uncomfortable leaving Mr. Kim sitting in the car while I ran errands and explored the city, but because it made me feel less isolated to have another adult around. Especially one who spoke Korean. It's good practice for learning English, I told him, as if I were doing it for *him* and not me. In Asia, this is called "saving face." I was becoming culturally acclimated.

Most days, Mr. Kim took Ruby to preschool in the mornings, dropped me off at the gym, and waited in the van, reading *Playboy* magazine for the articles.

"For to learn English," he said.

"What'd you learn today, Mr. Kim?" I asked, climbing into the back of the van after a workout, sweaty, too lazy to put my street clothes back on, wearing only leggings and a tank top, cluelessly underdressed.

When he saw me, he blushed. "Where you go now?" he wanted to know.

That's when I blushed. It was embarrassing that I didn't have anywhere pressing to go. Maybe Gee was right: I lacked the adventure gene. While having a driver was a huge convenience, it was also a straight-up reminder of how little I had to do all day.

So I joined the American Women's Club, mostly because I wanted to have somewhere to tell Mr. Kim to take me while Ruby was in school and Rio was with Mi Chung. And that's where I was introduced to the tagalong scene. I thought it would be easy to make friends, but the tagalong ladies didn't invite me into their expat homes, because I wasn't going to be in Seoul long enough to be worth the friendship investment. I call this tagalong math. Later, I would come to understand this algorithm; in Paris, I would be on the other side of this survival strategy, not wanting to extend myself to women who wouldn't be around long enough to reciprocate. It wasn't just that I didn't want to waste time getting to know other moms who would be gone before I could memorize their kids' names; it was also because I didn't want to lose people I'd come to rely on as friends. Good friends. Women with whom I shared the day-to-day experience, the ups and downs, the frustration over not knowing how to get things done; women in whom I confided, with whom I commiserated; women who made me laugh. And laughing while tagging along is nothing to sneeze at. So tagalongs get picky. The first question out of their mouth, almost before "What's your name?" or "Where are you from?" is "How long will you be here?"

"Welcome to Seoul." The woman sitting next to me at the American Women's Club monthly coffee meet-up said, "How long will you be here?" I was wearing jeans and a Newcomer Crack-N-Peel label. She was dressed in head-to-toe fake designer goods: Chanel tweed jacket and quilted purse with chain-link strap, Ferragamo flats in black patent leather. She looked like a throwback to a committee lady. She looked like my mother.

"Less than a year," I told her. She smiled, nodded politely, and never said another word to me. *These are not your people*, I told myself, to lighten the sting of rejection. Still, it hurt that they didn't extend themselves to me. Being a tagalong is a lot like being in high school: There are cliques, new girls, and own-the-school girls. But, to be fair, I was a short-termer. I wouldn't even be in Seoul long enough to attend the fundraiser they were all planning.

However, I *was* there long enough to take a vacation. A real vacation. Not just an overnight on Jeju Island—the Hawaii of South Korea—on a photo shoot for a high-end kids' clothing catalog. (I joked that Ruby and Rio made more money than I did that year.) Or a weekend in Busan, where someone fell into a bucket of halibut at the fish market and picked up a nickname they hated. Fish Butt! No, this was the kind of vacation travel magazines feature. We flew to Bali, with a layover in Singapore. Ate satay in the Night Market, had cocktails at the Raffles Hotel, where the Singapore Sling was created, visited the world-famous zoo, and took a family photo with an orangutan on our laps. Then we were off to Ubud, where a sacred monkey perched on Gee's shoulders and groomed his hair like they were long-lost siblings. We slept deep in a rice paddy at a luxury hotel with walls that were paper-thin and slid open to a lush expanse of nature, iridescent green and undulating. There was a sleek modern infinity pool, the water appearing almost black and falling off toward the horizon; fresh flower petals were strewn on the bedspread. At night we heard frogs mating.

Before returning to Korea, we stayed at one of those family-friendly resorts with a kids' club and babysitting. Gee and I sat at the bar, him in a batik shirt, me wearing a sarong. We ordered drinks that we paid for with beads from a necklace they gave us when we checked in, so that we wouldn't know how much money we were spending on alcohol. Ruby had her hair braided on the beach. A jellyfish stung Rio. Gee relaxed, and the two of us got our groove on. This vacation was the big payoff for our stint in Korea. It was meant to be a blowout, one-time-only Far East adventure. At least, that's how I saw it. Afterward, I was ready to go home and get back to reality.

PUDONG VS. PUXI

Gee's company sent us back to China, this time to look for a place to live. Modern apartments with killer views versus old-world charm. Convenience versus square feet. It's like being on a game show. Only on *House Hunters International*, the couples always end up compromising—that's because it was their idea to move to Lisbon or Buenos Aires. I'm being shanghaied, so I'm not so open to compromise. I want a nice apartment in a cool neighborhood with a great view, and it's Jake's job to make that happen.

Gee and I are sitting in the back of the van, on opposite ends of the seat, each of us hugging our own window, watching the city unfold, our hands meeting in the middle, palms squeezing. It's funny how holding hands without speaking can allow you to have two completely different experiences together. Just the physical act of intertwining fingers can mask divergent inner monologues. Probably Gee's thinking, *This is so fucking awesome*, and I know I'm thinking, *This is so fucking crazy*. He shoulda been thinking his wife is a saint to consider moving to China with him, but, knowing Gee, he's thinking about his job and how he has five hundred emails to answer so we need to wrap up this apartment-hunting thing so that he can get back to work. I'm wondering who my friends will be. Will I walk to the wet market, casually pass the bullfrogs packed in mesh bags, and buy those green beans that are as long as jump ropes? Will I be happy cooking? Will cooking fill the hours of the day that I used to spend working?

We aren't holding hands with Jake, but there is an element of hand-holding in his job description: make the *lǎowài* feel comfortable about moving to China; help them find an apartment, open a bank account; hook 'em up with cell phones and metro passes; teach them to carry their own toilet paper and watch out for cars, because pedestrians do not have the right of way; show them where the expat hospital is, just in case. Don't forget to point out the Pearl Tower—that iconic, Jetsonian, "the future is now" landmark that flashes neon at night. Shanghai is touted as the Pearl of the Orient, and it does shine bright after dark. It's a city made for vampires, but in the dull light of day, there's a crumbling veneer of dirt, grime, and mildew.

"Why does everything look so ravaged?" I wonder out loud. Most of Shanghai was built in the past ten or twenty years, so why does it all look so preternaturally old?

"Accelerated decay," Gee says. The result of harsh environmental factors, coal burning, and sneaker factories. Not just shoes, obviously. Purses, textiles, auto aftermarket, agrochemicals, disinfectants, furniture, pharmaceuticals . . . You name it, most likely some part of it is made or glued together in Shanghai. Everything for sale cheap in the States blowing toxic smoke out of chimneys in China. No regulations. You can't call it deregulation because the Chinese have never even tried to keep the place clean. Our "sweet spot," Gee says, is apartment buildings that have been built in the past two to eight years. Before two years, there's off-gassing, glue and paint leaching, like a homegrown chemical spill, and after eight years, you deal with high-speed degeneration.

"I wonder what that does to the body."

"What?" Gee responds, like he can't quite make the cognitive leap from factories to flesh.

"Accelerated decay," I repeat. "I wonder how that impacts the human body."

"It's only three years, doll. Besides, you're not a high-rise," he says, pinching my thigh for emphasis. I don't say anything else. I've learned to keep my fears under wraps. He'll just dismiss them anyway. But also, I'm hoping he's right. That we'll get a free pass for three years.

■ ■

Since we've been married, we've lived in five cities in four countries across three continents. And that doesn't count the times Gee has moved overseas without the family, leaving me alone with a full-time job and a kid or two. This is not a normal life. Maybe it sounds spoiled and petty not to be wowed by our good fortune, but in a way, the good fortune is all his. Every time we relocate, I quit my job; every time we return, Gee moves up a rung on the corporate ladder. It's asking a lot of employees to uproot their lives and move to a foreign country. But that's what Gee signed on for—he works in project management, and he goes where the job is, whether that means a few months on a cruise ship to Alaska or a year building an expo in Osaka. It's asking more of *me* to tag along. In the past, this meant pulling the kids out of school and quitting my job; this time, it will mean shuttering my consulting business. Theoretically, I'm willing to do that, but so much rests on our ability to find a place that feels like it could be our home—clean and safe, convenient and comfortable.

No, that's not it—that's not nearly enough. Our house in Los Angeles is all of that and more. It's a 1950s postwar bungalow that we painstakingly renovated into an enviable hang. That's the thing we do best, me and Gee: fix up places. I work in the design industry now, and Gee's handy with a power tool. Our house is not grand but not shabby, *pas mal*, reasonably good: palm trees, kidney-shaped dipping pool in the backyard, friendly neighbors, and an unofficial off-leash dog park a few blocks away. On weekends, Gee fires up the grill and people come to chill. We have a life in LA, a good life, so in order for me to give it all up, an apartment in Shanghai will have to be way more than comfortable.

Jake throws the wow at us big-time. Apartments so ritzy, I joke that Gee must be a big shot now. Maybe that's why his jaw clenches so much on this trip. Gee's worried about this gig in China, but not the in-China part—he's worried about deadlines and budgets; he's worried about nuts and bolts. And he's worried that I might refuse to come, because this time I really am on the fence. I'm up there, swaying. Will she or won't she?

Jake is pushing Pudong, with its private elevators, marble floors, and gold-leaf powder rooms, so outrageously excessive I'm almost tempted to say yes just for the sheer, outlandish fun of it. For the social media bragging rights. You could roller-skate from the bedroom to the kitchen in a place this big. But we don't have little kids, and a formal dining room that seats ten will just make me feel their absence more acutely.

Anyway, Mina says we'll like Puxi better. This is how she explained the difference between Pudong and Puxi: Pudong is close to the international schools, but Puxi has the culture and great restaurants.

"You and Gee will be happier in Puxi," she assured me. "It's more authentic."

Such a polite way to say, *Now that you're empty nesters.*

Only we're not really empty nesters. Our kids haven't exactly moved out; they're just not coming with us to China. They're millennials. Rio is sort of in college, and Ruby is kind of working. They both have a revolving-door relationship with our house in Los Angeles; whenever one of them is in between jobs or schools or apartments, they move back home for a soft landing.

"I'm worried about leaving them alone," I tell Gee.

"They're adults," he says, reminding me that we were on our own at their age.

And it's true. We were in our twenties when we met. We fell hard,

like every love song ever made rolled into one. Birds chirping in sur-
round sound, the earth moving under our feet, we had Love On The
Brain. Six weeks later, Gee packed his bags and moved clear across
the country.

"Come with me," he urged, standing so close you couldn't slip a
piece of paper between us. "It'll be an adventure." He was in cutoffs,
hair bleached and spiky, wearing a ripped-up Slow Children T-shirt
(that's the name of the garage-punk band he roadied for), while I
leaned into him, whispering, "Baby, please don't go." Years we spent
trying to make a long-distance relationship work. I thought when I
finally followed him to California that Los Angeles would become
my new home—not just a home *base* or a place to store our things
while we lived overseas.

Puxi versus Pudong?

I hold on to what Mina says like it's solid science, because I need
to trust someone and I'm not sure we can trust Jake. Don't get me
wrong, I like Jake; he's chatty and easy to be with. But it feels like he's
hustling us, trying to fast-talk us into an apartment we'll end up being
miserable in for the next three years. We chat in the van in between
stops. He tells me how he met his wife during college in the States;
they got married in Vegas and moved back to Asia to cash in on being
Chinese and speaking English, but now his wife and kids are living
with her family in Taiwan and he's living alone in Shanghai, working. The lure of big bucks. So, in a way, we have similar lives. Global
nomads. Although my guess is that Jake lives in a shoebox outside
the city. I'm careful not to sound spoiled when turning my nose up
at these over-the-top luxury apartments. I politely tell him that we
don't need so much space. I want something that will feel like home,
not a game show. But more than that, I want something I don't have
in Los Angeles, which is urban life; I want to be able to walk out my
door and stroll down the street to a café or a museum. If our nest is
empty, I want our lives to be full. Maybe this will be a chance for me

and Gee to reconnect. To find out if, when we strip away the kids or a bathroom remodel, we still have something left to say to each other.

But Gee and I are just a file on Jake's desk; he's not concerned with our marriage. Jake has his own agenda—it's more about doing business with his real estate buddies than finding us our dream apartment. Jake and his pals high-five each other as they shuffle us into elevators in half-empty apartment buildings, speaking Chinese all the way to the fifty-second floor. These exchanges are called *guanxi*, which officially means "relationships that facilitate business dealings." In the States, we'd call them kickbacks.

"Wow," Gee says when he sees the view on our next stop. It makes me feel woozy. I close my eyes and dig my nails into my palms. Once, I was on a business trip in New York and got stuck in a hotel elevator for hours. It was crowded, too, everyone freaking out in different languages. At least it was glass; the entire hotel could see us suspended in air, so I knew we'd get out eventually. But these elevators are dark and small, and this is China.

Gee leans over the balcony in amazement. "Look at the river, Em. I bet this view is spectacular at night."

"It's a nice view, but then what?" I say. I don't tell Gee it makes me nervous to be so high. Instead I say, "I feel like Jake is trying to slam-dunk us into Pudong."

"Yeah," Gee agrees. "There's nothing but high-rises in Pudong. It's overbuilt and expat-friendly."

"That's why they call it Pujersey behind its back," I joke.

• •

I'm holding out for something charming. This is potentially the fourth relocation that Mina has handled for us. She gave me the lowdown on neighborhoods when she dropped off my visa and itinerary. Gee was already in China on an extended business trip. Mina stopped by our house on her way home from work. It was getting dark outside, and she looked worn out. I hear the company is moving hundreds of families for Gee's project. We were sitting on stools at my kitchen table, a restaurant-quality, stainless steel–and–butcher block work surface. This is the table where we do everything: carve turkeys, blow out birthday candles, play backgammon, work from home, and sometimes work out our differences. It bears the nicks and stains of our lives. I mention our kitchen table because it's something (else) I would have to leave behind, along with our kids and pooch, if I say yes to China. I know it's just a table, but it needs to be noted that I wasn't sitting in LA, thinking, *Damn, I've always wanted to visit the Great Wall and see those terra cotta warriors.*

"You and Gee will like Puxi," Mina said, as if she knows us—even though the three of us have never been in one room at the same time. She rattled off Puxi's advantages like a travel agent: art deco architecture, museums, and restaurants. "It's got everything," she said.

"Everything," I repeated. Let it roll on my tongue. Tasted the sound of it. And immediately, sight unseen, I knew that was where we should live.

■　■

Based on what Mina said, I have my heart set on the Former French Concession (FFC), on the Puxi side of the Huangpu River: storybook quaint; wide, tree-lined streets; boutiques and galleries; noodle shops and organic markets.

Jake shakes his head doubtfully, as if finding us a nice place in the FFC will be difficult. Instead, he shows us some crummy apartments, cramped and boxy little flats that would be perfect for a grad student. I don't even have to nix them; I can see Gee's jawline sharpen—there's that clenching again—when Jake tries to sell him on this complex by telling him how many of his coworkers will be living there, including his assistant. Gee's ego doesn't flare often, but this rankles him. And then Jake takes us to a building in the heart of the FFC that I nickname 4100 Cockroaches; I nix that one. When we suggest that he dig deeper, Jake says that maybe the FFC isn't in our budget and I say, "That's good to know, because I don't want to move to China anyway." That's when Gee smiles. He likes it when I get tough, as long as he's not the target.

"Maybe we should look at a serviced apartment," Gee suggests, "in case Em decides not to move to China." He squeezes my hand tight as he says this.

So Jake shows us a serviced apartment in Pudong, which is basically a bachelor pad with housekeeping. Functional and spotless. It has a bedroom, bathroom, couch, and TV, plus a kitchenette. Even a washer-dryer. It would be like living in a hotel for three years.

"I could do this, Em," Gee says. "You don't have to come."

And I don't. Nobody's holding a gun to my head. But three years is a long assignment. I'm having a hard time being okay with making Gee live here alone, and I know how hard separation can be on a marriage. And my design consulting business isn't nearly as lucrative as this opportunity for Gee, so it only makes sense that I should accompany him. Marriage is a partnership. That's what partners do. I just wish his success didn't always come at the expense of mine. That's happened slowly, over time; the decisions I've made along the way have not always been considered and logical. Life is complicated. It's not like he stole anything from me; it was more like a gift than a theft. I gave him my thunder, just handed it over. *Here, take the remains of what I hold dear.*

"We'll find something we love," Gee promises. He's talking about apartments. And then, really quietly, so Jake can't hear, he whispers, "We just have to push back harder than they push us."

■ ■

Here's what I know: Jake may not care about whether I move to Shanghai with Gee, but he does care about pleasing his boss, whose name is Kimberly. And Kimberly, well, she doesn't give a hoot about the status of our marriage either, but Gee's company is her cash cow, and that makes Mina *her* boss. And *Mina* says we'll like Puxi better than Pudong, and Shanghai has the good air, and what she doesn't say, what she doesn't need to say, is that it's her job to make sure Gee's company maintains the appearance of family values. That means keeping us together, as opposed to breaking up a marriage.

ÇA NE MARCHE PAS — IT DOESN'T WORK

I suck as a tagalong wife. The thought occurred to me as I was walking home late one night, so late it was nearly morning, the streets so quiet, the only sound was the click of my heels on pavement. Real heels, not sneakers or rubber soles like I wear in Los Angeles. We're talking boots, buttery leather, the kind that pull up and hug your calf, soft and tight, almost second skin. Bought them during *les soldes*. The rest of the year, I walked around the Marais, nose pressed against shop windows, eyeing architecturally designed white shirts and handmade purses, making mental notes, waiting patiently for the sales to begin; that's when Frenchwomen pounce. Only tourists pay full price. And I was not a tourist. I was not an expat, either. I was something in between: year two of a four-year overseas post—not long enough to speak proper French, but just long enough to know how to shop like a real Frenchwoman. In Paris, the best sales only come twice a year: January and June. Talk about pent-up desire.

It was the wee hours, when all good wives are tucked into bed next to their husbands, and there I was, stumbling along back streets, my dress wrinkled, smelling like a wine-soaked ashtray. I was gonna pretend I sucked because I had no real homemaking skills, which is true, but that would be a skim-over. I wanted to slip it in on the sly, the whole thing about the poet. How I ran around with him during the day, drinking half a carafe of rosé at lunch, Côtes de Provence, then showed up at school late on the back of his moped. My kids waiting in front of the ivy-covered entrance on Rue du Ranelagh, Headmistress V. standing between them with an arm draped over each tiny shoulder. The three of them glaring at me.

I wanted to gloss over my struggle to do the simplest household tasks, like how to work the appliances or write a check for eighty-five euros without needing a dictionary to spell *quatre-vingt-cinq*, which explains why I paid the electric bill and the gas bill in cash, scheduled a repairman in person, and spent an entire morning standing in line, as the salesman in the BHV appliance department asked questions and I repeated, "*Ça ne marche pas*" over and over, like some mad-housewife mantra. *It doesn't work, it doesn't work, it doesn't work*, and no, I can't describe in French the exact malfunction: that it starts and stops and sputters, sometimes making a high-pitched whining noise; that other times it clunks and clangs so loudly, I'm afraid the neighbors will complain. All I knew how to say was, "It's not working." *Ça ne marche pas.* And you know we're not talking about washing machines anymore, right?

We move around a lot, on account of Gee's job. Most often the focus is on what we stand to gain. And usually, it's financial. But also, you lose things in a move. It's inevitable. Sure, some of it is just stuff, books and kitchen gadgets, but some of it is more ephemeral. Things you can't hold in your hand or pack in a box. Sometimes you don't even know what's at stake.

Year one was a mess. I sad-sacked around Paris, living my life like it was a jail sentence. Trying to keep it all together. Trying to get the family settled, open a bank account, learn the language, and understand the layout of the city. Trying, above all other things, to make my marriage work and raise well-adjusted children. Often these goals seemed at odds with each other. The kids had been happy in Los Angeles. Paris was exciting for about ten days, like any vacation: *Kids, look! The Tour Eiffel!* And then, pretty quickly, the shine wore off. The Eiffel Tower was just something we passed on the way home from the international school, when we got off the metro at Trocadéro and walked through Champs du Mars toward our temporary housing, an old and musty apartment with little light and even less heat. Every day Ruby and Rio dropped their backpacks at the door and immediately ran to their room and crawled under the covers. The apartment was dark; the children, exhausted from trying to fit in at a new school, regressed into afternoon nappers. I spent my days hunting for an apartment, preferably one with lots of light, and shopping for little gifts for the kids, just so I could see them smile: a new Lego set for Rio, a bedazzled Paris T-shirt for Ruby. I'd make mac and cheese for dinner. With ice cream for dessert. No veggies! No Daddy, either—Gee's commute was long; usually he came home after the kids were asleep.

Year two, I got busy with the PTA and the tagalong crowd: three-hour, Michelin-star meals in the middle of the day. (There's an expat tip for you: When you go to Paris, forget about fancy dinners and splurge on lunch at the best restaurants instead; they offer amazing set menus at affordable prices.) Spent every euro Gee made eating and shopping. And I took a writing class with one of the other moms from the kids' elementary school. "It'll give us something to do besides eating." She laughed, tugging at the waistband of her slacks. She had an engineering degree from MIT that put my business degree to shame, and she was not an ounce overweight—she was bored. I was bored *and* lonely, so I decided to join her. As it turned out, I have a knack for storytelling: A few of my pieces were published in a literary journal, and I was invited to read at a club near the Bastille.

Gee couldn't make it—something about an executive team dinner. We were living in Paris together in only the most basic sense: We shared a bed, but our lives had gone in different directions. I was in charge of cooking, cleaning, and kids. He was bringing home the bacon. That wasn't the deal when we got married. There was no deal, no prenup on my career aspirations; we just fell in love and got married. We were both in the music industry. I never imagined that his job would trump mine. Or that he'd *ever* choose dinner with a bunch of suits over a live gig at a club. Especially one that was headlining me.

"You'll have other readings," Gee said. "I'll come to the next one," he promised. But this was my first, and it wasn't just a big deal—it was a once-in-a-lifetime, bucket list sort of thing. I wore a beret and read a story called "Chloe Has a Bad Day," a piece I wrote about pre-sexualized girls in LA and parents who weren't paying attention. I worried, it being Paris, that people wouldn't care about spoiled California girls. But they laughed. I was standing behind a podium in a bar near the Place des Vosges, reading my story out loud, and the room was humming along with laughter. A person could get high on a thing like that.

Gee wasn't around to share the experience, but the poet was there. His hair unkempt, kind of disheveled, like he had just tumbled out of bed. His presence reminded me to slow down. "You're going too fast," he noted time and again when coaching me for this reading, trying to get me to deliver a more theatrical performance. He was grinning at me from the back of the room, as if I were his protégée. His undiscovered talent.

"You're like a mushroom," he once observed. When I asked why, he said because they grow in the shade. He held this idea of me living in the shadow of my husband's international career. He called me Madame because I was married, sneering ever so slightly when he said it, just enough so I knew he was being sarcastic. I called him Bleu because he wore blue shoes; it seemed a sartorial choice. Later, I realized he bought those shoes on sale, like everyone else who wasn't a tourist, because they were all he could find in his size. Blue shoes.

We celebrated my literary debut at Le Petit Bofinger: classic French decor, crisp linens and cherrywood banquettes, on the ceiling a flying saucer–size Tiffany lamp, all fragmented glass and mirrored walls. "What will you have, Madame?" Bleu asked, his voice low and deep, a saxophone dipped in molasses. He spoke just above a whisper, forcing me to lean in to hear him, compelling me to stay there to respond.

"Everything," I said. "I want it all." I didn't fancy myself the kind of woman who made the kiddies dinner, put them to bed, and waited for her husband to come home with tales of corporate intrigue and ten-course meals. I had my own dragons to slay.

We ordered the raw platter, french fries, and a carafe of chilled Chablis. And *mi-cuit au chocolat.* Molten chocolate cake. Hot lava cake. The kind of cake that is meant to be shared and eaten with a spoon. We were upstairs, tucked away in a back booth. He smelled of cigarettes and dirty laundry. I knew sex with him wouldn't be tidy. We weren't having sex; I was just thinking that if someone did, with him, it wouldn't be. And if someone were going to, well, this would be a fairy-tale beginning.

His smile said, *I know what you're thinking.*

I shot back a look that said, *Show me.*

It was like the time my brother stood in the middle of our parents' living room, holding a Mexican cherry bomb in one hand and a match in the other, and my sister dared him to light it. For one brief moment, after he blew up the stained-glass windows and before we knew how much trouble we were in, I looked at him and said, "That was awesome!" We were singed, glowing from the inside out; his fingers were hot to the touch. That's how it felt with the poet. After dinner, I stumbled home and slipped into bed next to Gee. He draped his arm around me reflexively, without even waking. He's a sound sleeper.

CORSICA

If this were another kind of expat story, I'd be telling you about all the places I've seen, the stamps on my passport, the slide show of my life. FYI, that's the reason expats have such a hard time repatriating: because their friends back home don't really care about their road trip through the South of France, sleeping in funky castles. Or that the monkeys in Ubud will come right up to you, sit on your shoulder, and groom you if you let them. If you want to hear about riding elephants in Chiang Mai, the street food in Hanoi, or the jungle ruins in Siem Reap, there are plenty of other books you can read.

But let me tell you about Corsica. Corsica is an itty-bitty island in the Mediterranean that's technically French, surrounded by Italy, and attracts a ton of German tourists. And us. Me and Gee. On holiday while living in Paris. We dropped the kids off for summer camp at a run-down château in the Loire Valley and flew to Corsica. Landed in Ajaccio, on the wrong side of the island, and had to drive all day to the apartment in Bastia I had booked for the week.

I thought Gee would shoot me. But here's the thing about him: He's pretty easygoing. So we rented a car and made our way through dense forests and wild horses and backwoods country so beautiful that Gee said it was the best mistake I'd ever made. At one point we had to stop and wait for a herd of sheep to cross the road. We got to Bastia around dusk, drove by our flat on some ancient cobblestone street, looked at each other, and shook our heads no, deciding to explore the beach instead. So we dumped the flat, forfeited the deposit, and headed south to find a place that was so beachy, we woke up with waves slapping at our sliding glass door. We were in heaven.

I'm gonna come right out and admit that if this were opposite day and Gee had planned that trip and we had landed in the wrong city and had to drive eight hours across the island to a flat in a walled-in medieval town that we didn't even want to step foot in, let alone sleep at, I might have been pissy. But not Gee. He woke up happy.

"Let's go find coffee," he said, giving me a morning hug.

Gee and I have always traveled well together. No plans, no guidebooks, no agenda, content to wander aimlessly. A few days of that, and I was falling in love with him all over again. We ambled south to Porto-Vecchio, hitting every beach town on the way, lying in the sand, slathering sunscreen on each other's backs.

I'm a pretty good swimmer, but Gee's a beach potato. He grew up in Maine, where all they do is sit and watch the water ebb and flow, like an animated postcard, the ocean too cold to wade in. I grew up in the Mitten, where you get dirty-sweaty wet canoeing in rivers and swimming in lakes, so I went out way past the buoys, where the water was still like glass, beautiful and calm, and then—boom—sharks!

Do they have sharks in the Mediterranean? I wondered.

Maybe that was why the buoys were so close to the beach. My heart started to race; my mind filled with pointy teeth lurking just under the glassy surface. I turned and headed toward shore, but then I thought how silly it was to be afraid of sharks in this most idyllic and calm paradise, so I turned around and started swimming farther out, past the buoys, again. Alone. Freestyling. Occasionally diving like a dolphin, my hair slicked back straight, black like oil, when my head came up for air. I've got a swimmer's body: broad shoulders, my torso an inverted triangle, lean hips and legs. I'm completely at home in the water, but I'm used to the Great Lakes and lap pools, no undertow. Or sharks. Then the whole shark thing popped up in my head again and I circled back toward the beach, slagging myself for being such a weenie. Around and around I flipped, a few strokes farther out, followed by a sudden retreat, at war with the monster in my mind, eventually coming to a dead stop, treading water, doing 360s, my head and body whipping one direction and then the other, before finally and in a complete panic I made a mad sharks-on-my-tail dash for the beach, heart pounding so loud I could hear it thumping when I lay down next to Gee.

"Sharks," I said.

"I know," he replied. "I was watching you."

Gee knows better than anyone the misfire in my brain. Knows but doesn't understand. I was still in that second-honeymoon fantasy, thinking our marriage would work if I just asked for what I wanted, so I sat up and said, in the sanest, most rational voice I could muster, "I need you to sit behind me, straddle my body with your legs, wrap your arms around me, and whisper, just whisper into my ear, 'There are no sharks.' Tell me I'm safe."

"There are no sharks, Em," he said in that flat, facts-only tone of his that shattered the fix.

"Please, Gee."

"It's all in your head, Em."

"I know, Gee. I know there are no sharks. Of course it's all in my head—that's why it's called anxiety. But I didn't bring Xanax to the beach. So I need a hug. Please."

"I'm not going to pander to your neurotic fears," he said, listing them under his breath, as if to emphasize the ridiculousness of it all—cockroaches, elevators, spider bites, small spaces, and now sharks—before returning to his LA-noir gumshoe-detective story.

In all fairness, Gee doesn't believe in God, either. Things you can't see, touch, or weigh don't exist in my husband's world. I curled up in a tight ball, arms wrapped around my legs, head tucked into my knees, and rocked back and forth, hugging myself, feeling crushed by the whole *Should I stay or should I go?* question of us, the clash, the dead end of me going back to an empty well, over and over again. *Just breathe*, I told myself, digging my fingers into my own flesh, until the only pain I could feel was real, until I could see the imprint of my nails on my skin. My mind focused on the sensation of the sun burning the back of my neck. *You're okay*, I assured myself. *There are no sharks.*

REPATRIATION BLUES

Moving home is never as easy as it sounds. I was standing in a supermarket, holding a purple vegetable in the shape of a giant teardrop, trying desperately to remember the word for *aubergine* in English. It was summer in Los Angeles, and even though it was hot outside, the market felt like a walk-in refrigerator.

"Eggplant!" I blurted out loud like a crazy person. No one noticed.

I missed the shops on Rue Bretagne, the street vendor who sold *rôti* chicken on a spit, potatoes broiling in fat dripping beneath the birds. Cheese shops and wine shops and baguettes so warm and crusty, the kids devoured them like candy. I had to buy two at time: one to savor fresh, the other to save for dinner. Forget about keeping them overnight—they'd be stale by the next morning. This memory made me want to go home, and I don't mean our rental in LA. Putting the eggplant in my basket, I grabbed a bottle of wine to take to Nadia's. She was hosting a welcome-back dinner for us, and I had promised to bring this vegetarian caviar dish I learned how to make in Paris.

■　■

Let's back up a few months, to when we found out that Gee's overseas assignment in Paris was coming to an end. I called an emergency family meeting at Chez Omar, the Moroccan restaurant a few blocks from our apartment in the Marais. Nothing fancy—couscous and shish kebabs—but they didn't mind that we brought our pooch, Chandler, and let him sit on his fuzzy sheepskin pad by our feet, eating table scraps. We had gone native. It happens to expats. We weren't just living in Paris; after four years, we fancied ourselves locals. Tourists walked up to me on the street and said *excusez-moi* before asking directions in really bad French.

"Guys," I said in total seriousness, "we cannot move back to Los Angeles."

Round the table we went, taking turns imagining where we should go next. Rio said he wanted to stay in Paris. That's so Rio; he does not like change. Ruby said she wanted to move to Ohio. Ohio! She's never even been to Ohio. Said she wanted a house with a white picket fence and a yard for the dog to play in. It hit me that Ruby was describing my own childhood. We gave her the world, but all she wanted was a normal American life. Gee was the only one who said Los Angeles. Not because he wanted to go back to LA; he just wanted me to get with the program and accept reality. I said Spain, because my Spanish is better than my French. But of course, Gee was right. We were moving back to Los Angeles.

.　.

"You really fucked up," Nadia's husband said to us as soon as we walked in the door of their house for dinner. *I know*, I was thinking. *We never should have come back to the States.*

"Never shoulda sold your house in Silverlake," Willy continued.

It was an odd sort of greeting, just this side of gloating. *He's so American*, I thought. *Big and dumb, no boundaries.* That's how they view us overseas. He was wearing a retro '50s flowered shirt, tailored, not oversize—kitsch elevated to Los Feliz cool.

"Your house in the hills," Willy continued. "What'd you sell that for?" Like a dog with a bone, he was not going to let our real estate fiasco go unnoticed. For years, we lived in the hills and they lived in the flats. That irked them big-time. They paid attention to stuff like that: who has what, shops where, lives in the hills or the flats.

"We did okay on the house," Gee said, sidestepping the conversation. My husband does not like to talk about finances in public.

"Well, whatever it was *then*, you could never afford to buy it back *now*." Willy laughed.

Nadia gave me a hug. "Good to be home?" she asked.

Nadia and I were friends through our daughters, Zoey and Ruby. We carpooled, babysat each other's children, and traveled together as families so the girls would have someone to play with. She was a fashion editor, the kind of woman who kisses your cheek and inhales your whole outfit—shoes, hair, and clothes—in one breath, doesn't miss a thread, then passes judgment before you've even had a chance to say hello. During awards season, she freelanced as a stylist. I suspected she spent a lot of time on her knees, pinning hems and sucking up to celebrities, so I let it slide. The constant comparisons. The backhanded compliments. The jealous, bitchy shit.

"Ooh! This is nice," she said, fingering my brightly colored cotton blouse with bell sleeves. "Where did you get it?"

"Senegal," I told her, relieved to have passed muster.

"Whaaaaat! Senegal! When did you go there?"

"Last year," I said. "On the kids' winter break. I wanted to go somewhere warm. . . ." My voice faded out—she wasn't listening anyway. She didn't care *when* I had gone; she was just registering that I had gone somewhere so exotic, somewhere so *not* Mexico or Hawaii. Somewhere fabulous where she hadn't been. My living in Paris was bad enough, but Senegal? It was too much for her to handle.

"You're too much!" she exclaimed. "Senegal!"

She didn't ask a thing about the trip, so I didn't bother telling her that we stayed in Somone, a town so off the grid that goats ambled down Main Street. Not a word of English spoken—just Wolof and French. I had tons of pictures of the kids all over the world, looking like little bored travelers: ho-hum—another church, another castle. But this was an adventure. *Kids! Look! A bird sanctuary! We're in Africa!*

We stayed a block from the beach at the most unpretentious, totally chill hotel called Club Djembé. At night it had drumming and dance performances with tiki torches. It was authentic, too, not a tacky, hipster, Hollywood hangout. But Ruby and Rio were not happy on that trip, even though Ruby got to go deep-sea fishing and Rio collected cool stamps for his school project. We had to taxi to M'Bour, the only nearby town big enough to have a post office, to buy the stamps. It was packed with women wearing colorful headdresses and men in long flowy garb. The kids were out of their comfort zone, they huddled together on a bench in the back, pouting.

"Kids, c'mon—we're on a family vacation!" I tried to cajole them later over soft drinks and chips, hoping to rally their spirits.

"It's not a family vacation if it's just the three of us," Rio said.

Gee didn't come. He practically has to be forced to take time off work, especially overseas. By the time he gets sent to a job site, the clock is ticking and the project is on a deadline. But that only partly explains Gee's workaholism. It has more to do with his father's being an artist, creative but not particularly motivated to make money. There were a few years when Gee was growing up that his dad was out of work and the whole family had to live at the grandparents' house. Hamburger Helper and Jell-O pudding. A rough patch like that doesn't just stay with you; it forms you.

Ruby sulked in Senegal too. But not because it was just the three of us. She didn't like our hotel; she complained that it was another thatched-roof hut in the middle of nowhere. Zoey's family always goes to Hawaii, she reminded me; they stay at a fancy hotel with a giant pool slide and room service. Why couldn't we ever stay someplace like that, she wanted to know. "It's like you intentionally find the crummiest place on Earth," she whined, "and that's where you take us." She folded her arms across her chest in protest.

Zoey came running into the house, shadowed by Ivy, her new mini-me—her Ruby replacement.

"Where's Ruby?" I asked.

"In the pool," Zoey said flippantly. And then, reading my expression, she added, "She didn't want to come. True swear."

Zoey and Ruby had been best friends before we moved to Paris. They did everything together. Wore matching outfits, giggled in the back seat of my car, and practically lived at each other's houses. They were like sisters. That was four years ago. This new version of Zoey was standing on the staircase in a bikini top and short shorts, on her way upstairs to her bedroom with her new best friend, who was wearing a see-through mesh top over a black bra and tight jeans. Eighth grade going on eighteen. The girls turned and ran upstairs together, legs and hair flying.

Willy laughed, saying, "Zoey can be a mean girl." It was half apology, half proud papa. Nadia always nurtured this side of their daughter; she thought it meant Zoey would grow up to be a strong woman. I wished they hadn't invited Zoey's new best friend to Ruby's homecoming dinner. It seemed insensitive, at best.

"Do you want me to go upstairs and talk to Zoey?" Willy offered.

The last thing I wanted was for Zoey's dad to force his daughter to be nice to mine. Instead, I went outside to find Ruby; she was in the pool with Rio. "What's up, kids?" I asked. Ruby didn't answer. She didn't need to; I could imagine how she was feeling. Her old best friend had a new best friend. It must have hurt like a broken heart. And on top of that, she'd had to leave *her* new best friend in Paris. She climbed out of the pool, wearing a T-shirt over her bathing suit to cover up her changing body, fleshy and self-conscious, and stood there, sopping wet, eyes red. I wondered if she'd been crying, but it could have just been the chlorine.

"Do you have another top?" I asked her.

"Nah," she said, wringing out the corner of her ISP T-shirt,

International School of Paris, like it was a security blanket she didn't ever want to take off.

"Can we go home?" Rio wanted to know.

■   ■

Repatriation is hard. They don't tell you that when you move overseas. The company warns you all about culture shock and provides global sensitivity training, but it leaves out the worst part: coming home and not fitting in. Here's what happened. I'm just gonna give you the CliffsNotes on how our first year back in Los Angeles played out. Willy was right: The real estate market was sky high. We couldn't afford a teardown in our old neighborhood, much less buy back our dream house in the hills—the one we sold because we wanted to enjoy the expat life. We were living in the now, baby! That house paid for our trips to Senegal, Italy, Morocco, and Amsterdam.

"You're in multiple bids," our real estate agent told us over the phone, international long distance. We thought that was a good thing. Multiple bids! Really, it just meant we had something everyone else wanted. Something we undervalued. A real home. In a desirable community. Where we knew our neighbors and our kids went to school with the kids down the street.

When Gee's project ended, we moved back to LA, tails between our legs, as renters. And we leased the Barbie house. In the Valley. Not just in the Valley but in the flats, no winding canyon streets or hillside views, instead we heard cars screeching and helicopters overhead. That house had all the rooms we needed. It was real cozy, just miniature in size, like a dollhouse. In a way, it worked for us. Being an expat can bust up a marriage or make you a tight-knit family unit. We came home snug and smug, woven together.

Repatriation gave us a bunker mentality. Sure, we couldn't touch our old neighborhood, but we didn't want to live there anyway. We may have become renters, but we were also Euro snobs: fresh produce, good wine, quality over quantity. Paris had ruined us for LA. The food, the fashion, the architecture, the art. The metro system, for God's sake! Even the weather—wrapping up in coats and boots and hats and drinking hot cocoa at Angelina's, where the chocolate is so thick you can stand a spoon in it. It was hard to move back to the States after living in France. We knew Target wasn't French even if you pronounced it *Tarjay*, like Nadia did. And we had no appetite for cruff, a word Rio made up that refers to the crappy stuff Americans buy to fill up their lives. We said "Americans" as if they were not us and we were not them; we no longer belonged. Anywhere. Our cachet was crashing; we didn't have that hipster pad in the hills, no longer could anyone introduce us as "our friends who live in Paris."

I won't even go into detail about every uncomfortable phone call with so-called friends who were too cool to visit us in the Valley. The excuses so lame, you wouldn't believe: "It's so far"; "It's too hot"; "The traffic"; "I grew up in the Valley!" Meaning, *I couldn't wait to get out.* Or how Ruby's old friends disappeared into thin air and how Rio's school had me on speed dial because he was having "adjustment issues." Everybody expected us to come home from Paris the same as we were before we moved. To pick up where we'd left off, unchanged. Or, worse, changed in some fabulous way. "Ruby must be sooooo sophisticated now," Nadia exclaimed on the telephone when she invited us for that welcome-home fiasco. She meant transformed, like Audrey Hepburn in *Sabrina*, into a gamine, pixie dream girl. *That* kind of sophisticated. As if somehow living in France meant girls could skip over the awkward middle-school phase. Ruby *was* sophisticated, in ways that weren't so easy to see. She was worldly, well traveled; she spoke French with an almost flawless accent. She didn't look like a Cali girl anymore. She seemed younger, more innocent; she dressed more modestly than her American friends. That's because she'd been living in an international environment where young girls were not influenced by Hollywood culture. She went to

Paris an LA girl, and she came back a TCK (third-culture kid)—not French, not American, totally comfortable in a room full of global nomads. The kind of life experience her girlfriends in Los Angeles didn't understand or value.

■ ■

"You need to make new friends," Dr. B. Queensly suggested.

"Add that to the list," I laughed. "I've got to get my kids situated in new schools, update my résumé, reboot my professional network, and somehow get a job. *And* you want me to make new friends?"

"What I mean is, you need to make an effort to reestablish community here in Los Angeles," she advised. "Expand your social circle. Reach out to people with whom you've lost touch. Four years is a long time, and you've fallen off their radar. Maybe join a book club. How does that sound?"

"It sounds like a lot of work."

It would have been easier if I had actually been *from* Los Angeles. My roots there would have been stronger. I'd have family. All I had was Gee. And he wasn't much help. He didn't have the same issues when we repatriated. Sure, he had the superficial "Lost in the Supermarket" stuff, but—let's get real—he came home from an overseas post, took a week or two off work to get resituated, and then Monday morning, bright and early, he was back at the office. With the same boss, the same team. It was the kids and I who floundered. And on top of the whole real estate debacle, there was the financial reality that without Gee's expat package, we needed a second income. So I had to get my life together—fast.

My life. Two one-syllable words. Huge concept. I needed a job.

■ ■

"Come work with me," Andra offered over coffee served in paper cups. With plastic lids. Even though we were not taking it to go. We were sitting two feet from the counter where we'd ordered our drinks. Andra was working at a media rep firm that handled a hot new architecture-and-design publication. The kind of magazine that featured beautiful people running around gorgeous modern homes barefoot, in linen. "Design is the new rock 'n' roll," she joked. "All you have to do is run the office, answer phones, and maybe help with pitches and proposals—the sort of thing you can do in your sleep, Em. It's just part-time. It would be a huge help to me, and we'd get to work together again!"

It was perhaps the least professional job I had been offered since I'd graduated from college, barely a smidge above being a secretary. But I grabbed it. We needed the money. And I wanted the flexibility—the kids still had to be dropped off and picked up. Anyway, I was pretty sure they were sending Gee back to Japan in a year. It wasn't even worth it to put my résumé together and look for something more substantial. That could take months. By the time I found a professional position with flexible hours, I'd just have to quit. And, to be honest, I couldn't wait to get out of LA.

GOMEN NASAI — SORRY, NOT SORRY

"I'm not moving to Tokyo!" Ruby screamed, flying down the hall and slamming her bedroom door, before blasting Linkin Park on her boom box.

Rio headed to the kitchen. "What's for dinner?" he asked.

It was like the kids had switched bodies. Rio was my constant concern when we lived in Paris, but now he was all chill about Tokyo and Ruby was the one having a full-on meltdown.

"You know how she gets," Rio said, his face in the fridge. "She's just being a drama queen; she'll get over it. Want some?" he asked, pulling out a box of leftover pizza.

I shook my head no.

"Don't do it!" he yelled at the back of my head as I followed Ruby down the hall into her room.

Rio was right; I shouldn't have barged into Ruby's room. I should have given her space, should have let her cry it out, should have respected her emotional process. You know what else I should have done? I should have let her live with Celia. Let her stay in Los Angeles and move in with her best friend's family. I didn't even consider that as an option, even though she begged me—they both did, Ruby and Celia, two against one, promising to focus on school and get good grades—but no, I had to keep the family together. What was I thinking? I was thinking, *Ruby's sixteen, and before you know it, she'll be off to college and it will never be the four of us again.* I wanted the family to be together, even if it meant moving to Japan, and I needed Ruby to get with the program, so I barged into her bedroom.

Her room looked like a tornado had blown through: moldy dishes in her underwear drawer, half-empty cans of soda littered on the desk, cookies and magazines scattered, her entire wardrobe balled up and dropped carelessly. It's embarrassing to admit how many times I have screamed, "Clean up your room" at that girl, mostly because I know for sure that somewhere there is a picture of me at about the same age, holding a teacup pup in my lap, making that silly excuse for a dog wave at the camera like my very own fur baby. In that photo, I'm wearing a peasant blouse, rocking an Acapulco tan, and smiling the most blissfully blind teenage smile you can imagine, while less than two feet away from me, on the floor, is a dirty little rock-hard dog turd. Ruby and me, we're like the apple and the tree.

■　■

When Ruby was a little girl, we were almost preternaturally connected. She used to climb into my bed in the stillness of morning and snuggle up close. One morning when she was about five years old, we were lying there and I was stroking her hair, thinking, *She is the same age I was when I broke my leg.* That morning, with Ruby curled up at my side, was the first time in my life that I ever considered the accident from my mother's perspective: how frightened she must have been to find her baby on the front lawn, broken; the sheer panic that caused her to throw me into the back seat of the car, not realizing an ambulance to the hospital might make more sense. Maybe she couldn't bear to stand by, waiting helplessly. She must have been in shock, out of her mind, unable to think anything other than *Please, God, let this not be a big deal, let this be something the pediatrician down the street can fix.* Or maybe she was tipsy. That's a possibility too. I was at home with the housekeeper and the handyman while Mom was out playing mah-jongg with the girls when it happened. Not that I judge her.

Okay, what a crock of shit—we all judge our moms, our girl-friends, our daughters. And ourselves. Judge and compare. But, that morning, for the first time, my heart felt the depth of my mother's fear. I don't know where she found the strength. I'm not sure I could handle a Ruby crisis. Andra says you get the shit you can take, like it's custom-made, which is just a hokey way of saying, "You rise to the occasion or the adversity." My full-body cast catapulted my mother into supermom mode. That's what I was thinking about when Ruby interrupted my thoughts to say, "That must have hurt, Mommy."

"What, honey?" I asked. We hadn't even been speaking.

"When you broke your leg."

Being a mother is mysterious. The connection between Ruby and me was beyond sight and sound. It was subterranean. It lived at a cellular level. I telepathed and she received. That's how close we were. *When she was six.* Ruby at sixteen was a whole other kind of relationship.

• •

"Why can't Dad go to Tokyo and we stay here?"

"Because, Ruby, I want the family to be together."

"I hate this family," she screeched. "Why do we always have to move? This is not normal—you know that, don't you? This is not a normal life."

Then she burst into tears, like it was the end of the world. She was wearing her deep blue and silver one-piece competition jumpsuit.

"I'm gonna lose my spot on dance guard," she cried. "It's all your fault."

"That's not fair," I told her. "It's your dad's fault; it's his job that's dragging us to Tokyo, not mine."

"You always do that—" she said, "blame Dad. I get that it's his job and he has to move; I'm not stupid. What I don't get is why you have to go too."

"I'm just trying to be a good wife," I said.

"Why don't you try being a good mother?"

"I'm trying to do both, Ruby, but it's not easy."

"What about your job? You're just going to quit, aren't you? What is wrong with you, anyway? It *is* all your fault, because *you're* going to follow Daddy and that's the only reason Rio and I have to go too. I don't understand why Daddy can't move to Japan without us."

"Well, there's a lot you don't understand," I said.

I wasn't going to tell her the reality, scare her off marriage and destroy the Disney princess fantasy she swirled in, layers of tulle with powder blue butterflies. "That's the dress I want to wear to my wedding," she said at ten years old. We were window-shopping in Paris, and no doubt she could describe that dress in perfect detail today, that dress she has committed to memory. Unlike French. I bellied up to her pity party, saying I knew just how she felt, that I didn't want to go to Tokyo either. Tried to make it sound like we were in the same boat, girlfriends waiting for the phone to ring—laying it on thick, cajoling, commiserating—but in the end I reality-checked my daughter.

"We're moving to Tokyo, Ruby. As a family. You're coming, and you don't have a choice in the matter."

"I thought life was all about choices," she snapped back. "Every time I leave the house, it's 'Make good decisions, Ruby.' Not 'I love you' or 'Goodbye, Ruby; have a great day, Ruby'—it's always 'Make good decisions.' Why don't you practice what you preach, for once? Celia's mom says I can live with them. Just because you don't have friends or a job you love doesn't mean I don't have friends and a school I love. You're ruining my life."

And that's when I said, "Ruby, honey, c'mon; it'll be an adventure.

Tokyo!" And when that didn't work, I went with increments of time. "It's only a year," I said, sounding just like Gee, like I had Stockholm syndrome, channeling Patty Hearst, Tanya in combat fatigues with a machine gun, sleeping with her captor.

"It'll be fun," I said.

"For you, maybe."

"For us. We're a family."

"I'm not going," she whined. "You can't make me." She curled up in a fetal position and began to twist her hair around her index finger for comfort, signaling that she was done with the conversation. As I was leaving her room, she slipped in one last dig. "Oh, and Mom," she said, not even looking at me, "those pants . . ." meaning my new skinny jeans, camo-style, with zippers at the ankles.

"Yeah?"

"You're too old for them."

■ ■

Someday Ruby will pull these international experiences out of her back pocket at a cocktail party and she'll thank me. That's what Andra always says. It's like money in the conversation bank. Andra is my biggest supporter, and she loves Ruby, but what she knows about parenting can fit in a bottle cap. She shows up for the fun stuff, birthdays and BBQs, and the kids love her. But she was wrong about this. Japan was life-defining for Ruby, and not in a good way. She dug her heels in, cut-off-your-nose-in-spite angry. When she wasn't eating or moping about the house, she was barhopping in Roppongi—karaoke and smoking *shisha* with the expat kids. She had a boyfriend in the navy. I know this only because I snooped and found pictures of her with a sailor in her desk drawer (one of those black-and-white strips that spit out of a photo booth). She didn't actually use that desk, just the drawers. She failed almost all of her classes that year. Even French. Four years in Paris, and Ruby flunked French at the American School in Japan. Failing was her way of saying "fuck you" to Gee and me. Only it was eleventh grade, so she was really saying "fuck you" to college. Someday, she'll cut me some slack and stop blaming me for the year she got dragged to Japan, like I stopped blaming my mom for the accident, but I will always feel responsible for the fallout.

■   ■

"Why don't you just stop someone and ask for directions?" Andra asked.

It was cherry blossom season, and Andra was visiting us in Tokyo, sweating, blisters forming on her pampered toes. She was wearing the wrong shoes, her purse the size of a gym bag, way too heavy for traipsing around the city—the kind of purse you throw in the passenger seat of your car when you only have to carry it from there to the office. It was full too. She was prepared for anything but being lost. She was packing a phone, a travel guide, a notebook and pens, a wallet, makeup, tissues. Eye drops. Hand cream. Aspirin. Gum. Hand sanitizer. She was a mobile drugstore. And now her shoulder *and* her feet were killing her, but she looked great.

"Brazilian blowout," she told me. "Best beauty treatment ever—wash and go."

I kinda missed her big hair; it was statement hair. It said, *She wild; she up all night dancing.* Now it said *slick and corporate.*

I was trying to find this ramen restaurant I went to once with my friend Mebae. The thing is, I didn't know the name of the restaurant or exactly where it was. Usually I could find it on foot, which eventually we would have. Usually I had nothing better to do than wander up and down back streets in Shibuya until I spotted this particular noodle shop, with the indigo curtains flapping in the doorway. But Andra and I were out of sync. She was jet-lagged, starting to look at me sideways, like she was about to lose her shit. She was not impressed with my basic survival skills, my ability to experience being lost as an opportunity to explore the city, and I could tell she didn't like Shibuya, which admittedly can be overwhelming. The first time Gee brought me to Shibuya Crossing, I burst into tears. *No way can I live here*, I thought. Too many people. The largest, craziest intersection in the world; it split in five directions. Huge video screens mounted on every building, advertisements everywhere I looked, lights flashing, and enough people to fill a stadium. So congested, I felt like I could lift my feet and the smash of human bodies would carry me across the street without my toes ever touching the ground. After a while, I got used to it and just went with the flow. But now I deferred to Andra's sore feet and we stopped to eat at the next noodle shop we happened upon. It had laminated menus with pictures of ramen bowls.

"How do you live like this?" Andra wanted to know—meaning, perpetually lost. "You have a favorite restaurant," she said, "and you don't even know the name of it or what street it's on. We just spent an hour and a half walking in circles, and it doesn't faze you. Nothing does. You don't even care what shows up on your plate."

It was true. I pointed to the veggies and Andra pointed to the pork, but when our bowls came, mine was loaded with shrimp and all I did was shrug.

"That's not what you ordered," Andra said accusingly, like it was my fault that the waitress messed up my order, but really what she meant was, *Send it back!*

While she was pointing out how I'd become a spineless, aimless shell of my former self, the waitress returned and swapped my soup bowl. Presumably the other person, the customer who *could* speak Japanese, got my ramen dish and complained, *Hey, where's my shrimp?*

"See? It all works out." I shrugged.

"Can you ask for hot sauce?"

"Nope. I know maybe twenty words in Japanese, and hot sauce isn't one of them."

Andra flagged down the waitress and did some wacky pantomime fanning her mouth whilst pointing to the soup bowl, and damn if the waitress didn't nod and smile and even bow a tiny bit before bringing her a bottle of spicy stuff. Andra is used to getting and doing exactly what she wants. She doesn't just like her routine—she's married to it. But let's face it: "Routine" is a soft word for "high-maintenance, ironclad, willful diva set in her ways like my grandma." Andra is single. She skips breakfast, walks slow, talks loud, spoils her dog, pampers herself, works late, takes long baths at night, and sleeps in on weekends, and when she goes to bed, she crashes—lights out, eye mask, earplugs, day over. She does not have to pick up after anyone or answer the phone in the middle of the night, in case it's a kid stranded in Roppongi. She never has to go a *movie* she doesn't want to see, let alone *move* overseas.

A: Seriously, Em, how can you live like this?

E: Like what?

A: Never getting what you want.

E: Maybe what I want isn't as good as what I got; maybe the soup with the shrimp would have been better.

A: Are you okay? This iteration of Em, this go-with-the-flow girl, it scares me.

E: Turns out I'm good at adapting. It's the thing I excel at, like how some people are good managers and others are computer geeks. I'm a great mover. Sure, I'm a pretty good marketer—I can develop creative campaigns, plan events, sell sponsorships, woo clients, and close deals—but you know what I'm really amazing at? Moving. Yep. Thought I was a mover and a shaker, but it turns out I'm just a mover. Not a whole lotta shakin' goin' on. No heavy lifting, but labeling boxes—what to take, what to leave—that's my wheelhouse. I write an excellent resignation letter. And you can throw me in the middle of any city anywhere in the world and I can remake our lives in less than a month. I am especially good at friend selection; it's like speed dating. Show me a welcome coffee, and I will make five new best friends. Don't be jealous, Andra—they're just temporary, like human placeholders. And when my new best friend leaves (because repatriation is inevitable; it's the flip side of being a tagalong), I'm really good at saying goodbye. Not so good at keeping in touch, though. Hanging on, that's sort of the opposite of adapting, but letting go, I'm fucking great at that. I can let go of almost everything. Not you, or Gee and the kids, my inner circle, but to anyone or anything outside it, I'm waving and smiling like the queen. Sayonara.

So there you have it—my surprise life skill is being adaptable. Like right now, I just don't give a shit that the waitress brought me shrimp instead of veggies, because it doesn't matter, and if it does, if it's something I don't like, like bean paste, I'll learn how to avoid it. Take *onigiri*, for example, those rice triangles wrapped in seaweed—they're tasty and convenient, you can get them everywhere, but sometimes they're filled with weird stuff, so I learned how to read two words in katakana—"tuna" and "chicken." *Et voilà*—no more surprises, no pickled plum. It's quite a talent, when you think about it: adaptability. It's like shape-shifting: Where once I was a career woman, now I'm functionally illiterate. I've gotten real good at simplifying conversations, asking questions that have only a yes or no answer, and as long as I don't have to use the telephone—as long as I can point or touch, make faces, sketch cave drawings, smell food in the market, squeeze generic packaging to see if it's sugar or flour—I can get by. But you want to know why I really succeed where so many tagalong wives get derailed? It's because I'm okay being by myself. All day. Ruby and Rio are in high school now, and they can get there by themselves. So I'm pretty much on my own, almost every day, except once a week when I wash my hair and teach English to rich Japanese kids whose

parents want them to go to Stanford. That's me smiling through pro-
nunciation drills, even though my brain is leaking potential. Yeah.
Adaptability. It's totally my strong suit.

A: Oh, honey. You're breaking my heart.

Andra reached over our ramen bowls and grabbed my hand, her
eyes wet with emotion. She does like a good cry. "Why don't you
move back home?"

That right there is why it's so much easier to make friends with
other trailing spouses than trying to explain your life to people who
really know you, or think they know the real you. Tagalongs bond
fast, and not just over a shared language or home country, and for
sure not over politics or religion, which are totally taboo in Tagalong.
It's one simple thing, one question tagalongs never ask each other:
Why do you do it? Tagalong wives accept each other's choices at face
value because we understand, in the marrow, how those decisions
were made.

A: Are you okay, Em?

E: I'm okay, Andra. I keep busy. I'm writing a lot.

A: You should blog about living in Japan.

Everyone assumes you're some sort of travel writer if you say you're
writing when you live overseas. Mostly I wrote about growing up girl
in America. The things that happen to girls, how all girls are at risk,
how as Americans we like to see ourselves as the leaders of the free
world but in reality we are prisoners of fear, looking over our shoulders, double-chain-locking our doors, worried about stranger danger
and not letting our kids go to a park by themselves. I felt safer overseas
than I ever did in the States. It was kooky and crowded in Tokyo, I
wouldn't want to live there forever, but I liked being there as an expat.

A: Remember when we worked at the radio station and you came to
Tokyo with the Romantics? Did you ever think you'd be living here?

E: No, not in a million years.

●   ●

There's a picture of me backstage at the Romantics in Tokyo, my own personal *Cheap Trick at Budokan*. I'm wearing pink glasses and this super-cute dress I bought at the 109 building in Shibuya, boutique heaven; it's flowy, with tulips. I'm the only girl in the photo, surrounded by the band, the president of Sony Music, and our DJ, Arthur P. We were taking press photos with the listeners, six contest winners and their plus-ones: moms, best friends, and one couple who'd gotten married the day before.

"Do I have to go to the wedding?" I whined to Andra during our nightly update phone call.

"Fuck yeah, you do," she said. "With flowers and cake. And take pictures. This is our Valentine's promo. You're not on vacation, girl— this is work."

And it was—a lot of work. I put together the whole promotion. It took months of planning, cooking it up with the band's manager. After the press photos, he came up to me and said, "We're going out to dinner."

"Cool." I smiled. This was the payoff for all that work. Dinner with the band.

"The thing is, Em," he added meekly, "you can't come. Sony is entertaining the band at a hostess bar in Shinjuku. No girls allowed. I'm sorry," he said.

I'm sorry? *Gomen nasai.*

That's what I said at the bar with my winners later that night as I threw down my corporate credit card and got righteously trashed. We all did.

"*Gomen nasai,*" I said—"I'm sorry"—every time I stepped on some guy's foot, plowed through him, bumped into him rudely, knocked him out of my way, and it happened a lot. The dance floor was small.

Bars are small in Japan. People are small. Japanese girls are delicate. Not like American girls. American girls are tough. *I'm sorry I body-slammed you just then. Did it hurt?*

   Gomen nasai.

I AM NOT A GEISHA

My last job before moving to Tokyo was with that trendy, hipster design publication where Andra worked. It was a glorified assistant position that didn't do much for my self-esteem, but it did fill the gap between Paris and Tokyo. That's pretty much where my career had landed—a string of downward-spiraling, in-between jobs. Mostly I answered phones and proofed advertising proposals. They threw me a bone and let me manage their one-off, less prestigious resource guide. A few months later, we moved to Tokyo and I had to grovel, beg, demand, pester them like a harpy for my piddly little commission check, which arrived, at last, a year after I worked for them. Too late for Christmas, too late for Valentine's Day, too late for spring break in Vietnam. Too late to enjoy, the check sat in my Japanese inbox, tainted money, reeking of my puny insignificance and bruised ego. I concocted elaborate schemes in my head over what to do with it, now that I had too much pride to cash it. Donate the money to charity? Build a house in Nepal via Habitat for Humanity in the name of the publisher who tried to stiff me?

This debate was still brewing in my head as I dressed for the Tokyo American Club charity gala. Black on black on black: flats, slacks, and jacket. The only thing that separated me from the waiters was a string of pearls. It had been my job to solicit donations for the gala auction. Director of sales, annual fundraiser. That's what I put on my résumé to bridge the gap when I got back to Los Angeles. I did not explain that it was volunteer work. Or mention my coffee klatches with Veda, another tagalong wife, who was my partner on the sales committee. Or elaborate that really all I did was secure in-kind donations for the auction. Art and antiques, travel and hotel accommodations in exotic locales.

It's a strange thing, calling on businesses in Asia. Phnom Penh. Saigon. Laos. Guam. The names alone are loaded. I know them because they used to be either army bases, or the United States was bombing the shit out of their villages. They evoke girls in hip-hugger, bell-bottom blue jeans with the sun embroidered on their pockets. Peace signs. My aunt had a copper bracelet, the name of some MIA soldier who never came home engraved across it. Her wrist turned a greenish black from the cheap metal reminder that some Americans were dressed in real camouflage. Things were different now. At least in Southeast Asia. The United States was doing big capitalist business with the same countries it carpet-bombed in the '60s. And everyone was playing together real sweet-like—a kindergarten teacher's fantasy.

Konichiwa from Tokyo!

Greetings from the Kingdom of Cambodia!

Join us for nine holes in Laolao Bay.

Enjoy a cruise on the Mekong Delta.

Thank God for short-term memory loss and long-term financial gain. The hotels in Nha Trang did look fabulous. They served chocolate martinis in swanky restaurant bars. And the beaches in Nam were to die for, although I'm not sure that's a good use of metaphor.

Also, I was thinking how nice it was that these people didn't hold a grudge against Americans. They took my calls; they returned my emails with warm greetings. Everything was blue skies and clear waters, palm trees and seventy degrees. They all wanted to do business with the lady from the Tokyo American Club.

And they gave.

Ocean-view hotel suites with continental breakfast and cultural performances, airport transfer included. The donations were pouring in, and the tourism dollars were spreading like jam on toast. I was thinking Vietnam looked pretty damn inviting. Maybe someday we'd be invited back to Kabul, sit in rooftop cafés and watch the sunset while sipping mint tea or some Kabulian concoction. Maybe we'd cruise the Tigris, stop for lunch in Mosul, enjoy ethnic dancing in Baghdad; we'd throw dollars around, play desert golf, shoot toy rifles at dummies in burkas for a few dinars. We'd drink and laugh, and they'd let us pay them to forget.

I was thinking there were worse things than fudging the truth on your résumé. We raised a bunch of yen—that's what I'd say if anyone asked me in an interview. And the money was used to fund social programs in support of underserved women and children—which, honestly, I felt pretty good about. And I padded my CV with global brands like Hilton, Four Seasons, and American Airlines. It made me sound legit, and it wasn't a lie, more like a half-truth. My résumé is filled with little deceits like this. Some women fret about dates, about whether anyone will do the math and figure out how old they are. But since Gee started traveling, pretty much everything on my résumé is just this side of a fairy tale, as if I could get a real job in a foreign country, with no working papers, language skills, or connections; as if I had been paid in yen, instead of coffee, croissants, and tickets to charity balls. Technically speaking, I wasn't even a guest at that black-tie dinner, didn't get to choose between prime rib and pan-seared salmon. In the back room, they fed the volunteers chicken roll-ups, potato chips, and bottled water. But they gave me a paddle for the live auction, and that's where the painting I secured from an artist in Kyoto named Daniel Kelly showed up. Official description: *I Am Not a Geisha*, multimedia print on washi paper.

It's big, an oversize blowup of a Japanese girl with a tattoo sleeve, staring straight into the lens. The photo is black and white, washed out and fuzzy, flowers vividly hand-painted in an intricate tangle of color that snakes up her arm like a vine. It's edgy and modern, with a small vintage geisha postcard glued on as a reminder of how things used to be. To be clear, geisha are not working girls; they are considered female companions, paid performers, decorative objects in whiteface on stilt-like platform shoes, hobbled, swaddled in fabric, inching along, their eyes shaded from sunlight or direct gaze by a parasol. But this girl, this young woman with the almond eyes, the one in the photo, her head is not bowed; she's looking straight into the camera, chewing the lens.

You know how art speaks to you? Well, this piece screamed at me. My arm flew up with the opening bid. There was a flurry of activity. A fat man with a bald head, a chunky gold wedding ring, and diamond cuff links raised his paddle. He gave me a look that said *back off*, like I was the help, and for a moment I vacillated, standing against the wall in my working-girl blackout wardrobe meant to make me invisible. Normally, this type of purchase would be a joint decision in my family. Gee and I acquire art as a team. And this piece is substantial. We're talking a big chunk of art. Bold. Out of my league. The stakes were rising faster than I could do the math: twenty thousand yen, fifty thousand yen, a hundred thousand yen . . . How much is two hundred thousand yen in dollars? Veda stood next to me, egging me on.

"Don't let him win," she whispered. Back home in Atlanta, Veda was an executive for a high-profile nonprofit. She had her own ax to grind. My paddle kept flying in the face of this businessman as he sat at the head of the table, pasty and bloated, his wife at his side, expat package bulging in his pants pocket. I stood my ground. Literally. I had to—I didn't have a seat. I could hardly afford the dinner, let alone the art. There was, however, that commission check, that two thousand dollars spoiling my inbox. A surge of adrenaline pumped through my body, and before I had time to breathe, let alone think, I raised my paddle one more time and stared him down. *You don't know me, old man, but I'm a dog with a bone to pick, and that girl is mine.*

I did not acquire this piece of art—I fought for it, tooth and nail, blood, sweat, and tears, baby. I did not merely, discreetly, or easily buy her. I reclaimed her and took what was meant to be mine. I am not a geisha either, dammit.

MAKING SMOOTHIES
IN TOKYO

But what if instead of writing broken, torn, pissed-off essays that sound a lot like rants, I was to write lyrical, expat-slice-of-life travel pieces about living overseas. Like this:

Stopped for lunch in a park in Hiro-o, plugged into my iPod, listening to Black Eyed Peas. Took a path up some wooden steps past a man sprawled on a park bench, reading a book, kids wading in a pond, a girl painting in watercolors on an easel. Where is the love? The path wound and twisted, opening onto a clearing with a small garden near an arbor where I sat on a bench to eat lunch—*onigiri*: seaweed-and-salmon triangle—my soul drifting. In front of me sat a Japanese woman with gray hair, playing with a goose the size of a small dog, red bandanna tied around its neck like a collar. Balancing the goose on her knees, she held it in her palms, flat on its back, spindly legs and webbed feet stretched out in ecstasy as she kissed its beak, bouncing it up and down like a baby, rubbing its feathered tummy, nuzzling its head. Then she held that goose midair, hovering above the grass, and blew on its belly until it peed. Carefully, she set the goose on the ground; it rose up on its haunches and spread its wings in play. She retrieved some toilet paper from her bag, picked up the goose, gently wiping its belly and privates, and meticulously cleaned the ground. I don't know how long I sat there, in that cocoon of a park, in the middle of Tokyo, letting the afternoon wash over me. Unplugged my earbuds, letting the air fill with the music of cicadas. The woman opened a book; her pet goose waddled about contentedly. Felt like my veins opened up and America drained out.

Or this, haiku:

Woke up, made the kids
a power smoothie, took a
walk in Shibuya.

Or maybe this, a day in the life, fragments:

I'm hugging the edge of the bed, leg dangling, my hand resting on the floor. He's been dogging me all night. I can feel his heat, his heartbeat through my T-shirt, know he wants something, can't keep pushing him away. The alarm goes off. *It will have to be quick*, I think, turning toward him. The comfort of him takes me by surprise, the rhythm of us like home, Motown, loose and sexy. It triggers something deep and primal, Marvin Gaye and Tammi Terrell. Me and my guy. Afterward, we kiss, a gentle fusion.

"Breakfast!" I yell upstairs to my high school children, who are not little anymore and don't like to be yelled at in the morning, don't even like to talk in the morning, at least not to me—especially not to me.

"What's in the smoothie?" Rio asks, wrinkling his nose. "You put that weird stuff in it, didn't you?" he says accusingly.

I shake my head no, lying.

He sips and frowns.

"Just OJ, banana, and yogurt," I tell him.

"You forgot to mention the weird stuff," he says.

"Tomorrow you can make breakfast."

"I'm just saying"—he circles back—"seeds are not food, that's all. I'm not saying I don't love you."

Rio makes me laugh; he is so cheeky and perfectly comfortable in his skin, slouching around in baggy jeans and high-top sneakers, smelling of rubber and dirty socks, ink and grease. I wonder if the girls at school love this boy, with his ponytail; his wispy, never-been-shaved mustache; his smart mouth and marshmallow center.

Ruby ignores the smoothie entirely. "About this weekend," she says. "The *ryokan*. Will there be beds?"

"Couldn't get beds," I tell her.

"Don't say you *couldn't get beds* if there are no beds."

"Guys, it's a *ryokan*. There are no beds. By definition. There will be mats on the floor."

Ruby crinkles her nose.

"Please come," I beg. "It'll be fun, a family trip, an experience, something to recount someday about the time you went to the Japanese *onsen* nestled in the snowcapped mountains, bathed in natural hot springs, and slept on the floor."

"Outty on that," she replies. "Nori says I can spend the weekend with her."

"I just like to tease you. You know that, right?" Rio says, kissing me goodbye as he follows Ruby out the door to catch the school bus.

I drink the power smoothies with flax, hemp, and chia seeds; I make them for myself anyway. Hours later, Gee calls to firm up details for Kita Onsen. It's centuries old, in the middle of nowhere; getting there will require trains and buses and a taxi ride. Our Japanese teacher, Saya-san, is coming, with her American boyfriend, the one who works with Gee. I tell him we are one for two on the kids.

"Cool," he says.

Hanging up, I realize that was my first actual conversation since breakfast. A red-and-blue-striped Mardi Gras mask pops up on my laptop. "You have a call," Skype informs me; it's my mother, calling from Detroit. I put on my headset and press "connect."

"How are you?" I ask the party mask on my computer screen.

My mother is getting older. She's got arthritis, gout, diverticulitis, and God knows what else. She takes more pills than a rock star, and these days she's more likely to trip and fall than go to a costume ball, but her Skype screen icon is a Mardi Gras carnival mask. I tell her I'm coming home this summer and ask if I can bring our dog when I visit her.

She hesitates. "That drooling, farting, snoring creature?" But she eventually relents.

We haven't seen each other in more than a year. Gee will visit his family; I will visit mine. Home leave is never long enough to do everything we need to do—that's the official explanation for his-and-hers family visits. It works better this way. After Paris, I stayed with Gee, but I gave him back all rights to his mother.

The street is strewn with cherry blossom leaves, pale pink, the sky a blanket of white. If this were LA, I'd say it was overcast, that it would burn off by midafternoon and the sun would come out. But I really don't know Tokyo at all. It occurs to me that I probably couldn't point to Japan on a map. I live here but don't know where *here* is. Where is home, anyway? Where you sleep, where you're from, where your dog is, where you find yourself, where you left the biggest piece of yourself behind?

I have a new student, named Shota. "I lived in California," he tells me.

"I have a house in Los Angeles," I tell him.

"Is it a McMansion?"

What am I going to teach this kid who looks Japanese but opens his mouth and pitch-perfect American slang spills out? Nothing, maybe. Maybe he's just taking my class to feel comfortable; after-school

English is a safe zone for kids who look Japanese but aren't, not experientially. My students are kids who have lived overseas, Japanese boys and girls, from six to sixth grade, from barely verbal to fully bilingual, with one thing in common: They were expats, and now they are misfits in their home country. They're like my children in reverse. The term "third-culture kids" makes me think of *Third Rock from the Sun*, like they're Martians or something, kids who are comfortable anywhere in the world except where they're from, who stumble over the simple stuff like "Where do you live?"

I stop in a boutique on the walk to Shibuya Station. A tiny pink vinyl skirt and jacket hang on a store mannequin. I touch them, feel their slickness, admire the rhinestones and decals: a decorative high-heeled slipper and a cherry red lipstick tube. This is exactly the type of outfit I used to buy Ruby when she was little and looked cute in everything, candy sweet, all kisses for Mommy. I touch the skirt and let it go.

Ruby is on a no-carb diet, in addition to being a vegetarian. The vegetarian thing is definitely about not wanting to eat things with a face that you cuddle, but the no-carb thing is all about the prom, I suspect.

Ruby, Rio, and I sit down to dinner: rice and tuna sashimi from the market in the basement of the metro station.

"Where's Dad?" Ruby asks.

"Working late," I say.

"Aren't you glad we all came here so we could have family dinners together?" she says, sarcasm dripping.

Ruby recounts her challenging day with mean girls at the American school. "I was a mean girl in Paris," she admits. "Then we moved back to LA and I got dumped by all my friends back home."

Rio recounts middle school social architecture: There were the blondes and the nonblondes, and the subgroup of nonblondes: Asians and geeks. "I was a geek," he says.

Ruby laughs. "You *are* a geek."

When Gee's here, we talk about school projects, but when it's just us three, we talk social groups. It's like we're best friends. Almost. It's almost like being home. Her room is almost clean, his math is almost done, my husband is almost home, I'm almost happy.

After dinner, Ruby coils up on the couch like a kitten, twirling her hair around her finger, sucking her thumb.

"Stop that," I scold her.

"I found a prom dress online. They could ship it," she says hopefully, getting her laptop to show me.

It's a V-neck, halter-top party dress with full skirt that looks like it would be pretty on her. But she's worried.

"Nori says prints make you look fat. What do you think?"

I think she is soft and beautiful and that she should wear what she wants, but high school isn't that simple. Neither is living in Tokyo. It's hard to find clothes that fit American bodies. It's dangerous to buy a prom dress online, I say, offering to take her shopping instead. Relief spreads across her face; she is still my baby for another nanosecond.

The international man comes home late, eats leftovers, and climbs into bed next to me. I pretend to be sleeping; he falls asleep instantly, snoring lightly, reminding me of my dog, Chandler, who is home in Los Angeles with Andra. Princely Chandler. Who is getting old while we are away. *My dog's getting old*, I think. Limping, farting, slowpoking old. I turn on the light and jot that line in my journal. Then I scribble "old dogs" and underline it. I'll write more tomorrow. I curl up next to Gee, rub a strand of his hair back and forth between my thumb and index finger, and close my eyes. I don't know where I am from one year to the next, but for now this man is my home. Sometimes it's enough. Almost.

■　■

It's that time again, of boxes and lists, organizing my life into piles.

The things I need to take with me on the plane: laptop, favorite jeans, a bathing suit, T-shirts and sweats, driver's license. The things that can be shipped: art, books, puffy down jacket, and gloves. Travelogues on Japan can be given away. Or can they? There's a rumor floating about our possibly coming back in a year or two. Do I pack my navy suit or ship it by sea? What I mean is, how long can I wait before looking for work? And does it fit anyway? Sushi is fattening. No one told me that. Maybe it wasn't the sushi; maybe it was the ramen. Here's a list of stuff I want to do or get before I go: buy chopsticks, and T-shirts in Kanji; visit a stone spa, lie on hot rocks, and sweat. Detox. Say good-bye to teachers and students and my one tagalong friend, Veda from Atlanta, whom I'll probably never see again. Host the American-style barbecue I've been promising for Aiko, Mebae, and Terada, the Japanese ladies who taught me how to cook that cucumber thing with warts.

I want to tell people in LA we're heading back, but I get stuck on the verbiage: Am I coming (or going) home? Coming or going? Is LA my home or a stopgap between one relocation and the next? I have a home in Los Angeles, but I'm not *at home* there anymore. How many going-away parties can you throw—sushi, sake, sayonara, baby!—and still be missed? How many birthdays, bar mitzvahs, and graduations can you not attend before you aren't even invited at all? I'm that old friend my parents had when we were growing up, the guy who did business in the Orient (that's what they called it back then) and married a Japanese woman. For a few years, they came to dinner whenever they were in town, he and the wife, delicate and shy, but then we lost track of his comings and goings. He wasn't at my sister's wedding or my father's funeral. He fell off the radar. I'm that guy. I don't even remember his name anymore.

CRACK ME OPEN

Crack me open, and there's a *D* tattooed on my heart and a map in the shape of a mitten, Great Lakes coursing through my veins. Motown albums next to Eminem CDs. A ticket stub from Patti Smith at the Second Chance Bar in Ann Arbor, where I hung so close to the stage that her spit hit my cheek. A frayed Michigan T-shirt belonging to that guy who lived on the third floor of my dorm freshman year, whose name I've forgotten. A string of music-industry jobs taped together with bumper stickers, designed by Andra and me, radio "it" girls—her in stilettos, me in leather. She was the sexy one, but I had swagger, a sassy hip sway you could recognize from behind. Not to be mistaken for a limp, ever.

This walk of mine is the result of a childhood accident. I was climbing a cement planter, when it fell on me. The handyman who was cleaning the windows warned me not to climb on the flower box, but I didn't listen to him and there was no one else watching us—me and the girl next door, whose name I do remember, but I'm not gonna mention it because her mother threatened to sue mine after the accident. And all she had were a few bruises! I was the one who wound up in the hospital. In a surge of adrenaline, the kind you see in the movies and think never happens in real life, the handyman lifted the concrete and someone pulled us out from under it. Later, when my mom hired the handyman to come back and remove the flower box, he couldn't budge it. It had to be busted up into pieces. Fortunately, I was only busted up, not in pieces.

My recovery was documented in black-and-white stills and home movies. There's a picture of me, my leg in traction, surrounded by a stuffed-animal zoo. Lions and tigers and monkeys hanging off the bar I used to hoist myself up and greet guests. The room was filled with a steady stream of well-wishers and an embarrassing amount of gifts for a five-year-old with only one friend, the girl next door. She didn't come to see me. But my grandmother had been a longtime volunteer at the hospital, so I was a legacy patient, showered with visits and presents from all the old *bubbes*. My mom made me give away most of the toys and stuffed animals to other kids in the hospital when, two months later, I went home in an ambulance. That was the only way to move me—I was in a full-body cast that extended from my armpits to my toes on one side and down my thigh to my knee on the other. My mom had a hospital bed installed in our breakfast room, where my siblings would hang out, pretending my cast was a table while eating peanut butter and jelly sandwiches on my plaster torso. Okay, that's not true, but it makes for a good image.

Here's what *is* true. There's a home movie of me on the deck of my dad's motorboat, surrounded by Rat Pack–y men and women in wide-brimmed straw hats, Italian-movie-star pretty, holding cocktails and smoking cigarettes. My sister pretends to be camera shy while my brother makes silly faces, hooking his index fingers into the corners of his mouth to stretch his lips, tilting his head to the side, and crossing his eyes. Then the camera pans to me, a papier-mâché kid wearing nothing but a pair of plastic sunglasses, spatchcocked on the deck like a Thanksgiving turkey, no life jacket.

What if there was a wave?

That's what I was thinking when my mom pulled out the home movies to show Gee and the kids. We were on home leave from Paris.

"Home leave"—that's Tagalong for taking your vacation in your home country. We couldn't go "home" to Los Angeles because our house had been rented to a bunch of twentysomethings with Indian bedspreads tacked to the walls and mattresses on the floor. So we went to Detroit instead. My mom broke out the movies, and everyone waxed nostalgic about the good old days. Everyone except me.

I was struck by how many things were wrong with that film footage. First, how did they even get me on the boat? They must have thrown me in the back of a station wagon and prayed they didn't have to brake fast. And then what if I'd had to go pee? *Hold my cocktail for a minute, Nan. I need to get a bedpan for the kid.* What kind of parents drag a plaster-cast child on a boat outing? That's what adult me wants to know. One big wave, and I would have slid overboard and sunk to the bottom of the lake like an anchor.

"Why did you take me on the boat?" I asked my mother after we watched the movies. I was having a glass of wine while Gee put the kids to sleep. My mom was sitting on the living room couch, drinking a vodka, straight-up, no ice. She was wearing a kaftan, chunky jewelry, her blondish hair cropped close to her head.

"Oh, Emma," she said with a sigh, as if it was so obvious it needed no explanation: "You wanted to tag along."

My head nodded yes, of course, little broken sparrow didn't want to be left behind. It made perfect sense. No kid wants to lie in bed alone all summer long while everyone else is outdoors, playing hopscotch. But the tagalong spouse in me shook her head no, not buying it. It wasn't that I didn't want to be left behind; I wasn't the decision maker. I was only five years old. It was that my dad didn't want to sacrifice a glorious day on the water because of his clumsy kid with a broken leg. And, to his point, the summers are short in Detroit. You spend all year fantasizing about that one perfect boating day. Like girls and weddings. Only I'm not the kind of girl who dreamed about wedding dresses and bridal bouquets. I dreamt about leather jackets and bands on tour. A corner office and rocker-chick cool. Music was more important than boys. It was the language through which I experienced life.

I grew up in the Motor City; it made me wanna holler. Made me wanna get up and dance. Made me wanna prance and pose and preen from the moment I held a cheap plastic guitar in my hand and played along with my big sister's rock 'n' roll singles. It seemed as though the very air we breathed was filled with Motown grooves and pop hooks. We listened to vinyl records and waited, in screaming anticipation, for bands to come through town.

The first concert I ever saw was with my mom and my older sister. She went berserk, standing on her seat, tears rolling down her cheeks, pulling at her frosted blond hair, screaming. The roar of thousands of teenage girls was deafening. I held on to my mother's hand the whole time, taking it all in.

"Did you like it?" Mom asked afterward.

"It was all right," I said. *All right*, like if my birthday and the Fourth of July collided with walking on the moon, like riding a bike downhill, no hands. I intuitively affected the air of nonchalance that would see me through countless backstage, celebrity-shuffling, coke-snorting years.

•   •

"This is not a test," the facilitator said, handing out multiple-choice questionnaires. She was wearing a smartly tailored kelly green blazer that had lost at least a decade earlier any style points it might once have had. This was the era of shoulder pads and oversize jackets. I was wearing jeans and a Rock the Vote T-shirt.

"I think she shopped my mom's closet," Andra whispered in my ear.

"I think she *is* my mother," I whispered back.

"Think of this as an icebreaker," Blazer continued, shooting us a cease-and-desist glare. "I'm just trying to get to know you, and hopefully we'll all get to know ourselves better in the process."

Here's who we were, me and Andra: radio promo girls, *not* party girls. We threw the party—conceived, planned, and executed it. Sound check, backstage, after-parties, and the mother of all parties, the block party. That was our baby—balloons and bands, fortune tellers and street dancers. No mimes.

"Mimes are not rock 'n' roll," Pax said. He was the program director, which meant he was in charge of the music. Ten thousand listeners came, plus Andra and I, standing in front of an eight-foot stage, clipboards, headsets, big hair, and megawatt smiles.

Two days later, we were in Northern Michigan at a team-building retreat, having breakfast in the lodge under deer antlers.

"Do I have anything in my teeth?" Andra asked.

"You're good," I told her. Andra was my boss, but it felt more like we were best friends. We worked together all day, and at night we attended events together. When we weren't working, we were sleeping. And now we were roommates.

"It's like living in the dorm," Andra said, wincing at her half-eaten spinach omelet.

I was nervous about the seminar, but Andra said not to worry, you can't embarrass yourself in a room full of radio people.

"The worst that can happen is that you've got spinach in your teeth. And we don't." She smiled, showing me her teeth again. "Plus, we're superstars, Em. We totally rocked the D. Ten thousand listeners came to an event that we threw. We made it into the newspaper!"

"Yeah, but," I pointed out, "that article was all about how a car got trashed and someone got stabbed."

"Front page, Em," Andra repeated. "Above the fold. Superstars."

∎ ∎

First question on Blazer's questionnaire: *How much time each week do you spend at the gym? Circle the best answer: 10 percent? 20 percent?* All the way up to 100 percent.

That was easy; I circled 0 percent because I didn't need a gym. My job was like running a marathon 'round the clock and holidays—especially holidays: Rockin' New Year's Eve Bash, Thanksgiving for the Homeless. The last time I had dinner with the family, it was a Saturday night. My brother and sister were there, and I ordered hamburger in a skillet; it's like a Coney Island loose burger, only upscale at my parents' golf club, which means minus the chili and with grilled onions and steamed tomato instead. My dad said how great it was to see me, and my mom agreed, saying it seemed like I was always working. That's when I realized, *Fuck, I am working. Tonight!* Ticket winners, the station van, bumper stickers to pass out at Harpos on the East Side. How could I have forgotten?

"So sorry, gotta run," I said on the fly. "Rain check."

"What about your dinner?" Dad wanted to know.

"Can you cancel it?" I asked, grabbing my purse.

"But it's Saturday," my mother objected, as if work and weekends were mutually exclusive.

"Love you," I shouted over my shoulder, blowing her a kiss.

And I did. Love my mom. But I loved my job more than anything. That job was everything—my paycheck, my social life, my pride and joy.

• •

How much time each week do you spend working? I circled 95 percent, because a girl's got to shower. I was thinking I had this test down solid because I ate, slept, and breathed my job. Then we all stood up and Blazer started to weed us out.

How much time each week do you devote to community activities? "If your answer is over 20 percent," Blazer said, "please sit down." One person took a seat. *How much time each week do you devote to family? Friends? Self-care? Volunteer at your kid's school? Spend time with Grandma? Walk the dog? Read something other than work-related materials? Pursue a hobby?* Andra, Pax, Timmer, even the shy girl in traffic and the creepy engineer, they all sat down, dropping like flies. And then came the last question: *How much time each week do you spend with your spouse or significant other?*

For a smart girl, I could be pretty thick sometimes. I thought sitting down meant you were out of the game. But no, it meant those people had lives outside work. Salsa lessons. Dinner for two. Kids. Even Andra was married. It wasn't as if that came as a surprise; it's just that I never gave it much thought until they were all sitting down staring at me, the last one standing. Alone. My cheeks started to flame. It was like that nightmare, the one where you show up naked at a party, only worse. Naked, I could handle. Naked, I looked okay. But feeling this kind of exposed, married to my job, unloved, unfucked, unbalanced—that hurt. My fridge was empty, and now everyone knew. "I have a cat," I said defensively. I had a mad crush on the sax player in the Urbations; he passed out on my bed fully clothed after a show once. Maybe he took off his bandanna. *What percent of your time is spent in pursuit of unrequited love?* How come Blazer didn't ask that?

Plus, there *was* a guy, a roadie in LA; he called me in between gigs and girlfriends. He was geographically undesirable, but other than that, we got along great. Once every year or so, we spent 100 percent of ten perfect days together. Tower Records on Sunset Boulevard, Venice Beach, margaritas at El Coyote. It was a long-distance relationship; that should count for something. Sweat pooling under my arms, my shirt starting to stink, my eggs moldy, I could smell myself, and it wasn't pretty. Turns out you *could* embarrass yourself, even in a room full of rockdogs. There *was* something worse than having spinach in your teeth: You could be twenty-nine, without a hobby. And when Blazer talked hobbies, she really meant a normal life. Minivan and a man. I hadn't realized what I was missing before, but now *I wanted it so bad.*

All of a sudden, everyone was trying to fix me up. Andra's husband had a best friend named Hal, toothpick skinny, with bad skin.

"He likes you," she said.

"I'd marry you if I was into girls," Timmer said, trying to make me feel better. He had this amazing head of hair: bleached, almost pure white curls; dark roots. And great taste in music—old soul, like the Delfonics and the Dramatics.

"Please," I begged, "can't you reconsider the whole being-gay thing?"

Pax threw me a bone and offered to send me, in his place, to Los Angeles to interview a headbanger band on satellite radio.

"Isn't that your job?" I asked. "You're the PD, the on-air dude; I don't know anything about heavy metal." It was a total mental pass— Ozzy came on the radio, and I punched out.

"You go, Em," he insisted. "LA's not my thang."

"How can LA not be your thing?" I joked. "We're in the music industry; it's everybody's thing." Pax's scheme had all the markings of Andra playing matchmaker again.

• •

You told him, didn't you? I asked Andra. She was sitting at her desk, surrounded by stacks of bumper stickers and T-shirts. Photos of her with rock legends lined the walls. Her office was a fangirl fantasy.

A: What? Who?

E: Pax. You told Pax about the roadie in LA.

A: Go to LA, Em. Have some fun, get laid, and come home with a tan, girl.

E: You know if this plan of yours works, if true love awaits, you may
   need to get a new assistant.

A: Em, I say this as your best friend and not your boss—if you're in
   love with this guy, you should be with him; this is just a job. Really.

E. It's the best job ever, though. Us. We're a team.

A: It's still just a job, Em, and it's not like you won't find work in the
   biz in Los Angeles.

E: You sound like my mother.

"You girls can have it all, Emma," my mom always said. Everything
she had, plus everything she wanted. "You girls are lucky." She didn't
mean Andra and me; she meant our whole generation. She made it
sound so easy.

■   ■

A month later, the roadie and I were sitting on the edge of the pool
at the Sunset Marquis in West Hollywood, dangling our feet in the
water. I was still in the dress I'd worn to the radio station: inky, with
a raw-edged hem, kind of cool, kind of hip vibe. I was the only girl in
the press photo. Everyone else was either a program director or with
the band. There were no girl PDs; girls ran promotions, we threw
the party, but we didn't program the show. The roadie had his jeans
rolled up, and he was wearing an X T-shirt.

"You're so LA now," I joked. I told him about my day: interview
with the band; group photo for the trades; drinks in the back room of
an Italian restaurant in Santa Monica; car and driver; and this hotel,
the Sunset Marquis, hush and lush.

"I think Mötley Crüe is staying here," I whispered. This was a hot-
shit rock 'n' roll day for me, and I told the roadie everything, every
little detail, even that my voice had been shaky on-air and my interview questions were lame.

Who are your musical influences? How did you come up with the name for your band?

All day long, I had been worried I'd say something (else) stupid and they'd figure out I didn't know anything about heavy metal. Sitting next to the lead singer, who seemed much taller in person—his pants striped the long way, black and white—I'd been too nervous to eat pasta, worried I'd get spinach in my teeth.

"This is the most relaxed I've felt all day," I admitted, as we leaned back on the concrete, just me and the roadie, night-sky gazing, the air balmy.

I guess I should come clean about the fact that the roadie was Gee, and Gee's not really a roadie, not anymore. He was a roadie when we first met, but after he moved to Los Angeles he started running lights and sound for fashion and auto shows. I teased him about being a weekend punk. He didn't cut his hair, though, so I could still twist his rat tail around my fingers when we lay down. I liked how safe I felt with him, even riding on the back of his motorcycle in the rain, as if nothing bad could happen to me when we were together. Gee liked being with me, too, although he had a hard time articulating feelings.

Once, we were walking down Melrose and this wildly awesome woman passed us, tall and thin, with a mess of dreads, yellow blond, piled high on her head like a pineapple. She was pierced and tattooed, ripped and torn. Fierce looking. I was looking at her, thinking, *I don't know if I can compete in LA. It seems like a lot of work just to get dressed in the morning.* That's when Gee said, like he was reading my mind, "You know why I love you, Em?" When I asked why, thinking he was gonna say that I made him laugh or that he felt comfortable with me, this is what he said—he said he loved me because I was normal. He said "normal," but I heard "average." He said "normal," and he meant it as a compliment. He said "normal," but I'm pretty sure what he meant to say was that he felt comfortable with me. I punched his arm playfully and acted all insulted. He fumbled over his words, trying to walk it back. I made him squirm too. Let him twist on that word choice all day. But I knew what he meant: I wasn't that girl with a pineapple on her head, wearing a costume, living life like live theater. I wasn't the girl *with* the band; I was the girl working the phones behind the scenes, making sure the band had a crowd to play to.

"I'm starved," I said. Gee suggested Tommy's (the original, on Beverly and Rampart) since it was open twenty-four hours, because I *am* the kind of girl you take to Tommy's for a burger with everything. At the end of the day, even a pinch-me day like that one, you want to come home to something real. Something grounded. Me and Gee, we grounded each other, we lived in each other's back pockets like touchstones. A few months later, I moved to LA.

∎ ∎

Nah. That's not what happened, not even close. That's the feel-good, book club version of Gee and me. In real life, we were sitting on the edge of the pool at the Sunset Marquis, our legs dangling in the water.

"A girl could get used to this," I said, rubbing my foot against his.

"You should come to LA, Em; you could totally get a gig in the music biz, easy."

When I asked if this was his way of inviting me to move in with him, he didn't say yes. He said, "Sure, why not? You could live with me and Armin."

"As what?" I asked.

I wanted clarification, because I had a roommate in Detroit, named Lulu. She was an artist—she made strangely compelling soft sculptures out of beads and found materials—and we got along really well. I wasn't looking for a roommate situation, and I already had a great gig. I was looking for something I didn't have: a life partner. We'd been dancing around this idea of my moving to LA for years; usually it was me on the fence, and mostly because I had a job that

I didn't want to give up, but this time it was Gee who had cold feet, giving me the 'ex' girlfriend needs a place to crash treatment.

The rest of the trip was pretty much a disaster. As bad as it gets. I checked out of the fancy hotel the radio station put me up in and moved into Gee's apartment in Koreatown, the one with cockroaches of all sizes, babies and big fat mamas—whole communities of roaches—living in their bathroom. I jumped up and down, screaming *eeewww* so loud the boys thought there was a dead body.

"Don't be a girl," Gee sniped at me.

Then he disappeared, poof, into the wind, saying he was working, even though it was the weekend, and his roommate, Armin, babysat me, taking me to breakfast at Dukes on Sunset and later to the Hollywood Bowl to watch the orchestra rehearse for free. At night it was the three of us, me and Gee *and* Armin, at Coconut Teaszer on the strip, for catfish and live music. We stayed up late, the three of us talking music and drinking beer. Then we crashed, in our clothes, the three of us. The next morning, Armin offered to drive me to the airport, the three of us again, and by the time I landed back in Detroit, I was pretty sure Gee and I were stuck in the just-friends bin. When Armin wrote me a love letter saying that Gee was a fool for not appreciating me, it was official: me and the roadie were over, kaput. I grabbed my address book and crossed his name out with a black felt-tip pen.

A few months later (after he broke up with the girlfriend he hadn't admitted to having when I was in town), Gee called and said, "Hey, Em, I've been thinking about you. . ."

And that's when I told him I was getting married. I don't know where this came from—perhaps a fierceness that reflected a deeper sense of my own value than I consciously knew myself to possess, my inner pineapple headdress. "This is the year I'm getting married," I informed Gee, like it was my New Year's resolution and if I said it out loud, I could make it happen.

I hope it will be to you, but if it isn't, it'll be to someone else.

I didn't tell him I had options, didn't mention the Paper Bag Man, the guy my mom was rooting for, a proper suitor, wooing the hand of his intended by enchanting her mother like a character in a turn-of-the-century romance novel.

"That man is in love with you," my mom said, not to mention (but she did, lots of times) paper bags are big business, Emma.

I liked the Paper Bag Man, but I wasn't in love with him and I didn't want to marry him. He scared me. When he said I was the one, I worried he meant I'd *be* the one, *the only one of us*, to fix dinner, or, worse, that he'd want me to quit my job as soon as we had kids. Basically, I was afraid the Paper Bag Man would try to shrink me. Not just change me—shrink, twist, rearrange me.

I thought the guy least likely to turn me into my mother would be the roadie. If I told you Gee was on the plane two days after that phone call with a ring and an offer of true love forever, you'd probably smell a bullshit Hollywood ending, and you'd be right. What he did was disappear, for weeks—radio silence, like he forgot my number—but the next time he called and asked me to come to LA, he said "please."

"Please, Em, I love you and I don't want to lose you."

So I quit my job and followed Gee to LA. I didn't know, at the time, that I was establishing a life precedent.

THE HOLE

The first conversation I had with V was week one at the international school in Paris, and it was about Ruby, now in fourth grade.

"Of course, we don't *require* a uniform," V said, stressing the word "require" as she stared disapprovingly at my daughter's miniskirt and crop top.

"Oh, c'mon." I laughed. "All the girls in Los Angeles dress like this."

She smiled and nodded, didn't even have to point out that we weren't in LA anymore. That's how V operated: She tricked you into stating her case for her, and then she nodded in agreement, like it was your idea in the first place. *That slick.*

This time, she pretended she wanted to talk about Rio.

"There have been several incidents we should discuss," she said when she summoned me to her office and placed the blame squarely on my shoulders.

It's always the mother.

So maybe I *was* a little out of my league, putting my kids in a tony private school in the sixteenth arrondissement, but there was a lived-in, ramshackle, vine-covered, *Madeline* feel to the place that appealed to me. Kids bursting out of classrooms, spilling chaotic energy on the playground, and I thought, *Yes, my children will be comfortable here.* I did not choose the American school, with its sprawling, suburban grounds and football field; I did not even consider St. Mary's, with its nuns and state-of-the-art science lab. I picked the international school, while sitting at my kitchen table in Los Angeles, from a selection of brochures, having never met V Strickling, or anyone like her, before. The V is for Victoria, like the queen.

■ ■

Let's back up a few months to when Gee was standing in our bedroom in Los Angeles, a towel wrapped around his waist, having just returned from eight months in Italy. I came home from work and found him freshly showered, suitcase open on the bed, unpacking. I was torn between wanting to rip the towel off him and giving him a proper welcome home and expressing just how hard it had been without him. I wish I could tell you I went with the towel idea, but instead I said, "Gee, this isn't working. You need to get a job in LA."

"Jesus, Em, I just walked in the door."

It was the sort of fight we could do on autopilot. We just started hurling complaints at each other, like paintball, like you can shoot that bloodred, shocking-pink, deep-purple shit at each other and it'll wash right off.

He said I was being a bitch.

I said he was never around.

He said I was the one who wanted more money.

I said we'd have more money if we didn't spend every dime I made on after-school care and babysitters. If I had a coparent to help with the kids. Toward the end, the fight petering out, Gee complained that I'd taken over the whole closet, and I said it made me feel sad to see his side bare, like how my mother must have felt when she looked at my dad's side of their closet: empty, no suits hanging.

"I'm not dead, Em. I'm traveling on business." And then he said, real quiet, "Em, this is my job."

"Can't you do something else?"

"I'll try."

I thought he meant he'd try to get another job, one that was based in LA, but what he did was get another family relocation overseas.

"This way, you don't have to work while I'm on the road," he said. "It's a management position, Em. Put your eggs in my basket," he pleaded. "Just for a while, so I can move my career forward." So that's what I did. Because I wanted my husband to be successful. I wanted *both of us* to be successful. But I admit, despite all my complaining about how important my career was, a year in Paris did sound like fun. And then after a year we could come home and I could get a new job. A better job. A year is like a sabbatical—it's no big deal; it could even be a career boost, add to my cachet. The zoo threw me a bon voyage party; they had a cake with a caricature of me standing in front of the Tour Eiffel, wearing a beret and carrying a baguette under my arm. When I saw that cake, joy rippled silently through my whole body. A year in Paris!

A month later, Gee was already gone and I was overseeing the movers. Literally, the movers were *in the house.* The kids and I were packed and ready to go—boxes labeled with magic marker: "Keep," "Ship," "Give Away"; the house sitter arranged; our cars in storage— when the relocation manager called Gee in Paris.

The two of them conferenced me in on the call.

"Good news," Mina announced. "Your stay in Paris has been extended."

Just like that, a year in Paris turned into four years abroad. Four years is not a little time off to refresh—it's career suicide. After she hung up, leaving just Gee and me on the phone, he didn't ask, "Are you okay with this, Em?" He said, "You need to sell the cars, call the insurance company, cancel the house sitter, and hire a real estate manager. Ship everything you think we'll need: books, toys, furniture, kitchen items."

Mina arranged a last-minute rental car to be dropped off at the house, as a courtesy, so that I could facilitate the change in plans. "Your life is like a permanent vacation," she joked.

I smiled politely, controlling the urge to snap at her, because Mina was my official interface with Gee's company and I didn't want to be labeled a "problem wife." I always tried to keep it friendly, but we were not friends. And moving to Paris was not a vacation. When I go on vacation, I like there to be sand and a beach, straw hats and flip-flops. I like to plan that vacation myself, pore over websites, looking for the most dropped-out, dope, off-the-grid place I can find. Yelapa—it's a tiny little cove in Mexico that I shouldn't mention because it's a best-kept secret. You can't even get there by car. You have to take a boat from PV. There's no dock; they just throw your bags on the beach and you wade in after them. A week, maybe ten days later, totally destressed, mañana, baby, you grab that ferry back to civilization and return to work. A vacation has an end date; that's what makes it a vacation—that round-trip ticket back home.

That night I was taking the kids out to dinner, backing out of the driveway, when I hit the side of the garage and heard a metallic *crunch*. Oops. *This car is bigger than mine*, I thought, putting it in drive, gently stepping on the gas while the passenger side scraped against the garage again. For a minute I forgot how to drive; my brain couldn't send a message to my hands. *Turn the wheel, Em!* We were rocking back and forth, like when I was driving in Detroit in the winter, stuck on ice, trying to get some traction, only it was August in LA and the kids were in the back seat, wearing T-shirts and shorts.

"Mommy," Rio yelled, "you're smashing the car."

"I know."

"Are you gonna get in trouble?" Ruby asked.

"No, sweetie, Mommy never gets in trouble. She gets stuck some-times, but mommies don't get in trouble. Besides, Daddy's company has insurance."

• •

So there I was, summoned to the headmistress's office, feeling awkwardly like my teenage self, like I'd gotten caught smoking in the john or talking back in class. V was smiling. She had this perpetual smile, a red slash, like it was painted on; she was wearing a tweed pencil skirt, pumps, and a creamy, silky blouse with one too many buttons undone—a little too revealing for primary school, if you ask me, but this was Paris and it was I who was underdressed. *Sloppywood.* Jeans, sneakers, and a moto jacket. Outplayed from the get-go.

She smiled, so I smiled.

She crossed her legs, and I crossed mine.

She mentioned Columbine, and I lost the battle. Right there. Had to apologize for my son's taking a protractor to the park, hiding it in his sweatshirt pocket so he and Andy could dig a tunnel from Paris to China. Of course, she didn't actually mention Columbine or Sandy Hook or Parkland or any school shooting. She didn't have to—it's there, in the ether, when you talk schoolyard aggression in an international environment, and I was willing to fall on that sword. I get it. How the world views us. How, in my second-grade, American boy's hands, a protractor could be seen as a weapon. But she wasn't willing to leave it at that.

"Sometimes," she said, "when children have a hard time adjusting, it reflects a deeper problem. How are things at home?" she wanted to know, and then, not waiting for an answer, she followed up with a second query. "How are *you* doing, Emma?"

"I'm fine," I lied, shifting in my seat. No wonder the kids were intimidated by her. I searched her office for something to diffuse the tension—framed family photos or student art projects. Then I spotted a pair of boots and a whip in the corner.

"Do you ride?" I asked her. Of course she did—she was British. I could easily visualize her astride a quarter horse, making it do figure eights, holding the reins tight, slapping it with the crop.

"I've been headmistress here for some years now," she responded, ignoring my question, her smile unchanged, her hands poised in her lap, recrossing her legs for emphasis.

Is "headmistress" one word or two? I wondered, still imagining her in those boots with the whip. *Maybe it's hyphenated.*

"And," V continued, "the children who struggle most are often the ones whose mothers gave up satisfying jobs to follow their husband's careers overseas."

Boom. She zeroed in on me.

"Did you work, Emma? Yes, of course you did." She answered her own question, using the past tense. "Rio tells me you worked at the zoo."

"Marketing director," I confirmed, feeling the need to defend myself with a professional title. "Worked at the zoo" was too vague; the kids used to tell their teachers that Mommy took care of the sick animals. Even after Bring Your Daughter to Work Day, when Ruby sat on the floor in my office, coloring, while I typed on the computer, she still told people I took care of baby animals. Because this one time the zoo had a litter of wolf pups whose mother had abandoned them, and I got to play with them, tails wagging, nipping at my fingertips.

"Failure to nurture," the keeper said, so the baby wolves were moved to the nursery with a litter of newborn German shepherd service puppies, and the nursing mama fed them all, wolves and puppies alike.

"How long can they stay together?" I asked.

"We do have to keep an eye on them," the keeper answered, petting a baby wolf. "One day, it's like a switch flips. Instinct kicks in, and these wolves will kill all of these dogs. Nature versus nurture."

Why was I even thinking about this? One day the wolves were sleeping with the puppies, and the next day they ate them. Too close to home, I guess. Why was V talking to my son about my job, anyway? She was sneaky. Then she said something about my possibly mourning my career and how it would be understandable if that were the case.

"It sounds like you had a big job," V said, trying to flatter me into saying more than I should.

I started to perspire, under my arms, between my breasts, in the small of my back, but I didn't say anything, afraid that if I opened my mouth, the whole fucking dam would break. Next thing you know, she'd be getting me to admit how I'd lost my shit last week on the way home from school, had a total meltdown, crying, begging the kids to please just behave, sixteen metro stops from Rue Ranelagh to République, the three of us standing the whole way, squashed and jostled while I tried to hang on to both their hands.

"Why don't we have a car?" one said. "When can we go home?" the other wanted to know, and she didn't mean home to our apartment in the Marais. I practically had to pull them up the stairs four floors to our flat, no elevator, my backpack loaded with groceries.

"Why don't you do the grocery shopping when we're in school?" one asked. The other complained his backpack was too heavy, dragging it behind him, letting it clunk on every step, saying he was tired, plopping down on the landing between the third and fourth floors. "It's too heavy, Mommy."

"Andy has an elevator," he whined. Ruby pointed out that if I did the shopping *before* I picked them up, I would be able to carry Rio's backpack.

They blamed me for all of it: the metro, the stairs, Paris. I was the bad mommy for making them move. Yet I was just barely holding it together myself.

"Buck up," I told my grade-schoolers. "This is where we live, this is where Daddy works, this is our life now," and all the while I was crying and pulling them up the stairs, pushing them through the front door. As soon as we got into the apartment, that's when I really lost it, collapsing on the floor, kicking the door shut, punching Rio's backpack, wailing on it like I was at Gold's Gym. Ruby kept her distance, staring at me like I was a scary monster; Rio crouched on the floor, covering his head, just in case I missed the backpack.

A week later, Rio *accidentally* gave the little Japanese girl in his class a black eye, nearly causing an international incident. And V requested this meeting with me.

"You'll need to fill that hole, Em," she said.

She was referring to the hole that quitting my job at the zoo left in my psyche, in my identity, in my day, the nine hours between nine and six when I had nothing to do. Which wasn't entirely true, I had plenty to do. Domestic chores took longer in Paris. Multiple trips back and forth to the market, carrying groceries on my back because I was too stubborn to break down and buy one of those caddies with wheels, like Gee suggested. The ones that came in plaid or polka dots—so cute, they were supposed to make you think it was fun to go to the market. "It won't solve the problem," I said. "The cart will be too heavy for me to carry up the steps." When Gee insisted it would be more efficient, if I just . . . I stopped him with the palm of my hand, saying, "It won't solve the fucking problem."

"Why don't you join the PTA?" V asked. "They could use a woman with your abilities. And it would be good for the children to see you participate in school activities. It might be good for you, too, don't you think?"

That's how I got recruited for the PTA. Newcomer welcome coffees and bake sales. I was about to go all Niagara Falls—I could feel tears welling up—but I didn't let on, or we'd be flooded out of V's office, down the hall, spilling out into Rue Ranelagh. And I was already late for coffee with the tagalongs at Café Mozart. I thanked V politely for her time, for her concern about me and the children. Then, because I don't know when to stop and I always have to close the deal, I agreed to the whole PTA thing.

"I'm so glad we had this talk, Emma," V said.

• •

She was right. I did miss my job. But if I'm being completely honest, work was stressful and sometimes a break seemed like a good idea. It wasn't that I didn't like my job. It was a good job. First and foremost, the zoo was in Griffith Park, which was practically across the street from the kids' school in Silverlake. So it was convenient. Commuter convenience is a big plus in LA. And then there was the job itself, overseeing the radio-advertising budget, so even though I never got back into the music industry after Korea, I did (almost) get back into radio. Radio adjacent. And I was good at that job; I knew exactly how to develop promotions that would be on-air-friendly, like *Hog Wild*. That was my boss's idea.

"Give the pigs some love," she said.

Pigs are not the sexiest animals in the zoo. Kids don't tug on their mommy's shirt, saying, "Pleeeze, can we go see the pigs?" They're farm animals, the lowest rung of zoo critters. I needed to somehow make wild boars sound fun, so I got a bunch of radio stations to each sponsor a pig, and they got their listeners to come to the zoo in droves to vote for their favorite pig. It was hilarious, DJs competing with each other, like having the most popular pig at the zoo would get them some serious bragging rights. I'm goooood at that stuff. I loved my job. Working with animals never gets old.

I'll tell you what does get old, though. The culture wars. Married versus single; stay-at-home or working mother; daycare or nanny; kids or dogs; lean in or tag along. One thing I learned at the zoo is that animal people are not necessarily kid-friendly. Every time I left work because Rio was sick or Ruby was in a school play, there was a closed-door chat with Bosslady about how my being a breeder couldn't get in the way of her departmental rules.

"Emma," she said, "it's not that *I* mind, but it's not fair to the others." And then she'd say, "We all make choices in life."

I'm tempted to say she was a bitch—a big, unattractive woman with a shrill voice on a power trip, and that her not getting married and not having kids was probably natural selection and not a choice— but that's the kind of thing you should say only to your girlfriends when you're pissing and moaning about your job. Bosslady had a personnel file on me that was bulging with memos.

When Rio, barely six years old, was recovering from surgery, I told Bosslady I had to leave work early to go to the hospital. Rio was a trouper. We dragged him to Korea before he could even walk or talk, and from there to Singapore, Bali, and Phuket. Maybe because he wasn't socialized with other English-speaking kids, his speech was delayed. His first word was actually a full-on sentence, a complete thought: "Go home now." I was pretty sure he wouldn't want to wake up in the hospital alone.

"Emma," Bosslady said, "it's not life-threatening. He'll probably sleep all day. Why don't you wait until after work to visit him?"

And I said, "Never mind."

An hour later, I sent her an email that said I felt ill and had to go home immediately. Another memo in the file. There wasn't enough personal time, vacation days, comp hours in the world to make that situation work. I was drowning in my mother's dreams. Everything she had, plus everything she wanted. And the math didn't add up, either. Childcare cost a fortune: early drop-off, after-school programs, and a babysitter to pick them up after the after-school programs. Then came Tuesdays. Half days in the middle of the week! It was almost like it was intentional, like being a working mother was not supposed to be manageable. Add to it that Gee was always somewhere else, on a gig in the Bahamas, or living in London for months at a time. No more long-term overseas posts, I told him after Korea. So, instead, he just took short-term gigs and left me home alone with the kids and a full-time job for months at a time. Which is really why I said yes to Paris. And agreed to put my eggs in Gee's basket.

BALANCE VS. BLEND

"Mais oui . . . There is an alpha in every couple, n'est-ce pas?"

"Yes," I agreed, "but I always thought it would be me." This got a laugh out of Pascal, a French colleague of Gee's. He leaned back, exhaled a cloud of smoke, and settled in for an engaging conversation. We were talking about the shifting balance of power in expat marriages, the loss of career, community, and financial independence for tagalong wives.

"We had a corporate training recently—" Gee chimed in, lighting a cigarette, holding it in his front teeth while he lit the match, so he could keep on talking, "and the new term for 'work-life balance' is 'work-life integration.' It's all about harmony. Forget about the balancing act, two partners trying to do it all—that concept never worked anyway. The new idea is to coordinate or blend all the parts into a functioning unit."

"That sounds a lot like how we don't refer to the US as a melting pot anymore. We're supposed to call it a salad bowl now," I said, slathering *taramasalata* on a piece of fresh crusty bread.

"What does that mean?" Pascal asked.

"Nothing," I mumbled, my mouth full of pink caviar.

It was Friday night in Paris; we were enjoying a delicious spread from the Greek shop on Rue Bretagne. Pascal had brought a bottle of wine for me and a bottle of Pastis for himself and Gee. They would be drinking and smoking at the courtyard window long after I went to sleep. Gee's not really a smoker, but in Paris the guardrails were off. The kids were watching a movie in the other room and ducked in occasionally to grab some food.

"It means," Gee explained, "that people from all over the world mix it up in the States, but they keep their cultural identities. Like how ingredients in a salad bowl blend together but maintain their original flavor." He was happy to have the topic move from women's issues to immigration and assimilation. But I was feeling feisty, so I didn't let it go.

"It's just PC jargon," I countered, adding that nothing changes for women or immigrants; we just change the way we talk about it. Then Gee said something about how language informs attitudes, and attitudes inform change, so it's a step in the right direction. And I said, goading him on, "Okay, so we're a *functioning unit*."

"Yep." Gee grinned. "If you look at it that way, Em, our marriage is actually quite modern. We're a functioning blend of work and family."

"Lemme get this straight," I responded, "just for the sake of clarification." The sporting disagreement among friends is a French pastime, but this was becoming something else—we were on the verge of slipping into a real argument. Fortunately, all we had on the table were cheese knives. "Are you saying the *functioning* whole may be the sum of unequal parts? Is that what this new term implies?"

"I'm saying," Gee said slowly, übercarefully, with the dawning awareness of someone who's just stepped on a land mine, "that each partner brings different things to the marriage. Different. Not disequal. Is that a word?"

"I don't think so, buddy, but grammar is the least of your problems."

"Bah! You are lucky, no?" Pascal concluded. "You experience a different culture. So, you don't work. This is no malaise. This sounds like blah-blah-blah—more whining."

• •

Maybe I did sound like a whiny, white-privilege bitch. Poor me, I had to live in Paris, Tokyo, and Seoul, not just overseas but global capitals. So what if my residence status was attached to Gee's working visa and I wasn't allowed to work? I get it; it was a fucking First World problem if ever there was one. But the thing is, I couldn't succumb to that way of thinking. If I allowed my voice to be shut down, it would be like being twice annihilated, first by my husband's career and then again by my own self-awareness, by the silliness of my so-called predicament. A passport stamped *non travaille pas*. After all, a woman without a career is like a fish without headphones. It's not really a dilemma, is it? Especially if that woman is married with kids—oh, for God's sake, isn't that enough? Greedy little bitch wants everything. Marriage, kids, *and* a career. Well, yeah, that was the promise, but the promise turned out to be not so much a fantasy as a setup for failure, so now the women's magazines, the tied-up-with-a-bow online articles, are saying that you can still have everything, just not at the same time. Sequentially.

Only nobody says that to men.

At first I felt guilty for not deriving pleasure from following my husband around the world. Then I felt conned by feminist ideology and began to self-identify as an antifeminist. It took me a while to figure out that wasn't supposed to work. That's the point. Make women miserable enough *doing* everything, instead of *having* everything, and we'll retreat back into the home, where we belong. It's systemic. And it could pretty much be fixed with one thing: affordable childcare. Which they have in France. But I digress. This is not a feminist story. Or is it? I used to stare at my pay stub and calculate my actual take-home, net pay, less the cost of daycare and after-school babysitters. It didn't add up to much. If you're Sheryl "Fuck All" Sandberg and you're the COO of Facebook, you can lean in till you're flat-out horizontal on the massage table at the end of the day, because you can afford a nanny with legit paperwork who drives a Volvo, can even have her do the grocery shopping and cook, but for the rest of us, it's a grind and Pollo Loco for dinner. I was basically working full-time as a placeholder just to keep my résumé current. Who wouldn't quit and run off to Paris for a reprieve? But once you've had a career, you just might have an existential crisis and wonder, *Who am I if I don't work?*

• •

"You must be Gee's wife," the guy in the green felt hat said, extending his hand to shake mine.

"Must I?"

"Huh?"

"Must I be Gee's wife? I mean, it's a fair question."

"Maybe I'm mistaken," Green Hat said. "I thought Gee pointed at you."

I scanned the bar, looking for Gee, and spotted him nose to nose with a green-streaked blonde.

"Him?" I asked, pointing at the two of them, so close their foreheads were almost touching. My husband. *The man you say I "must" be married to.*

Green Hat got this look on his face like he couldn't get away from me fast enough. But I was just getting started.

"So, if I *must* be Gee's wife," I asked Green Hat, "who must be yours?" And I pointed to an emerald-colored dress. "Her?"

He started to back away from me. That's right, back away from the bomb. The one that's about to explode.

We were on a St. Patty's Day pub crawl. I was invited out with Gee's team, an appearance in the flesh of the bitch wife from hell. Untamed. *Non*compliant. Crazy. A woman now referred to as Must Be Gee's Wife. My name had mutated into The Wife Of, The Mother

Of. Gee took my coat when we got to the bar. A gallant gesture or a way of controlling my exit? And he bought me a green draft, even though I don't drink beer.

"C'mon," he insisted, before merging into the crowd. "Get in the spirit."

I caught a glimpse of him, over a sea of drunken conversations, holding court. An American businessman in Paris. I sipped the green beer while weighing my options: stand in the corner like a disapproving schoolmarm, or conjure a fake smile and charm his colleagues. To cope or leave. Someone yelled, "Next!" The crowd began to move, and I was swept up and out into Les Halles, en route to another pub. This time, I held on to my coat. Somewhere between the third or fourth bar stop, I disappeared.

Gee came home a few hours later, sloppy drunk, and climbed on top of me like an octopus, all arms and legs, smothering me with kisses. I was squirming under the weight of him, which he mistook as desire.

"Where'd you go, Emmy?" he asked, kissing my neck.

"Gee!" I exclaimed, pushing him off me, "I can't breathe."

TOM AND JERRY

"You are a woman in desperate need of adult conversation," Jerry said the first time we met. We were sitting on the couch, our daughters playing in the bedroom. It was the beginning of the school year, and we were both new to Paris. The couch was not mine, we were living in a temporary furnished apartment. Old and dark, not quaint. It had the musky smell of strangers.

"Will you be my friend?" I asked Jerry.

"Yes, of course, Em*mah*, but I'm not talking about that," she said. "You know what I'm talking about, don't you?" she asked, covering my hand with hers. She let it sit there for a beat too long, long enough that it was uncomfortable. Honestly, I didn't have a clue what she was talking about, but her daughter was Ruby's first friend in Paris, so I played along.

Jerry pronounced my name Em*mah*, real formal, in this fancy Jamaican lilt. She liked to put on airs, wore a proper pin-striped walking suit just to pick the kids up from school, her dreads hanging down her back, and spoke in this island-born British accent, even though she moved to Paris from the San Fernando Valley. We're talking deep in the Valley too. Strip malls. Jerry had an unnerving way of penetrating your most private thoughts and pulling them out to examine over afternoon tea. Always tea. She didn't drink coffee or wine, could not even tolerate the smell of tobacco. Why someone who didn't smoke, drink, or eat meat would move to Paris was a mystery to me. But her body was her temple, her Zen Buddhist shrine; she read the Sufi poets and was into love big-time, not the pumping, sweaty kind, but the touchy-feely, deeply spiritual stuff. Past lives and the universe. Rumi.

She said she'd come to Paris to write a book, but she wouldn't tell me what it was about. She said she was happily married, but she'd left her husband in California. She said she wanted her kids to be around French-speaking people of color, but she didn't speak a word of French herself. She started sending me messages addressed to Tom and signed her emails as Jerry. I thought it was cute, because I hadn't seen those cartoons since my own childhood and I didn't know Tom was the dumb one, and that mouse, Jerry, was always tricking him into jumping off the edge of a cliff, scrambling in air before he fell into the abyss.

I'd see her every day after school, picking up the kids, and she'd tell me how many pages she'd written. I stopped asking what the book was about; she wasn't gonna tell me. Thought it was bad luck.

"Meet me for tea," she suggested one afternoon.

■ ■

A few days later, we were at Mariage Frères, surrounded by gilded mirrors and fancy ladies, spoons tinkling on bone china, whispers floating like smoke in the air. I was dying for a cigarette. She wanted to know everything—about my marriage, my husband, and my kids.

"What's it like to be a tagalong?"

I told her how I missed working, how sometimes I'd drop the kids off at school, go back home, and crawl right back into bed. I was starved for girl talk.

"You need a man," she announced, staring deep into my eyes, way past the humor that charmed most people.

"I'm married."

"Oh, that," she replied. "What? Him? The International Businessman?"

•   •

"Tom!" Jerry emailed me in November. "We need coats!"

It was too cold for our Cali-gal gear. For a while I got by with just a jean jacket; then I switched to leather; then I layered up, with the jean jacket under the leather. That's my signature move, always trying to work with what I already have.

"Let's go to Galeries Lafayette," she suggested.

We must have tried on every damn coat they had in the store, giggling like schoolgirls. If this had been a movie, they'd have cued the montage. It was raining coats, peacoats, overcoats, and big, puffy down jackets. I had high expectations and no budget. That coat, it needed to do everything: fit over sweaters yet not look too bulky, keep my legs warm but not drag at the heels. It needed to be stylish, but also practical and not frivolous. I sensed that, only for me, did it have to be affordable.

I tried on this one coat: calf-length cashmere, greenish brown like my eyes, so soft it could have been a blanket.

"Pas mal," the saleslady said.

Pas mal? Not bad. At those prices, a coat needed to be more than not bad. It needed to be *super bon.* Oh, the things I didn't understand about Paris, about life—that *pas mal* was French for "pretty damn good."

The next time I saw Jerry, she was wearing a long wool coat, coffee-colored like her skin, and cinched at the waist with African print ribbon. It fit her perfectly too. I was jealous.

"You bought a coat without me!"

"Em*mah*," she said, "It's cold. I needed a coat."

A week later, she was wearing a puffy silver down jacket. And I was still standing there outside the kids' school in my leather jacket, freezing.

"Two coats!" I exclaimed.

"Em*mah*," she said, "you are impossible. You want one coat to satisfy all of your needs. Sometimes it's a bit chilly; sometimes it's bitter cold. Some coats keep you warm. Some coats make you feel special. One is not enough."

"Are we talking men or coats?" I laughed.

I ended up buying a wool coat at a resale shop. It checked all, or most, of the boxes—affordable, practical, warm, passably stylish—but I didn't love that coat. It didn't make me smile. It didn't even fit me. Rather, it fit only when I wore it over a sweater. So it was an overcoat. The rest of the time it was oversize, but not in a good way; my body got lost in it. Jerry was right: I expected too much from one coat. A few months later, after I'd worn that big, ill-fitting coat all winter long, I bought myself a second coat, gunmetal leatherette with black felt cuffs and matching collar, snug and chic. I looked good in that coat, I *felt* good in that coat, and I wore that coat whenever it wasn't actually cold out, because that coat did a lot for me, but it didn't keep me warm. That's how I discovered scarves. And silk long underwear and all the things French women use to stay warm while looking chic. But the thing I really learned, the takeaway, was, it's not cheating on an overcoat to buy a parka. Or, in my case, to acquire a second coat simply because it makes you smile when you slip your arm into its sleeve.

■　■

It was Jerry who introduced me to the poet, said we'd get along like peas in a pod. "He's in touch with his feminine side," she said. "He's like a girl. He's the male version of you—he tells everything. If he spent more time writing than he did talking, he might get something published." She let out a low grumble of a laugh. "If he spent more time editing than drinking, *I* might get something published," she added.

That last part wasn't a joke. The poet was editing her book of secrets. Jerry dragged me to a poetry event, somewhere on the Left Bank, to hear him read. The only other time I'd been to a poetry reading was in Detroit. Patti Smith was hiding out, living the married-mom life with Fred "Sonic" Smith, somewhere on the east side of the D. She was rumored to attend poetry readings, real low-key. So I'd frequent these underground dives in Hamtramck, hoping to catch a glimpse of her, alive and in the flesh, and convince her to do a comeback concert for the radio station where I worked. I'd sit in the back of the room, plugged into my iPod, searching for the High Priestess of Rock and Roll; when she didn't show, I'd leave. That was pretty much the sum total of me and my interest in poetry.

Until I met the poet.

He was standing at the podium, wearing suit pants, his shirt untucked, and those signature blue shoes. Which is why I started calling him Bleu. The place was packed; he was a bit of a local celeb, an enfant terrible. He had groupies too—this one girl, an angora pom-pom, followed him around in a pouf of pastel. He stopped by our table to say hello, but that girl was like a powder-puff magnet, pulling him away from us and into her web.

"I don't like that," Jerry said.

Jerry didn't like a lot of things. Like when I told her how the poet opened his front door looking like he'd just woken up, even though it was after noon, his shirt buttoned wrong, his belly showing above his pants, running his fingers through his hair, trying to make himself presentable.

"I don't like that," she said.

"What do you care?" I asked. "I'm the one who was there." I was the delivery girl, dropping off Jerry's pages and picking up the poet's edits.

"But he was expecting *me*," she said. So she took it personally. She thought it was unprofessional. It's disrespectful, she complained. "It's rude."

It was a ruse, that's what it was, just to get me and the poet to meet.

"How do you know Jerry?" Bleu asked.

"Our kids go to school together."

"Are you a writer?" he wanted to know.

No one had ever asked me that before. I didn't know how to answer. "Yes" would have been a stretch; "no" would have been a cover-up.

"Sort of," I said. "I write some."

"About what?" he pressed.

"Just stories, personal things, girl stuff," I told him.

"I'd like to read your work sometime," he said.

My work. As if my stories could be construed as *work*. It felt good, though, to consider them as something someone might read, as having a life outside my laptop. It made my pulse race and my cheeks flush. It was exciting, like rock and roll used to be, every part of me switched on. Alive. That's how it felt from the moment I met the poet. From the moment he opened his door—when I handed him Jerry's pages and he asked to see mine—I walked around in a fog of him. Dogs came up to me on the street and sniffed between my legs. I was oozing desire. I was practically drooling in some reptilian, club-waving, cave-girl, "me want him" kind of way. Every person, every conversation, every daily transaction, big or small, was an interruption of me thinking about him. I picked up the kids from school, Ruby excited about the school play, Rio upset by the substitute teacher from hell, me nodding my head, uh-huh, all the time thinking about him.

"You're not listening to me," they complained. They were miffed; I said I was sorry. She retreated into her shell. He went back to Gameboy. I returned to my fantasy—the one where I was a writer and the poet loved my work. And my writing, it was on fire, burning up the pages.

"I think I have a crush on a poet," I told Gee, hoping it would get his attention, hoping he might tap into some of the smoke that was leaking from my pores.

"It's just transference," he said. Gee was happy that I had found something to fill the hole. He was torn between the demands of his new position and the need to be present in our daily lives. My passion for writing made his life easier.

• •

The blood-type party was Jerry's idea. The Japanese believe you can tell a lot about people by their blood type, everything from personality traits to compatibility. Sort of a plasmatic zodiac chart. Kiko, one of the moms at the kids' school, told us about this, and Jerry thought it would make a perfect parlor game. She immediately set about hosting a blood-type party, an intimate gathering of expatriates and artists, two writers, and a Rastafarian DJ. The poet and me. No spouses. "Know your blood type" was all the invitation said, and it listed the invitees like a proper literary salon. I'm type O, universal donor. I get along with everyone. We sat on cushions on the floor, ate spicy Caribbean lentils and rice. Jerry was a laid-back hostess, cooking and serving, a brightly colored scarf around her forehead. She had recently cut off her braids and was sporting a bleached blonde afro. Kiko explained blood-type theory. Annari read a series of poems about love and loss. The guy with the dreads put Santana on the stereo. Jerry pulled everyone to their feet and started doing some sort of conga line. After we had exhausted our artistic selves, everyone started talking about vacation plans. Travel is the conversational staple among expats: who's going where, what to take or buy when you get there, when to go. Kiko was skiing in Chamonix, Annari was going to the UK to visit family, the guy with the dreads was going to Bruges, Jerry and her kids were meeting her husband in the Canary Islands.

"I'm going to Hong Kong," I said. Just me. No kids, no husband.

Why Hong Kong? They all wanted to know. Even for expats with loads of frequent-flier miles, Asia was exotic. That's when the poet put his head in my lap and said he'd never been to Hong Kong. His hair was soft and feathery.

"Do you want company?" he asked.

It may have been the most romantic gesture anyone has ever made in the history of me.

HONG KONG

For the record, Hong Kong wasn't my idea. I never wanted to go there. But nobody remembers that, not Gee or his mother; they remember only that I went. Or, rather, who I went with. Which is funny, when you think about it, because it was their idea in the first place; they shipped me off to Hong Kong and then when their plan backfired, boy, were they pissed.

"Oh, but you must go!" That's what Milly said when I told her that Andra was living in HK with the dot-com boyfriend. I was just making polite conversation. I didn't feel like talking about Gee's job, the kids, or the eighty-five different types of cheese they sold at the fromagerie on our market street, which was the sort of thing my mother-in-law liked to hear about when she called. Only I wasn't in the mood to humor her. Instead, I offered this innocent piece of gossip: Andra had just moved to Hong Kong with her boyfriend.

She swooped down on that like a hawk, insisting that I visit Andra, offering to watch the kiddies while I was away, like she'd be doing me a huge favor. Milly is the type of woman who always manages to make getting exactly what she wants seem like she's doing you a big favor. Truth is, she was dying to come to Paris. She's a total Francophile. The whole family is a bunch of snooty foodies, going on about the *rôti* chicken from Chez l'Ami Louis, that restaurant you have to book three months to the day in advance, insanely overrated, all the presidents go there . . . plus Gee's family.

"So, you're going to Hong Kong," Gee said, like it was a done deal, when he walked through the door that night.

This was my mother-in-law's version of the telephone game; I told Gee's mom that Andra had moved to Hong Kong; she hung up on me and immediately called Gee at work to inform him that his wife wanted to visit her best friend in Hong Kong. Before you knew it, he was emailing me to ask when, not if, I wanted to go. Milly was already packing her bags. Now my not wanting to go to Hong Kong made me seem unappreciative.

"What's with your mom insisting I go to Hong Kong?" I asked Gee.

"She's not comfortable around you," he said, "and you know how she can be. She just wants to come to Paris and spend time with the kids, and it would be easier if you weren't here, that's all." Gee can make anything sound reasonable, even kicking his wife out of the apartment so that his mother could iron his shirts and poach eggs for their kids. And it *was* his apartment, after all, paid for by his job. I was just the glorified nanny. There were times when I felt like a first wife in the making, like his side of the family was just waiting for me to get fed up enough to walk out.

Here's the thing about my mother-in-law: Everyone loved her. Andra loved her, thought she was arty, always in the kitchen, making something divine, or snatching up conversation pieces at Goodwill for next to nothing, a fake fur vest or some totally au courant military jacket. She didn't see the cunning side of Milly. No one did. And no one understood why Milly had a bee in her bonnet about me. Me neither. I mean, you can't hate your daughter-in-law for not being a good cook; it's a demerit but not a deal breaker. It had to be something deeper and more substantial, like she didn't think I was good enough for her son. Or maybe Milly didn't like how after Gee met me, it was all over for her. And after

I moved to California, it was set in stone: Her precious son was never coming home to Mommy.

"Em," Gee said, "don't make this into a big thing."

"But it *is* a big thing. Getting kicked out of the house by your mother-in-law is the definition of 'big thing.'"

"You're exaggerating," he said. "You're not getting kicked out; you're going on a trip, it's a vacation, and it's only a week. The two of you," he muttered under his breath, but loud enough so I could hear, acting like he was in the middle of a catfight.

I gave him the side-eye, a look that said, *How long will it take for you to choose sides? How long before your allegiance shifts from your mother to your wife?* The answer was that it should have happened already.

"You'll have fun," he said. "Besides, we've got miles."

• •

I was telling this story at Jerry's blood-type dinner party—about how my mother-in-law wouldn't visit us in Paris unless I vacated the premises, not just out of town but off the continent, on the other side of the world—milking it for all it was worth: the mother-in-law from hell and the bonus trip to China. That's when the poet put his head in my lap and said, "I'll come to Hong Kong with you."

We were sitting on the floor of Jerry's apartment in Neuilly-sur-Seine with the marble foyer and stone fireplace, listening to Ménélik. I like French rap, maybe because I can't understand the lyrics. It's like watching protesters march in Place de la République, which happened pretty regularly, the view from inside the expat bubble, no skin in the game, no real comprehension of the rage that boiled just below the surface. Protest as a kind of performance art, a visual experience, colorful signs floating by the café window. Unlike my mother-in-law—her, I understood. I knew exactly what she meant when she said, "Oh, but you must go!"

■ ■

A few months later, we were having dinner at Chez Pierrot on Rue Étienne Marcel with Gee's parents for their last night in Paris. It was my favorite restaurant, not fancy, not touristy. Gee told me the plan when he met me at Charles de Gaulle after my trip to Hong Kong, holding a bouquet of flowers. Like nothing had happened. Even though he read my emails and journals and maybe even found the mix tape I made Bleu and left in the tape player by accident.

Cheaters always get caught—that's what Andra says. A few years ago, before the dot-com boyfriend, she and I were lying on her ex-boyfriend's bed. The plan was just to return her key to his place— open the door to his apartment and drop it in a bowl on the table. But then one thing led to another and we started snooping around. Andra found some photos of the ex with his new girlfriend (they were in Big Bear for the weekend); then I peeked in his closet and found some of the girlfriend's clothes and decided to try them on. She had one of those dresses that buttoned down the front like a shirt.

"She must be preppy." Andra smirked. We raided his fridge for beer and collapsed on his bed, laughing. Me in his new girlfriend's dress, Andra staring at a picture of him and the new girlfriend, getting righteously pissed.

That's when she said, "Cheaters always get caught."

Technically, he wasn't cheating on Andra—he had moved on. But still, she felt cheated. And I wasn't really cheating on Gee, either; "cheating" makes it sound like I was sneaking around, hiding the evidence. This wasn't cheating; this was more like *Fuck you and how does it feel?*

■ ■

"I'm leaving you a painting in my will," Gee's mom announced at that now infamous Chez Pierrot dinner.

"Oh," I said, "which one?" Did I mention that the in-laws are col-lectors of sorts? Nothing worth much, but very art-school interesting.

"The one you admired last time you visited, darling, with the big, ballsy woman in the red slip, sitting on a chair, legs spread, smoking a cigarette."

I didn't even remember that painting, let alone ever saying that I liked it, but now it took on a whole new meaning. It was the Jezebel painting. I took a slug of wine; it was good, too, bloodred, robust. *She's got some nerve*, I was thinking, but here's what I said, what any good daughter-in-law would say in a situation like that: "Thank you very much, but I hope I don't inherit that painting for a very long time."

"Liar," she spat at me. Years of venom flew across haricots verts and foie gras. For a moment, time stopped. No one said anything. It was like the cat was finally out of the bag, sitting on the table for everyone to see. And it was mangy and ragged and stinky. Pus and crud. I opened my purse, pulled out a vial of Xanax right in front of the whole nasty lot of them, washed it down with a gulp of wine, and smiled. Didn't even try to hide it. Didn't excuse myself to go to the WC and discreetly take a chill pill like a lady.

■　■

According to her ad in *FUSAC*, the English-language expat weekly, DeeDee was a life coach, diet guru, and marriage counselor, but I called her the Divorce Doctor, on account of the fact that the first time we met, she said 85 percent of couples who seek counseling are really there to negotiate a divorce.

"Why are you here?" she asked us.

"We're in the 15 percent," Gee responded immediately.

I wasn't so sure. If you need to negotiate how to split the chores, who cooks, who takes out the trash, who pays the bills, and how much money to spend or save, I get the whole marriage-counseling thing.

But how was a marriage counselor going to help if you didn't like the flat, nasal sound of your husband's voice, or the way he walked with a forward tilt like he was always in a hurry and you were the one holding him back? I just wanted them all to leave me alone and let me hang out with the poet until I got bored. Was that asking too much?

"You're always trying to get me to give things up," I said.

"Like what?" Gee asked.

"Like my friends, my sense of community, my job; like our house in Los Angeles on stilts with a view of the canyon. That house was everything, and now you want me to give up Bleu."

"Maybe you need some time on your own," DeeDee suggested.

DeeDee's living room doubled as her office. It was very bougie: pastel colors and plump cushions. She had boxes of tissues everywhere—on the coffee table, on both sides of the couch, in the loo. It was like she *wanted* her clients to cry.

"You could use a dartboard around here," I told her.

"Typically," she said, "in situations like this, when one partner is having an affair, I request that he or she put that on hold while we work together on the marriage. Are you willing to do that?"

"Um, not really."

"Em, I know you're angry," Gee said, "but we need to deal with this. Please, I'm begging you."

"Oh, so *now* you believe in therapy. When you came home from Japan, stinking of that woman you fucked over there, you wouldn't have any part of it. I had to go solo to marriage counseling. Do you know how that feels, sitting there next to an empty chair, pointing at the air where your husband should be?"

"It sounds like you have reason to be angry," DeeDee said.

"Not angry. It's just funny how he's all about therapy *now*, now that I've found someone else, someone to talk to, someone who has time to spend with me."

"That's because your loser boyfriend doesn't have a job," Gee said.

"Neither do I," I pointed out. "Anyway, he's a poet. And he works. Sure, he doesn't make the big corporate bucks, but it's not all about the money."

"Easy for you to say when you're living off my income."

"What choice do I have? My passport is stamped *non travaille pas*."

"What do you both want?" DeeDee asked. "I tell my clients they have to figure out their personal bottom line. For some it's sex; for others it's money. Family. Love. Work. Intimacy. Security. What's your bottom line?"

"I want my wife back," Gee said.

"I want my life back," I replied.

I was staring at the wall, at this picture of nothing, just cool grays and soft pinks, lines, brushstrokes, colors swirling. It was meant to be generic and calming, but it pissed me off. Her art sucked. I sucked. I sucked as a tagalong wife. I was sucking it up and blowing it up all at the same time.

"I agreed to one year in Paris, and it turned into four," I said.

Sacrifice. Compromise. I had no identity. I looked in the mirror and saw my mother. The poet saw me. Not a partner who would handle the logistics of an overseas post; not a tagalong spouse to take care of the kids and keep house. He saw me as a woman. And also, *and especially*, as a writer. It wasn't even about the sex with Bleu; it was all about the cigarette after. The whole affair was like an extended postcoital smoke, meeting at cafés, talking for hours, dissecting everything: my marriage, his money problems, my writing. He loved my voice, the one on paper. It was like talking to someone wearing mirrored shades and seeing an enhanced version of yourself reflected back at you through their eyes.

"I feel betrayed," Gee said.

"Let's talk about Gee's feelings of betrayal—"

"The real betrayal," I interrupted, "is the *one* year that turned into *four*."

"That's a good place to start. Gee, can you hear what she's saying?"

"I want to. But I have a motherfucking full-time job, I have dead-lines hanging over my head, we are FUBAR—fucked up beyond all repair, over budget, on a tight schedule—and just coming here once a week in the middle of a workday puts me further behind. If I don't pull this project out of my ass, there will be no more expat package, no more fancy apartment in the Marais, her sitting in cafés all day."

"Can you see that he's under pressure, Em?"

"This was his choice, not mine. I would have preferred that we stay in LA, both of us working and raising the kids."

"I don't get gigs in Los Angeles, Em. I go where the gigs are."

"I'd like to circle back to Bleu. Can you put that on hold while we work on your marriage?"

"You're both being so puritanical," I said. "This is Paris. Doesn't everyone take a lover?"

"Em . . ."

"Yes, Gee?"

"I can't deal with this right now."

"I know. But I can't give this up, I can't give up one more thing; it feels like huge chunks have been carved out of me and I'm just trying to fill the holes."

"Maybe you should move out," DeeDee suggested. And I could see her point. I mean, I couldn't very well kick Gee out, since his company was paying for our place.

■ ■

Bleu thought it was a good idea for me to rent a studio. Jerry hooked me up with her real estate agent, and the three of us went looking for an apartment. We found a flat above a bakery on Rue Charlot—rhymes with "low"; the *t* is silent. Looks like "Harlot," but with a *C*. Every time I turned down my street, my mind said *Rue Char*low; *see* "*Harlot.*" Like a footnote.

I started to panic right there in the apartment with the real estate agent. Jerry and Bleu were checking out the kitchen and asking about rent. First and last.

"How many months do you want, Em?"

"Huh?" I hadn't heard a word; it was all noise and no kids.

Bleu came up behind me, put his arms around me, whispered in my ear, in that late-night jazz-musician voice, all rhythm and tone, "It'll be all right; everything is okay."

"You're in love, aren't you," Jerry said. It wasn't a question; it was more like a statement, maybe even an accusation: *You're not just fooling around; you're not like that, are you? You're not* that *kind of woman.*

But what if I am? That's what I was thinking, because I wasn't sure. I might just have been bored out of my mind and trying to claim something for myself from the French experience, something other than learning how to buy *jambon* at the *marché*. It was all happening so fast, it felt like being on a people mover. The path was in motion, but my feet were not actually taking any steps. I couldn't stop, jump off, or turn around. I wanted to close my eyes and make it all go away, all of them: Gee, Jerry, Bleu. I just really wanted to be alone. So maybe DeeDee was right about something.

■　■

I called the apartment Camp Mom, hoping it would sound fun, hoping to fool the kids into thinking it was a mini-vacation—like that was a thing, all the cool moms were doing it when they got tired or crazy and couldn't think straight or breathe anymore. But the kids didn't buy that for a minute. Kids are not stupid.

"You're too old for camp," Rio said.

"Where's the canoe?" Ruby asked.

Camp Mom was shoebox-small, the bed hung like a cloud suspended from the ceiling over a futon couch. The kids loved that the first and only time they slept over. I joked that you could pee, wash your hair, and make coffee at the same time. Camp Mom was close enough to our apartment that I could walk home, make the kids breakfast in the morning, take them to school, pick them up after school, feed them dinner, help with their homework, put them to bed, and then wait. For Gee to come home from work—which was *always* late, *intentionally* late. After dinner in Montparnasse; after drinks at the dart bar; after Pari Roller, the Friday-night skate that started at ten o'clock and went until morning. Getting my own place turned out to be more about Gee's gaining his freedom than about my having space. I was shackled to the kids.

Sundays were my day off. Mostly I just lay in bed, reading, or went to a movie by myself. I didn't write. I was too nervous to write, couldn't sit still, couldn't focus. And when I tried to write, my voice went sad. Maybe "sad" isn't the right word. Sadness is situational, Bleu said. It's temporary—your dog dies. Sorrow is something else—it's pervasive; it's your past, your future; it's today, tomorrow, and all of your tomorrows. When sadness is that heavy, it needs a weightier word to describe it. Paris can be depressing. No one has the nerve to say so, but all the buildings are all the same. The sky is overcast. There's no color. The whole city is a study in beige and gray, greige. I was terrified of losing the kids and ending up alone. I knew Ruby and Rio would stay with Gee unless I took them home to LA. But if I did that, I'd be a single, working mother with two kids. Which also terrified me. I couldn't support myself in Paris without working papers. I didn't want to move in with Bleu, in an apartment with a toilet that didn't work properly and halls that smelled of cat piss. He said I was venal. I had to look it up in the dictionary. I'm not sure it's venal to choose *not* to live in squalor.

"I'm living my life," he said. His observation, like Jerry's, was really an accusation: like I wasn't. You'd have to hear the way he said it, drawing the word "living" out for five extra beats, like he was Henry fucking Miller, living some grand artist's life in Paris.

▪ ▪

"How's Gee doing?" I asked DeeDee the next time we met; our counseling sessions were no longer as a couple.

"He's moved on," she said. "You should too."

"What does that even mean?" I asked her. But I knew what it meant. Since I was watching the kids mornings and evenings, Gee never had to come home, not for dinner, not for anything. It was therapy-sanctioned payback.

"What do you want to do today?" Bleu emailed me one Sunday after I had been living at Camp Mom for almost a month. He signed it "xoE," for "everything." I'm your everything, he told me, but he wasn't everything—he was just everything that Gee wasn't. It wasn't the same thing. We worked only as a threesome.

I want to go home, I thought. *That's what I want to do today.* I wanted to go home and do laundry, sit on the ugly, pink-and-green-floral couch, the one that Milly had talked me into buying, saying my taste was too severe, suggesting I go with something soft and pretty "for a change." I had buyer's remorse immediately. I hated that pinkish, poufy, so-not-me sofa so much that I painted the wall behind it pink—pink camouflage—hoping the couch would disappear into the wall. And then I shipped that couch to Paris, knowing it was never getting in the container back to Los Angeles. And now all I wanted to do today was sit on that butt-ugly couch that I hated, listen to Van Morrison, and read a book. It was Sunday, and I didn't want to do anything. And the only person I felt comfortable doing absolutely nothing with was my husband.

"Let's go to the Pompidou," I told Bleu.

▪ ▪

"You will not leave your husband," Ines said to me. "*Jamais*. You want your cake and eat cake too. Is that how you say it?"

"Usually we just say, 'She wants it all.'"

She was trying to master idioms. It was kind of endearing. We could be friends in another universe; she spoke in linguistic phrases, and I thought in song lyrics.

Ines was Bleu's ex, the mother of the daughter Bleu was raising all by himself, the girl who didn't like the way I laughed. Too loud and American. Ines worked somewhere in the South of France and came to Paris once a month to check in on her daughter. She was wearing low heels, slacks, not jeans, a tailored white blouse, and a scarf, managing to somehow pull off sharp and sexy, not severe. On this day, we were having lunch at Joe Allen's, a restaurant so American that only French people ever ate there: omelets and burgers, pictures of Hollywood celebrities on the walls.

"My gut is feeling that you are not serious." She meant about Bleu. Ines wanted to know if my intentions were honorable, and she concluded pretty quickly that they were not. That I was unlikely to leave my husband and kids, move in with her ex, and raise her daughter for her. And she was right—I would never do that. So I guess DeeDee was right too. You need to know your bottom line.

"American women don't understand love," Ines said. "They talk about being in love, but they don't want a man; they want a security blanket." And then she said *puh* the way Frenchwomen do: lips pressed together, blowing through the *p*.

I doubled down on her *puh* with a *humph*. And a Tina Turner song: "What's Love Got to Do with It?" When the lease was up at Camp Mom, I moved back to our apartment on Rue de Turenne.

SHARKS

My mother thought being alone was the worst thing that could happen to a woman, but she wasn't talking about being physically alone. In fact, she liked it when my dad traveled, nobody expecting her to get dressed or make dinner; she'd stay up late, watching TV, drinking and smoking, sleep all day. When I got home from school, she'd be just getting up, face puffy, shiny with sweat, wearing a lavender polyester nightie, cigarette holes scorched and hardened. It's a wonder she didn't go up in flames. Anyway, when she said being alone was the worst thing that could happen, she meant being single, no dance partner, like a coat hanging in the cloakroom after the joint shuts off the lights, nobody coming to claim you. *The leopard print, the one with the velvet collar, please—it's mine.*

She wasn't afraid of the bogeyman. That was my issue.

It started with a knock on the door. Which was a weird coincidence, because the tea-leaf reader on Tremont Street said someone was knocking on my door and that I should let him in, said she saw the letter *G*. But that was much later, when I was looking for love and had let my guard down. This time, someone was knocking on my door while I was sound asleep. Dreaming about having my picture taken. Flash, smile.

Later, I would realize my picture actually was being taken, only to be stuffed ceremoniously in a shoebox hidden in the back of a closet.

The knocking was incessant, rousing me from bed, so I went to the front door, mostly asleep, partly awake, totally naked, the door chain-locked from the inside.

I was staring at the chain drawn across the door, hooked into its groove, and I knew for certain that somebody else had drawn that chain. Because I never chain-locked my door. My first thought was *It's a surprise party! I'll just turn around, and a roomful of my friends will yell, "Surprise!"* And then my second thought was, *Oh, shit, I'm naked at my own surprise party.* Which happens in a nightmare, right? But by then I was fully awake and it was not even dawn and it dawned on me that there was a surprise, but it wasn't a party. Someone was in my apartment. And it wasn't someone I knew.

For one thing, I didn't have any friends in that city anyway. I had been there only a few months. Columbus, Ohio. Middle America. They test new menu items at fast-food restaurants there: deep-fried cheese. My first job out of college, promo girl for a record distributor. They gave me a company car, an expense account, and moved me to Columbus. My father was so proud of me.

"Don't scream," a voice from behind me said.

I couldn't scream, even if I tried. I had no voice. "Help me" came out as a breathless whimper. My legs Jell-O, I slipped to the ground.

He picked me up by the skin of my back. Later, there would be bruises; I would have to lift my shirt and show them to the company representative they sent to check on me when I didn't show up for work, couldn't speak, couldn't move, couldn't cry. Visual proof: *This happened.* The bruises would fade. I didn't know at the time that it would take years for the psychic damage to go away.

He carried me like a kitten, the tips of my toes scraping across the carpet, and dumped me on my platform bed. Queen-size, white sheets, black satin comforter, a graduation gift from my mom. It had seemed excessive.

"A double will be okay," I had protested. "It's just me."

But she had insisted, looking at me with something akin to longing, thinking, *If only I had been born in your generation, oh, the life I could've lived—the freedom, the career, the lovers, that body, my baby girl's body.* She was jealous of my youth and my independence. She did not envision me as a trophy in a box of photos.

He was wearing a black leather jacket, leather gloves, and a ski mask. He climbed on top of me, pinned me down with the weight of his body, covered my mouth with one gloved hand, and propped himself up with the other, pressing against me. I was thinking, *It doesn't matter, it's just a hole in my body, it won't be so bad, I've had bad sex before, I've been raped before.* That time, I knew the guy—he went to law school with my brother. We went to the movies, he spiked my Coke, and the next morning I woke up in his bed, cum between my legs. Afterward, when I asked my brother to come with me to see the dean and file a complaint, my brother said it was my fault—my skirt was too short, my pants too tight, my look too easy, the choices I made, blah blah.

But this time it was a stranger in a ski mask grinding himself against me, and I was wondering what my brother would say I had done to encourage this. Also, it was taking too long. It was taking too long for my rapist to get hard. And that scared me more than his being there, in my bed, more than the idea of him inside me. It scared me that if he couldn't get it up, things might get worse.

He took his hand off my mouth and warned me not to scream.

"I won't," I promised.

He used his free hand to rub his dick between my legs but still couldn't get hard. *Maybe I'm a lousy rape, maybe I'm supposed to be more scared, maybe I'm supposed to have more fight in me, maybe I shouldn't be so resigned. What if he gets angry? I don't wanna die.* "Please don't kill me," I begged. But he didn't promise not to.

And then I worried that if he didn't get it up soon, he was gonna make me touch him, he was gonna make me use my mouth.

My brother called me Mouth because I talked too much, said shit nice girls aren't supposed to say. The rapist couldn't get it up, and maybe I'd be able to laugh about this someday, but right then, real time, all I knew was, *This is getting awkward.* And when sex gets awkward, you need a cigarette. So I asked the rapist who couldn't get an erection if he smoked, and he said yes.

"Can I have a cigarette?" I asked, and he told me his cigarettes were in his pants, which were in the other room, so it was getting complicated. We were having this conversation like it was a date, because when a guy is rubbing his flaccid dick against you, it feels kind of intimate, his face so close to mine, though not his face, really—his head, covered by the ski mask. My hands wandered and touched the sides of his mask. I could feel his hair through the material, and considered ripping the mask off, just to see if I knew this guy, but then he'd have to kill me for sure. His pants were in the next room, and I realized he must have taken them off before he even woke me up. I saw his legs in the moonlight, and later, when the cops asked what color they were, I would say they were muscular and hairy.

"Are you alone?" I asked him. He was lying on top of me, his mask-covered ear hovering next to my mouth. We were still negotiating the smoke. Like, maybe if he had a partner, his partner could bring him the cigarettes. "Do you have a gun?" My follow-up question—my mind was conjuring worst-case scenarios.

He said "no" and then "yes." He wasn't alone, and he had a gun. He could have been lying—he was a rapist, after all. Again I promised not to scream, and he slid off me to go into the other room and get the cigarettes out of his pants pocket. I looked at the window and debated for a beat: *Should I run or should I stay? What if he's got a gun? He might shoot me in the back while I'm trying to escape. He might shoot me anyway*, I thought. So I flew across the room and jumped out the window into a snowbank.

When the cops came, they said I was lucky. They were sitting on my sofa, blue, faux Scandinavian modern, a hand-me-down from my sister.

"Did the intruder do this?" one cop asked, like he was my dad, surveying the mess in my living room. There were records strewn all over the green shag, promo posters, a box of pizza . . . Maybe it was the pizza delivery guy, or the guy in line behind me at the drugstore the day before when the clerk asked for my photo ID. I wasn't paying attention to him, but I could sense him, standing too close. It could have been anyone, really. He'd been wearing a ski mask.

They called him an intruder on account of the fact that he was impotent, so he didn't get to be called a rapist. But I don't make such distinctions. Couldn't tell them what color or size he was, either: black or white or brown, big or small. More distinctions I don't make.

"He was male," I told them.

"You were lucky," the other cop said. They had been tracking this guy for a while; he was a serial rapist, and most of his victims got beaten up something awful. That's when I realized that smoking saved my life. Which is funny. Not funny ha-ha, but dark funny.

• ▪

After the cops left me alone in my apartment complex, called the Shadows—you can't make this shit up—I called my mom and told her what had happened. She asked if I was all right, and when I said yes, she believed me.

"Gotta run—tennis with the girls. Nice chatting. I'll call you tonight."

Of course she was concerned, but she didn't offer to come to Ohio. So I decided to drive to Detroit. Right then. Couldn't get there fast enough. On the way, the cops stopped me for speeding.

"I'm trying to get home to my mother, Officer," I said. "I was just raped."

The cop asked if I had reported it to the police, and I said yes.

So he went back to his car and checked the records, and then he loomed at the window of my company car, a blue station wagon so I could cart all my promo posters and boxes of albums around with me. Cardboard stand-ups. Michael Jackson with the one glitter glove. Probably leather. *Thriller*? *Bad*? *Dangerous*? Not *Invincible*. Who knows? Who can remember? Details.

The cop said the report didn't say "rape"; it said "breaking and entering" and "sexual assault." A technicality. He didn't enter, not officially; he broke, though.

And then the cop wrote me a ticket for going so fast, so far exceeding the speed limit, that I couldn't simply pay it. It came with a mandatory court date in the middle of farm country somewhere between Ohio and Michigan.

"You were lucky," the cop said.

"Yeah, so I've been told," I replied. "Do you have a daughter?"

When he said yes, I said, "I hope that someday she will be as lucky as I am."

And then I took the ticket and drove away. By then I didn't want to go home to Mommy anymore, so I got off the freeway to turn around, somewhere in the middle of middle America, between Columbus and Detroit, and it was March. The ground was mucky. I was driving zombie, following a road that turned into a dirt path before it countrified into muddy tractor tracks winding around a farm, until I saw taillights again. It was a straight shot in front of me, only I was about five feet above the freeway, and between the freeway and me was a ditch. I tried to back up, but there was no way I could stay on the tracks in reverse the whole way back to the road, so instead I decided to gun it and fly like Supergirl, fully expecting to land on the highway and keep right on going, like in the movies. But I am not Supergirl, and the car landed in the ditch. It would have been funny if the same cop who had given me a ticket for *not* being raped, showed up to give me *another* ticket, this time for driving while in shock, but instead a truck full of farm boys pulled over, picked up my car, and set it right. Maybe chivalry isn't dead after all.

■ ■

When I got home, I put "I Shall Be Released" on the stereo. It was on the turntable nonstop when my boyfriend broke up with me freshman year—well, not exactly broke up, just stopped coming around, stopped scratching at my door. *This would be a great song to play at my memorial*, I thought. And then I got a yellow legal pad and started creating a memorial mix for myself in case I died young, or went to Hollywood and got a job as the person who made soundtracks for movies. My playlist began to take shape. "I Shall Be Released," Nina Simone. "It Isn't Gonna Be That Way," Steve Forbert. "Ghost Dance," Patti Smith Group. "Heaven," the Psychedelic Furs.

And then I quit my job and moved back home—to Detroit. In a stroke of either genius or super-bad parenting, my mother and father sold their house out from under me, forcing me to find my own place. Maybe they thought if they let me move back in, I would never leave. They were probably right, so I rented a duplex. It had two floors and a low-tech security system. At night I lined the windowsills and stairs with empty cans and jars, in case of an intruder. And then I pulled a trunk across my bedroom door, barricading myself inside. I didn't have a gun, so I slept with a hammer. I reasoned that I might not actually be able to stick a knife in someone's heart, but I could most certainly smash his head in with a hammer.

A year later, like the lady in the turban said, Gee knocked on my door and I let him in. He seemed harmless.

UNTETHERED

Two girls with dirty blond hair and trashy clothes were bumping and grinding onstage. This was Gee's idea for date night, so I let him run with it. So much of the personal side of our married life has always been handled by me: dinner plans; birthday parties; off-the-grid, thatch-roof, beachy vacations. I was the one who made a house a home, but our home was in Los Angeles and we were living in a fourth-floor walk-up in Paris. It was me who found us the newly renovated, centuries-old building with tons of windows and a cross-breeze in the heart of the Marais. There had been another apartment in the same building with a loft that promised privacy and romance.

"It's over our budget," Gee grumbled.

I begged him to push for the bigger place, but Gee didn't want to make waves. Gee is not a bigheaded, self-pumping American guy. That's why he's so successful abroad: because he doesn't intimidate people. In the States, he's easy to underestimate; overseas, he's got this unassuming thing going for him. A few years into the gig, he admitted that we could have gotten the bigger apartment if only he'd negotiated harder. So many lessons learned in Paris. Sharing one bathroom with two kids was the price we paid for Gee's not understanding the value of a romantic loft and private loo. There were other prices, other debts paid in Paris. Date night was one of them.

"Dress nice." That's all Gee would tell me.

Gee likes surprises; he doesn't seem to care that I find them selfish, that I think the person who plans the surprise has all the fun and the other person just gets ambushed. I put on my best night-out-in-Paris gear: black boots, black wrap skirt, and soft, silky top. Just a hint of sexy.

"Pigalle," he told the taxi driver.

Pigalle? Moulin Rouge, burlesque shows, and busloads of tourists? I kept my mouth shut, the silence between us almost weaponized. We were in this awkward place. I thought Gee didn't take an active role in the relationship; Gee said that when he suggested things, he got shot down. Date night was the marriage counselor's idea. We alternated planning activities; the only rule was, we had to go with the flow.

"*Ici*," he said, pointing to a strip club sandwiched between an adult-video store and a dirty-lingerie boutique. It must have been early for a place like this—we were the only customers—and the bar smelled like ammonia and lemons, the lingering scent of heavy-duty cleaning products. We ordered drinks and watched the girls do an uninspired, lazy, it's-a-job, tits-and-ass grind. This was Gee stepping out of his pocket-protector persona; it felt put-on, like he was trying too hard. He was jumpy, too, quaffing cocktails and looking around nervously. He got up to have a word with the proprietor, who seemed to know exactly what he wanted and led us into a private room. It was a peep show, without the glass partition. There was only one chair.

"I imagine they don't get many couples in here," I joked.

Gee sat down and told me to sit on his lap. A cheap red jersey dress walked in, plopped down on an oversize zebra cushion, and spread her legs, no panties.

The view was almost gynecological and reminded me that I needed to get a pap smear. We had yet to decide when our home leave would be, July or August, so I could schedule everyone's doctors' appointments. *Probably not a good time to bring this up*, I thought, as I felt Gee harden beneath me. He wanted more.

"*En plus,*" he said, his voice shaky.

Red Dress left and came back with a credit card reader. *Qu'est-ce que tu veux?* She and Gee negotiated something in French. The upgrade required a new room on another floor, up an unlit wooden staircase. Climbing the steps, Kat (that was the dress's name) got chatty with me.

"You want we make fun?" she asked. "You want we dominate him, *tu et moi, ensemble?*"

Gee said something about a *ménage à trois.* Clearly, he'd come unhinged. The new room had a beat-up fake-leather couch and a stained mattress on the floor, and I was wondering just how far Gee would take this. Kat left again, this time to get more drinks, and came back with Annabelle, so now there were two girls with long hair, bright lips, and sparkle nails. Kat and Annabelle. Katabelle. *Voulez-vous coucher avec moi?*

Gee asked if I wanted to play. *Tu veux jouer?*

There's a what-happens-in-Vegas aspect to the expat life—drinking, smoking, spending money like water—but this was some seamy shit, some date-night-gone-way-wrong sort of thing. It was like toxic shock syndrome. *Doctor, our marriage is sick and dying. Someone please call 911.* Someone needed to call "time out." There were two children at home, not babies but not yet teenagers, two children whose lives were being formed, who needed a mom who was paying attention and a dad who came home before bedtime, parents who would sit together at a piano recital or a school play. Two children who desperately needed their mother and father to behave.

There had been some sort of misunderstanding with the girls, and Gee seemed agitated. He didn't like it when people took advantage of him, and Katabelle had yet to deliver a live-action e-ticket experience. Maybe the threesome was supposed to include me, but that wasn't going to happen. I was planted on the couch, smoking. DeeDee had said to establish clear boundaries. A part of me wouldn't have

minded watching Gee have sex with another woman (or two); maybe
it would give me a new perspective on him. He's very handsome, my
husband, in a tan-khakis-and-blue-button-down sort of way. I'd say
J.Crew, but he bought his clothes at Costco.

Gee was on his third drink, I was on my tenth cigarette, the girls
were fast-talking in French, nothing made sense. This was so not the
kind of role-play scenario they taught at Berlitz. They started a girlie
pantomime, one rubbing on Gee, the other reaching out to me. I
was stuck like superglue to the vinyl couch, like I was at the movies,
minus the popcorn, watching my husband and two French whores
talk dirty to me.

Gee must have been cracking up. My husband was not mushy or
emotional; he loved me like a fact. I was the one who brought the
party, the joy, the humor, the pissy, or the preachy to our lives; he
was the anchor to my mood swings. But here was Gee, in a bordello,
swinging. The girls left us alone to figure it out. Gee threw a shocking-pink pillow at his feet and started to unzip his pants.

"You know what to do," he said.

I searched his face for some flicker of humor or humanity but
found none. He was like a human vibrator buzzing with sexual rage.
I was afraid to reject him. Again. Especially there. Anything could
happen in a place like that, and the American embassy would never
find out. He kissed me, slid my skirt open, yanked at my stockings,
slut-slapped me, calling me *salope*. This was Gee treating me like the
whore he thought I was, but also this was my husband lost in his
own head, imagining the wild sex his wife was having while he was
at work.

Maybe he should have come home for dinner once in a while.

I licked, I sucked, I did the laundry. I was bought and paid for,
like Katabelle. And yes, I hung out with the poet. What else was I
supposed to do all day with the kids in school, my career on hold—
take cooking lessons? I didn't even like to cook. Gee was the cook,

although he hadn't been in the kitchen since we'd moved to Paris. He was too busy working and, after work, drinking about work. He had his crew, I had our kids; we were leading separate lives. I felt trapped, handcuffed to my husband's international career. Sure, they were velvet cuffs. Business class on the company dime. But still, cuffed. All I ever wanted was a marriage that looked like what the magazine ads promised: his-and-hers careers, a couple kids, and a pooch in the backyard. We didn't even have a dog.

"Em," Gee wailed, "I don't know what you want anymore."

"Well, it isn't this," I said, burying my head in my hands.

"Please, Em," he wept. "Don't shut me out. I need you. I know I fucked things up, but I love you. I've always loved you. Please, Emmmeee, look at me."

When I opened my eyes, Gee was kneeling on the pillow, his arms outstretched, sobbing. We had become untethered. When you add up the true cost of an overseas post, I always put "date night" on the ledger.

∎ ∎

The next morning, Gee got up and made popovers like it was my birthday or something. The kids were crawling all over me.

"What did you do last night, Mommy?" they wanted to know.

"We went to a dance club," I said. Gee announced that he had a surprise for us after breakfast, smiling at me sheepishly as if to say, *This one you'll like, trust me.* So we took a walk on the Quai, along the Seine where all the pet stores were, and the kids chirped, "Please, Mommy," and Gee's eyes said, *Please, Em,* and there was this pooch, this big, funny-looking dog, in the discount bin, a French bulldog. He was huge, so he was no puppy, and his ears were floppy, so he was no prize, but we adopted him on the spot. That dog had every parasite known to man, all sorts of fluids leaking from his eyes, his nose, his bum; he was bleeding and rheumy, but the vet said it was all fixable with a few shots and some take-home meds. I was sure there was something fundamentally wrong with him, though, because he didn't like to walk, just stood there and dug his paws into the concrete while I pulled on the leash. *Têtu*—stubborn—the French said, laughing when they saw us on the street. We named him Raymond Chandler Bing, because Raymond Chandler was Gee's favorite author and Chandler Bing was the kids' favorite *Friends* character. There was seemingly nothing of me in that name, just a desire to make them all happy. It wasn't so bad a life, when you think about it, tagging along in Paris. It could have been worse, that's for sure. As the French say, *pas mal.*

PLAYING IT SAFE

I told everyone I was going on a yoga retreat at a dropped-out, laid-back resort in Mexico. Blue skies and ocean breezes. Which explains why none of my friends in LA understood my anxiety.

"I'm going on a yoga retreat," I said, wincing as if it were a risky medical procedure with slightly better-than-even odds. Maybe, I hoped, if I called it a "retreat," the experience would be more retreat-like. In truth, I had signed up for life training with a cliff-jumping, charismatic yogi. Think: *Survivor: Jungle Yoga*, then add a little rehab, a bit of touchy-feely group therapy, throw in some rock and roll kumbaya for atmosphere, and wrap it up pretty with a yoga teacher credential. I figured I would need something to do all day if we moved to China. The "we" was the iffy part. I was still on the fence and hoping ten days in the jungle would provide some clarity.

To be honest, most yoga studios make me want to scream. Incense and *om*. Joyous baby. Ferocious being. Innocent heart. It's like touching velvet—it's supposed to feel good, but it sends chills up my spine. The thing that drew me to this studio right from the start was the music. Throw-down playlists that rock the house. That, and the patter that seeps in while you're bent in half. The teachers riff about anything to divert your attention from the pain: about the gym shorts you bought at Target, the ones that shrank the first time you washed them, how the seams don't line up and they aren't comfortable anymore but you feel compelled to wear them anyway. You'll be in some outrageously twisted pose, dripping wet, muscles shaking, two seconds away from total collapse, and the instructor will yell, "Throw them out, already!"

Flip the switch, and you realize they aren't talking about your shorts anymore.

■ ■

So here I am, in Mexico, baby. Sea-salty infused winds mix with a din of rustling palm fronds that is so relentless, so pervasive, it feels hyperreal. As if the environment itself is streaming live from some amped-up broadcast system in the sky. Radio Bliss. Where the sea meets the sky in the jungle. It's scary beautiful. Like, really beautiful. And, also really scary.

Yogaman has been saying a lot of crazy shit on this jungle trek, much of it directed at me, like that I'm too "vanilla" to teach yoga, too old to become a yoga teacher, and too hung up on things that happened in the past. I've taken to wearing a hoodie and sunglasses indoors, so no one can see my face. Just trying to get through the training without having a nervous breakdown. Today's group activity is an afternoon hike, it's also a trust exercise, one that involves rope and blindfolds. I really want to nail this challenge because I totally blew it the second night here, when we had to climb an eight-foot ladder, cross our arms, tuck our chins, and fall backward into a human safety net.

Every year, Yogaman said, someone stands on top of the ladder, crying and whining, hooting and hollering, making a big-ass scene. Don't be that person.

And I wasn't, not exactly. I didn't cry or whine; I just climbed up and then climbed right back down, quietly stating that I'd prefer not to, like Bartleby's twin sister, hoping they'd run out of time or forget that I hadn't actually done the fool thing. Instead I stood there, watching everyone in my group—the supersize girl, the guy named Bear, and Lorca—climb and fall. Although Lorca didn't just climb and fall. No, she got to the top and owned it: the air, the altitude, the freedom, the power. She stood there and claimed the experience.

Lorca's my yoga buddy here. We're about the same age, both professional women. Only she's way more professional than I am; she's the woman I always meant to be. She has it all: the husband, a kid, and a corner office. And now she's standing on the top of the ladder like a lady wrestler. She's fearless and decisive. I can tell, not just because she's an executive VP at a global entertainment company, but because she summed up my dilemma in a nanosecond the first time we talked, saying without hesitation: go to China—it will be an amazing experience.

"What's to discuss?" she asked.

"The air," I said. And left it at that. She would never understand my life; her uncompromising nature gave me an extreme case of tagalong shame. I couldn't pretend to have a job that was so important I couldn't walk away from it—she'd see through that—and I couldn't whine about how I didn't have that job, because that would be lame, and anyway, "That ship has sailed" would be her response.

I was standing there, arms enmeshed with the group, catching yogis falling backward, one by one, having a total panic attack, the sound of my heart thumping against my chest amplified for my ears only. Staring at that ladder. When you paint the bathroom, you lean your shins against the ladder while you roll. But if you stand on the absolute tip-top of a stepladder in the middle of a yoga studio, there's nothing to press against or hold on to.

"I'm not scared," I insisted. It just seemed like an unnecessary risk.

■　■

That was two days ago. We're lined up shoulder to shoulder, the ocean behind us, waves lapping at our heels, air salty. We just snaked through a path in the jungle, blindfolded, a human chain connected by rope, so if one person falls, the whole chain goes down. There are about thirty of us yogis in training, all colors, sizes, and sexes, like a branding advertisement for soft drinks. Yogaman is stalking the line, his voice fading in and out with the wind. I can't see him, but I know what he looks like: cargo pants, muscle tee, dragon tattoo crawling across his bicep, red bandanna around his forehead, hair bleached and badly in need of a cut or hot-oil conditioning treatment. That's what he always looks like, except in class he's mic'd like a rock star.

"When I tap you on your shoulder," Yogaman says, "I will give you a message. That's your signal to drop the rope and run, screaming my words at the top of your lungs. There's nothing to worry about. The beach is clear. You don't need to see. Just feel the sand. Be in the moment. Shana will catch you at the other end."

Through the rustling palms, I hear yogis chanting:

"I am love."

"I am strong."

"I am beautiful."

"My body is a temple."

Yogaman taps me on the shoulder and whispers, "I will not play it safe."

Really? That's not even a positive statement; that's like when you offer someone a personal trainer for their birthday because you think they need to lose weight. It's a commentary, not a gift. But it's on the money. I did come here with a mission to play it safe; most of the other yogis are half my age, and my personal mantra, the one I gave myself coming into this retreat is *Just show up, don't keep up.*

"Well, that shit's not gonna fly," Shana said when I told her my mantra. Shana is the good-cop yoga teacher–studio manager. She looks like the fusion love child of a three-way between Alicia Keys, Bruce Lee, and Chrissie Hynde. Tough but caring. "It's not a retreat," she said. "You know that, right? People are gonna crack."

What's really freaking me out, though, more than the cliff-jumping, crazy Yogaman thing, is that when I finish this yoga teacher training, I will be that much closer to China. And I do not want to move to China. With any fiber of my being. The way I see it, *not* wanting to move to China is like choosing stand-up paddleboarding over surfing. It's common sense. Also, it's another exercise I fucked up. Paddleboarding versus surfing.

"You're playing it safe again," Yogaman said.

"I've lived in LA for years," I replied. "If I haven't slayed a wave by now, maybe I just don't want to." That's when he pointed two fingers at his eyes and then pivoted them at me, as if to say, *I'm watching you.*

I run, screaming, "I will not play it safe."

"Louder!" he yells.

"I will not play it safe!"

"Faster!" he demands.

And I'm trying, really I am. I'm running as fast as I can on sand, in trekking sandals, blindfolded.

"Run!" he yells. "Run like your life depends on it! Because maybe it does."

I'm running, I'm screaming, I'm pushing, I'm giving it my all, but also I'm now laughing, which makes me slow down and pitch forward, my feet clumsy, tripping over each other.

"You run like an old lady," he taunts me.

Yogaman has had it out for me ever since I refused to fall off the ladder. It's not about the ladder. This is about me not wanting to jump off the cliff with him. This is about me not wanting to go full-on into his jungle journey. This is about me resisting the man in charge. I run too slow, I read too fast, I talk too much. I speak up, I speak out, I talk back. Mouth. Strident—that's what Gee calls me when I push back. "Don't scream"—that was the guy in the ski mask and black leather gloves. I will not break; I only cry when the dog dies.

"Don't catch her," Yogaman calls to Shana. "Let her run into a tree. It'll do her some good."

This is insane, possibly even dangerous, closer than I ever thought

I'd get to drinking the Kool-Aid. I slow to a full stop and take off my blindfold, inches away from crashing into a palm tree.

"You weren't even running fast enough to hurt yourself," Yogaman says dismissively.

• •

At night, everybody shares. Sitting cross-legged on the floor, forming one big circle, knee to knee, in our jammies. It's like summer camp, and I'm the camper who can't wait to go home. Shana kicks it off saying, "Today was *awesome*." And then a chorus of affirmations chant in unison: *Aho*.

"I thought I was gonna pass out."

Aho.

"It felt so good to be supported by the group."

Aho.

"My mantra made me cry."

Aho.

And I say, "I feel like I've been called out for playing it safe."

Silence. Oh, man. You could feel the hush. You could hear the waves crashing. Couldn't I have just said it was awesome? But no, I dig in to my position. "Sometimes, playing it safe is an acquired skill," I tell the group. "It's a self-protective reaction to the dangers of life," I say, "a practical response to unnecessary risk." And then I shut up. Even I was beginning to hear how much bullshit comes out of my mouth sometimes.

• •

During the day, after yoga and breakfast, which is a yummy vegan spread of tofu eggs and chia seed pudding, we have Vedanta lessons. It's all very Socratic method. Everyone lies around on cushions in comfy clothes, listening to Yogaman teach the principles underlying the practice of yoga. It's a lot like what I imagine an AA meeting to be, or Sunday morning services at a Baptist church—all the sharing and testifying to your demons. The mind at war with the intellect.

In yoga-speak, the mind is ruled by emotion but the intellect is rational. According to Yogaman, most of us are just crazy ids running around, looking for a quick hit, a fix that can come in any form: sex, drugs, alcohol. Pretty much everyone at this yoga training is in bed with some form of addiction.

• •

The next morning at breakfast, a guy gets up and clinks his juice glass with his spoon, like you would at a wedding if you wanted to get everyone's attention before toasting the bride and groom.

"I just want to share my story," he announces. I don't know his name, but he is one of the guys who caught me when I fell off the ladder. (Yes, of course I did it; it was either fall off the ladder or pack my bags.)

He pauses for a moment, as if having second thoughts, and then his story pours out of him. Only the shaky tone in his voice lets on how hard it is for him to talk about his battle with gaming in public. His demeanor is awkward, not so much shy as lacking the self-confidence needed to state his struggle with Yogaman's swagger—Yogaman's mesmerizing ability to turn shit into schtick. Maybe because this guy is in pain, he's in the vortex, he isn't drawing on the distant memory of despair. He is talking about how he felt last week, holed up in his room with his laptop, when he couldn't be bothered to eat or shower, when he felt like life was happening online and real people were an interruption.

"And then I came here," he says, "and I feel surrounded by love. You guys. Every one of you, you've been there for me with a hug or a smile; we've been tied up and dropped from ladders, and always there is someone standing right next to me, every step of the way. This is so amazing. I don't ever want it to end."

What trip is this guy on? I wonder. Because I have been dreading every minute of every day here, except the actual yoga, counting the hours until the van comes to take me back to the airport. After he sits down, a sort of spontaneous burst of support comes forth. One at a time, yogis stand up and share their stories.

"I abuse cigarettes and drugs," someone says, wiping her nose, her eyes, smearing mascara across her face. "I'm only twenty-nine, and I feel like I've already completely fucked up my body and ruined my life. I don't know if I can ever get back on track, and it scares me. I'm scared shitless, but I'm here and I'm clean. Five days sober. It's not easy. Thank you."

"I abuse meth," the girl next to her says in a show of solidarity, a girl so pretty and thin she must be a model-slash-actress, both of them crying and holding each other's hands.

"I abuse money," Lorca stands up and announces. And then she kicks my shin under the table, like it's my turn to confess. So I stand up and say, "I'm married, with two kids and a dog; plus, I abuse chardonnay." I leave out Xanax. How I brought Xanax here with me, just in case, because I don't want Yogaman to confiscate my crutch.

• •

Here's the setup: We're in the yoga room, and we break into pairs. One person speaks for five minutes uninterrupted, and the other must remain silent; we can communicate only via energy, nonverbal cues.

"Use your eyes," Yogaman says. "Open your hearts."

"I'll start," Lorca says. "I'm in a postsex marriage. My husband and I haven't had sex for years. So I came here because Yogaman said he could help me sort out my life and make a decision, but so far it hasn't been all that helpful. Falling off a ladder. Big deal. I'm not seeing the point in these challenges. Sorry, Em, I guess you had trouble with the ladder. Should I go or should I stay? That's my dilemma."

Mine, too! I think, squeezing her hand.

Then she goes on for five minutes about how her husband is a weak link, a loser, a stay-at-home dad who's outlived his usefulness now that their kid can get to and fro on his own. *That's cold*, I think. But I sort of get it. Gee offered to be a stay-at-home dad once, when he came back from a gig that lasted eight months in Italy and I threw a hissy fit about his needing to get a job in LA.

"You go balls-out, Em," he said.

And I said, "Then what would I need you for?" But what I meant to say was, *Why is it always either/or?*

Okay, focus—Lorca's story.

"I come home," she complains, "and dinner is made and the kid is asleep, and all we do is sit on the couch and watch TV. Every time someone on my staff says they had a long night—wink, wink—I want to cry."

I've been looking at this woman the whole time we're on this retreat, on the hike and the ladder and the swim to the cove, eating basil-hummus burritos with her, listening to her talk about her fabulous career, feeling bad about my choices, thinking she's the woman I was meant to become, that this woman has the life I wanted. She has it all. And now I come to find out it's all a mirage.

No one has the best life. That's another thing Andra and I always say. We say it, but we don't really believe it. We said "no one has the best life" as a way of excusing ourselves for not having become everything we hoped when her career was booming and I was breeding. We say it to comfort each other for falling short, but we don't believe it, not for a second. Secretly, we both think having it all is possible and that we're fuck-ups for settling for less. For tagging along or going it alone.

Okay, my turn. Unzip and let it all out. "I don't even know where to start. I could hardly breathe when I rolled out my mat for our first yoga class in Mexico. Scared I couldn't keep up. Intellectually I know yoga is not a competitive sport. It's not about young hot bodies. It's not about them," I say, scanning the room full of toned and fearless yogis half my age. "I know this in the same way that I know I don't really have a brain tumor just because I passed out at airport security, which is to say—only partially, rationally but not emotionally. Yep, that was me: I'm the girl who passed out in the TSA line at the airport. People assume that I travel well because we do it so much, but I don't like to fly. I read somewhere there's a finite number of times you should go under anesthesia, and I worry that it's like that with flying, too, like I'm pushing my luck. But that's not why I passed out. I passed out because coming to Mexico makes me that much closer to *going* to Shanghai.

"Also, I was afraid to come on this yoga training, afraid I couldn't keep up or my back would go out; I packed three knee braces just in case. Speaking of packing, instead of actually preparing for this trip, I've spent the past few months nonstop nattering on about 'embracing change.' Mexico. The yoga retreat. Finding peace. Don't try to stop me. Lots of talk. Not much embracing. No packing whatsoever.

"Two days before our departure, in a total panic, I opened up a slew of emails from Shana that had been sitting in my inbox and finally started to pack my bag. *Going to Mexico.* There was that disclaimer; in case anything happened, I would be the only one responsible, which must be standard, but it freaked me out anyway. And then the packing list from hell: sunscreen, bug repellent, antibiotic cream, anti-itch spray, something for diarrhea, sunburn relief, muscle rubs, water trekking shoes, rash guard (my idea). And Xanax. I added that—I mean, I just don't travel without it. I learned that the hard way. A person with this much anxiety should probably not move to China. The list of things that scares me is getting longer by the day. I'm afraid of sharks. I'm afraid of losing my words. Sometimes when I'm walking the dog, I say the name of every object I see, out loud, counting the words until I screw up and call the trash can an ashtray or something. I can't watch movies where something bad happens to the mother. I'm afraid of every pimple, canker sore, lump, and bump on my body. I'm afraid of losing my teeth. And I panic in small elevators like they have in Paris, the ones with iron gates that close manually and look great in photos but fit only two people comfortably and are always jammed and get stuck all the time. Instead, I take the stairs, even if it means I'll arrive sweaty. I'm afraid of being the *adjumani*—that's Korean for 'oldest woman in the room'—only in Asia it's a term of respect.

"OMG, listen to me. I hate that about being an expat: If you open your mouth and speak from personal experience, it sounds like you're bragging. As if. Like anyone would brag about being a tagalong wife. *Hello, I'm attached to my husband's career.* Not exactly impressive. And now I've got Shanghai looming over my head. Yogaman thinks I 'play it safe,' he thinks I'm afraid to leave Los Angeles, but he's wrong. I'm not afraid to move overseas. I've lived lots of places. France. Japan. Korea (South, of course). China, though. That scares me."

●   ●

The end of the retreat is so close, I can almost taste the bus ride back to the airport in Puerto Vallarta. Bumpy and dusty, like summer camp. We'll be singing songs and recapping the highlights of the trip: Someone got a concussion surfing, Bear admitted to smuggling in coffee and cigarettes, and someone had a total meltdown and got kicked out of training. And the best part, the shocker is, it wasn't me! It was a hippie chick named Rain. All I have to do is make it through tonight's activity, and tomorrow we pack up, and then, finally, it will all be in the rearview mirror.

It's pitch black outside. Inside the yoga studio is flickering, the walls lined with candles. We are arranged in small groups on cushions surrounding a yoga mat. Yogaman floats in, wearing all white and carrying a guitar. Everything is communicated via eye contact.

"Respect the silence," teachers whisper to us on our way into the space. Shana is our group leader; she nods to Lorca and points to the mat, indicating that she should lie down. We all put our hands on Lorca, gently pressing her legs, rubbing her feet, stroking her arms. Yogaman plays "You're Beautiful" by James Blunt; then we silently absorb Lorca back into the group, rotating positions. It's all very somber and loving, *Into the Mystic*. When my turn comes, I'm biting my lip, trying not to crack up like a kid at a funeral.

I lower my body onto the mat, silently chanting, *Do not laugh, do not laugh. Whatever you do, Em, do not fucking laugh.* Close my eyes and feel my body covered by hands, blanketed, smothered. I'm still biting my lip when the first chord breaks and Yogaman launches into "I Shall Be Released." That's when I dissolve into a million little pieces, floating high above the room. This is the song I play when I'm sad, bruised, brokenhearted. It's the song I play when I'm alone and need something to soothe my soul. This is the song that I want played at my funeral, the first song on my memorial mix.

I wonder if that means I'm going to die. In Mexico. There's still one day to go. The thought doesn't even scare me, doesn't speed my pulse; it's actually sort of peaceful. It feels so good to get a foot and head massage at the same time. It feels timeless, out of body; it feels loving and supportive; it feels like . . . if this is dying, it might not be so bad; it might not be something to be so afraid of. What if dying is a candlelight massage, a peaceful send-off with "I Shall Be Released" playing in the background? Yogaman's comment from a year ago comes back to me. When I told him I was afraid I might have a heart attack if I took his Explosion Power Yoga class, he said, "Yes, you might, and wouldn't that be a sweet way to go?"

AQI RISING

Shanghai is like that bad boy in high school, the one who's smokin' hot and drives a beat-up muscle car, a gas guzzler, leaking fumes; it's a death trap, and you know you should walk away, but damn—those arms, that hair, the way he makes you feel nervous inside but also revved up. It's hard not to be seduced by so much eye candy, street fashion trendier than you see in Paris, pimped-out Chinese girls in see-through gauzy skirts strutting in mile-high sneakers, the mishmash of old and new, bamboo construction fences next to mega-highrises; it's wacky and dirty, possibly dangerous, but also the epicenter of the universe. Shanghai is so right now, so *très branche*. Plugged in. And really, so far, the air hasn't been all that bad. My eyes sting, but that's about it. It's summer, hot and humid. I'm more worried about my hair frizzing than my lungs.

We live here now. Found our dream apartment in the French Concession, walking distance from Green & Safe, which is like Joan's on Third, which everyone in LA says is just like Manhattan. I tell people Shanghai is like New York on steroids, only instead of having a Chinatown, the locals are Chinese and it's the Westerners who cluster together in certain neighborhoods. Upscale ones. The expat bubble. Two floors. A circular staircase. And four air purifiers. Gee's company bought them for us as a move-in gift. Just for the sake of comparison, when we were on assignment in Paris, our move-in gift was a magnum of French champagne. If Shanghai is the bad boy of relocations, that makes me the good wife for tagging along.

AQI: 0–50
Code: Green (Good)
Air quality is satisfactory.

First order of business is to get my paperwork straight. The man behind the counter eyes me suspiciously before speaking to Jake at length, in Chinese, gesturing first at my marriage certificate, then at my passport, and finally landing his finger on the residency permit application I just filled out, shaking his head emphatically no.

"Your signatures don't match," Jake says.

This is the first time I've seen him since the look-see and that awkward apartment search when Gee and I got up in his face and forced him to drop his kick-back *guanxi* scheme and find us the apartment of our dreams in the French Concession. So I worry that Jake doesn't like me, but he arrived clean, pressed, and professionally chatty, as always—bygones, no hard feelings.

"*Nihao*," I said, giving him a proper French greeting, air kisses on both cheeks. Let's get my residency status rubber-stamped. It's supposed to be a slam-dunk formality, since my living in Shanghai is attached to Gee's working papers, which have already been approved. All I have to do is show up with the necessary documents and swear to be married. But I'm learning that in China, nothing is easy. The signature on the form I just filled out does not match the one I used on my marriage certificate, so my identity is now in question.

This morning, Gee reminded me that we need to use up our furniture budget. He said "we," but he meant me; I need to finish decorating the apartment. I've ordered the essentials—beds, of course. And a hot-pink Egg chair that swivels. Like the one in *Sleepless in Seattle* that the two kids are squished in together, their feet tapping in unison as they turn toward the dad and say "H and G." Hi and goodbye. My kids would love this chair, but they won't be living with us. Rio is in college, and Ruby is house (and pet) sitting for us in LA.

I've always wanted one of those chairs. "Is it real?" I asked the store owner, whose name was Chad. Another American here for the gold rush, like everyone else. Or, to be more specific, his store sold disposable household furniture and knickknacks to the booming corporate-expat/tagalong market. Gee's company alone has hundreds of families temporarily posted here.

"This is China." Chad laughed. "Nothing is real. Have fun."

So I ordered the fake Egg chair and a fake-fur cube in shades of pink and purple to go with it, going with a sort of mid-'50s modern-boho vibe. Added a Chinese fainting couch in yellow bird print— that chaise is the definition of something you don't need and would buy only if you weren't paying for it. And, the pièce de résistance: an antique mantel to lean against the wall in the living room where there ought to be a fireplace but for some reason isn't one. I haven't gotten around to a dining table and chairs; that might imply that I have to cook, and I'm quite happy eating on the floor. Sherpa takeout from T for Thai.

"We need a dining room table," Gee insisted.

I laughed. "You bring out the Donna Reed in me."

You bring out the avocado counters, the fabric swatches, the T-shirt-folding, sock-matching, grocery-shopping wifey-poo in me. You bring out the blonde, the *Gosh, gee whiz, there's so much to do and I can't keep it straight*, in me. You bring out the Dorothy in me— click my heels, and where is home this time? You bring out the *Who am I in all of this?*

It's no wonder my signatures don't match.

I'm wearing the black-and-white-checked designer wrap skirt and matching sleeveless top I bought during the Paris sales. Why? Because in my mind I'm living in a movie, and that's the only way my life works: I dress up like a French movie star, and the driver takes me to the American consulate in Puxi before I go furniture shopping in Pudong on the company dime. The sunglasses are totally unnecessary; the sky is opaque, although there is glare. The driver, sadly, is for today only and specifically hired by Jake just to make sure I get to the consulate on time. So I'll have to find my way to the furniture warehouse on my own, which in itself is daunting. Still, who knows what the day might bring if I'm swaddled in agnès b.?

Jake hands me a blank copy of the application to fill out, which I do, this time using my optimistic just-married signature, thus forging my way into China. Yes, I swear, raising my right hand, I'm Mrs. Gee, and then I pay the guy fifty dollars. *Don't forget to get a receipt, doll,* Gee's voice replays in my head. That's what he said when he kissed me goodbye this morning—an uncomfortable, married-to-the-boss, daddy kind of kiss that made me bristle. He has this way of turning me into his assistant whenever we move overseas. And I feel like I can't complain because I'm not really working.

My original signature was so full of promise, every letter neatly, legibly inked on the official document. Signed, sealed, delivered. Now I just blow through my signature; sometimes it starts out strong and ends with a random flourish, as if to say, *Close enough,* or I just write "Em," big and bold, with a line after it, like I'm too busy to spell out the rest of my name, let alone my husband's. But now I wonder: Does it mean anything that I've totally dropped Gee's last name from my signature? Lately I've been thinking about taking back my maiden name. Just toying with the idea. Chinese bureaucrats can be nitpicky, but, to their point, my identity is a bit fuzzy on paper.

AQI: 51–100

Code: Moderate (Yellow)

Air quality is acceptable; people who are unusually sensitive may experience respiratory symptoms.

I'm invited to an orientation for newbies hosted by Kimberly, Jake's boss, for a group of women whose husbands all work for Gee's company. Which means it's mandatory. Or, as my mother used to say, a command performance. So I brush my hair, although brushing curly hair in this humidity can backfire into a mess of frizz. And now I look more like my unkempt, rebellious teenage self than a professional tagalong. I consider pulling it back into a ponytail but decide to go with the antiestablishment vibe.

Kimberly introduces us to the concept of Shang-*high* versus Shang-*low* days. Shang-low days are days when you can't cope with any of it—the air, the food, the water, the language. But then there's Shang-high! Fusion cuisine, fashion mecca, burgeoning art scene.

"Don't let the environment define your life here," Kimberly says.

Go!

Do!

Explore!

There's so much to see!

I'm trying to listen, but I can't help myself. I'm not thinking about ballet; I'm wondering about water. Which is worse? Plastic bottles, or those five-gallon dispensers? Pros and cons: Plastic is bad, obviously, but those jugs are breeding grounds for bacteria. I'm leaning toward bottled water, but which brand? Nestlé versus Nongfu. Locals swear by Nongfu; they say it's natural spring water, straight from the mountains in Tibet or something.

"It's shocking!" the woman next to me says. She's talking about how the Chinese girls dress on-site where our husbands work. Short skirts, no bras. Spandex. She's borderline matronly, hair blown, nails tastefully manicured; she's wearing a white blouse, slacks, and sensible shoes—the tagalong wardrobe. Her clothes tell nothing and everything about her. Tagalong apparel is the antistatement in fashion. It says, *I'm here, but it's not about me.*

You wanna know what I think is shocking? The water.

Here's my kitchen ritual: First, I rinse the veggies in tap water. Then I soak them in water that has been filtered through an eight-cylinder reverse osmosis system before it even comes out of the tap. For coffee, I use bottled water, which I filter through a Brita. For cooking, I double-wash, double-filter, and then boil.

"They should have a dress code," another tagalong says, agreeing with the woman sitting next to me.

Cities have a lifeblood that tagalongs are encouraged to tap into. In Paris, the relo team gave out copies of a resource guide called *Bloom Where You Are Planted*; it was all about finding your inner self, like tagalongs were seeds about to blossom into painters, poets, lovers. The title of Kimberly's PowerPoint presentation is "Beyond Surviving—Learning to Thrive." It feels a bit like bullshit, but I don't tell her that. I'm just getting my sea legs.

So why'd I come if I was so conflicted? The easy answer is that I'd run out of good excuses for not moving to China. For one thing, my mom died. When she died, the whole "I can't move to China with my husband because my mother needs me in Detroit" excuse fell apart. Overnight.

I was on the phone with Andra, telling her about my plan to move back to Detroit and take care of my mother. "She's been sounding frail the past few months, and I don't want to move overseas and be so far away from her," I was saying, when my brother beeped in. "I gotta take it, Andra. He's like the Grim Reaper: He only calls me when someone's in the hospital." Just like that, I lost my mother, and with her went my connection to Detroit as my real home, my forever home, the fantasy that I could always go back to the D.

Don't even ask about work; my consulting business in LA was barely limping along. Sure, we had clients, but they were a quirky mix of outliers. Like the architect whose passion was to build sustainable homes that were earthquake-, fire-, and storm-resistant; it was a noble cause, but the houses looked a lot like something you'd see in an illustrated storybook about a family of moles. The architect may have been passionate about concrete dome homes, but I was having trouble mustering the same level of passion for this pet project of his in particular, and for being a marketing consultant in general. Somewhere along the line, moving in and out of jobs, my career had lost its luster. No, it was more than that. My career had also lost its trajectory. Maybe in China I'd write something other than a press release or a sponsorship proposal. Maybe I'd get back to writing my own stuff. Also, and this is personal, maybe moving to Shanghai would spark Gee's and my love life.

AQI: 101–150
Code: Orange (Unhealthy for Sensitive Groups)
Members of sensitive groups may experience health effects.

We arrived just in time to celebrate our wedding anniversary. Not a milestone anniversary, but we're still together, which in and of itself is a big deal. So I wanted to surprise Gee with something sexy and fun. I traipsed all over Shanghai, looking for lingerie. I mean all over—on foot, bike, metro. I went to boutiques on Nanchang Lu that sold intimates for Chinese boy-chicks, girls with no tits, no ass, no body mass. In the States, I'm a solid medium—in China, I'm a triple XL. Out of desperation, I even went to Marks & Spencer, but all they had were the Queen's granny panties. Finally, I stumbled into Amy's Closet on Xiangyang, where nothing fit but they did have accessories. I bought a pair of pink furry handcuffs and a matching pink vibrator that didn't use batteries. *Kawaii.* That's Japanese for "cute." I didn't know any Chinese. And the old lady behind the counter didn't know any English, so she demonstrated how the vibrator plugged into a laptop. I was skeptical, which I demonstrated by scrunching up my face. She seemed to imply that I could return the lipstick-size sex toy if it didn't take a charge. Which it didn't. Well, it wasn't that it didn't take a charge, exactly; it just didn't hold one, to be more precise. So I decided to return it.

No oomph! The salesgirl laughs knowingly when I hand her the (slightly) used and repackaged vibrator. Her name is Ava. She's a gamine, pixie Chinese dream girl—short dark hair, shaved at the neck, bleached blond on top—and she speaks beyond-perfect English. She speaks the kind of English you learn only in bed.

"I told the old lady not to stock these," Ava complains. "They don't work for shit. Made-in-China crap! Nothing worse than a toy that loses its steam just when you're getting started. It's like making love to Chinese boys—they're done in two minutes. And when *they're* done, *you're* done. You know what I mean? Over and out. And you have to charge it in advance. That's stupid. Stupid, stupid, stupid. Too much work."

"Only it doesn't work," I remind her, "and the manager said I could return it."

And yes, I get that it cost only a hundred quai, which is maybe fifteen US dollars, but it isn't about the money; it's about selling stuff that doesn't work. I'm tired of things not working and no one taking responsibility. The whole buyer-beware thing is beginning to piss me off.

"You can exchange it for sure," Ava says. "We have better ones; they're made in Korea!"

Right away, she's on the upsell. *This is China, where nothing works, and don't even bother trying to get your money back.*

On my way out, I give her my telephone number. "Let's have lunch," I say. It would be nice to have a Chinese girlfriend.

I'm taking numbers and making friends. I join everything: the American Club; the Shanghai Expat Association; and a funky neighborhood yoga studio with open windows and an antique tea samovar, surrounded by oversize Indian-print cushions that gap-year yogis lay all over. I go to welcome coffees and happy hours. No one looks particularly happy, but everyone speaks English and they welcome me to the tagalong table like family.

My new friends have professional backgrounds in marketing or come from Detroit; they practice yoga or have children the same age as mine back in the States. We sign up for lectures on how to eat safe. Attend luncheons like the one at M on the Bund, very old-school British, high tea with a view, order the poached salmon. Over cake and coffee, we listen to the chef, an expat from London, talk about butterflies in gardens. Apparently, this is a good thing, an indicator of sorts.

"Butterflies mean no pesticides," the chef tells us. "You can get organic farm-to-table veggies online from Kate & Kimi." His patter is very down-homey and believable, because he's a dad and clean food matters to him too. We're all in the same boat, trying to stay healthy. I'm soaking up survival skills like a sponge, like when the marketing director at the hospital in Pudong said it was safe to exercise if the AQI is under 100. I'm surprisingly easy to convince that living here will be okay, because Mina said Beijing has the bad air and Shanghai has the culture.

Mina was right about Puxi and culture.

I go to the *Esprit Dior* exhibit at MoCA Shanghai. It's sublimely immersive: Rose-colored dresses float in floral-scented gardens, and there's a pristinely white atelier, complete with a Dior seamstress on loan from Paris. And an interactive digital surface, like I imagine they have in the CIA situation room: One swipe of the fingertip triggers a constellation of stars; click on a star, and it transforms into a red-carpet celeb in Dior and then fades to black. I've never seen anything this cool in LA.

My days are filled with outings and activities—adult daycare for tagalongs. The Chinese call us *tai-tais*, making us sound like we're umbrella drinks, but the term is actually derisive, more sneer than cutesy. *Tai-tais* are ladies who lunch—mani-pedi'd, empty-headed, pampered shopaholics. Housewives. It's amazing how easily I slip into this world. Not because I fancy myself a tai-tai, but because the alternative is to be alone all day, waiting for Gee to come home from work. I consider myself an expert at tagging along, having lived in Korea, Japan, and France. I now know, for example, that Gee and I need a social life as a couple. So I buy a pair of tickets to the pirate-themed cruise from a woman who is repatriating unexpectedly.

"Watch your eyes," she warns me, handing me her tickets. "My ophthalmologist in Texas said my eyes were getting wiggy from living here."

I nod, pretending to understand, while thinking, *How does one protect one's eyes, anyway?* It's not like there's an antipollution sun-screen for eyeballs. The chatter in the trailing spouses' Shanghai Facebook group this morning was all about dental concerns; at least with teeth, you can protect yourself by brushing with bottled water. I blew the eye warning off. There's only so much a person can worry about.

A week later, Gee and I are leaning against the rails of the boat, gazing out at the city, the Citco building, the Bottle Opener, the Pearl Tower. The cruise is a costume party, so we're decked out in swash-buckler gear. I'm wearing a worn-thin white ruffled blouse from the white-shirt store in Paris with a cheap black bustier from the com-modities market in Shanghai—the definition of high-low fashion. Gee's wearing an eye patch, a bandanna around his head, and a skull-and-crossbones ring. We're back on the expat trail. (I'm trailing.) He clinks his beer against my wine.

"It's kinda cool," he says.

"We'll be okay," I respond. Maybe if I say it out loud, the universe will hear me.

All kinds of Australians and Americans and Brits are dancing to '80s hits. Madonna. Bowie. Frankie Goes to Hollywood.

"Let's dance," I say. I'm a sucker for "Relax."

"After you, China Girl," Gee says, taking a pirate's bow.

•   •

Pretty soon we're at home in Shanghai, enjoying the faded old-world, art-deco charm of our neighborhood, the bustle of cars and taxis, quirky retail mash-ups like the vegan restaurant–bike shop, a guy who sells Prada bags in the basement of a back-alley tenement off Fuxing Lu. Perfect croissants. A coffee shop that plays collectable Motown LPs. A smoky jazz club. I get squashed in the metro and slammed by a bicycle. It's blissful. It's filthy. There's so much to do, so many things to worry about. Crazy cool. Insanely toxic. My head and my heart are on a collision course. At night, me and Gee cocoon on the couch with spicy peanuts and watch counterfeit DVDs that sometimes work and sometimes don't, much like the internet here; we look out at the Bund, lit up and twinkling, as we climb the circular staircase to our bedroom suite, with windows that span both floors, and I pinch myself, the view is so amazing. In bed, the air purifier humming on high, washed-out mulberry jacquard drapes pulled shut to block out the city lights, I curl up, pressing my butt into Gee's belly while he wraps his arm around my waist. He thanks me for being here; I tell him he's lucky to have me. This is the honeymoon stage. Textbook phase one culture shock.

AQI: 151–200
Code: Red (Unhealthy)
Members of sensitive groups may experience health effects.

The air goes from not so bad to not so good. All of a sudden, the open windows at my funky yoga studio lose their appeal, so I switch to the health club Gee's company pays for, where the windows are sealed shut *and* they have air purifiers. I'm riding the stationary bike when I overhear two international hotshots joking about air quality while lifting weights.

"Two hundred is the new one hundred," one says, and the other laughs.

The air is all anyone talks about. It's like talking about sex in college, complaining about your job in your twenties, bragging about your kids in your thirties, and after that, in your forties, whispering about all the sex you either aren't having or shouldn't be having. You talk about how the air looks like dirt, smells like a gas leak, and scratches the back of your throat like sandpaper. You don't talk about what you can't see, what it's doing to your body, the health risk of living here that you agreed to just to make bank, or, if you're a tagalong, so you could keep an eye on your mate or keep him company or avoid loneliness, or simply because it's become a habit to put your husband's career before your own needs. You for sure don't talk about how you shit five times a day. And the ladies who lunch, my new friends, don't know how much weight I've lost already, how my pelvic bones protrude like they did before I had kids, how my belly is a concave valley between my hip bones, which I kind of like but which worries me at the same time. Gee doesn't notice any of it: the air, my belly, my hips.

AQI: 201–300
Code: Purple (Very Unhealthy)
Everyone may begin to experience health effects.

The AQI is almost 300, and no one is joking anymore. No amount of rationalization can sweep away the fear, so I stop going to the gym altogether. Instead of exercise, I have outings with the girls; I meet a pair of tagalongs at elEFANTE Happy Restaurant & Deli, thinking a pitcher of sangria will do me good. Big happy in a chunky wineglass.

"The air is awful today," Yvette says, so we pass on the charming, Spanish-tiled outdoor patio, with lush plants in colorful pots, and opt for a table inside instead, then compare face masks. Mine is a free one they were giving away at Bank of China.

"Not good enough," Yvette insists. She shows me hers. Yvette is a woman who knows things. We call her the General. She's got an MBA and a no-nonsense haircut, and she's been in Shanghai long enough to carry some serious opinion weight on basic survival dos and don'ts. Yvette's mask has a carbon filter and a swooshy design pattern.

"You can get them on Taobao," she tells me.

"I wear two at the same time," Karen says, pulling them both out of her bag to demonstrate the layered look: a thin swath of polka-dot cotton, like the one I got for free from the bank, to cover up the industrial-grade face mask underneath. Then she shows a bump on her arm to Yvette. "What do you think?" she asks.

Yvette swats it away, saying, "It's nothing. Just a bug bite." Relief spreads across Karen's face, and she takes a gulp of wine. Turning toward me, Yvette says, "The mosquitos are brutal here."

I decide retroactively that the Dior exhibit was a Shang-*high* day and that yesterday, when I didn't leave the apartment because the air was iffy, was a Shang-*low* day. Today, my outing with the tagalongs is an information-gathering expedition.

Yvette says she never opens the windows; Karen says she runs home and opens the windows whenever it rains; and, in a related but contradictory piece of advice, Ian, a guy I met at the bagel shop around the block from my apartment, who is *not* a tagalong but *is* a scientist, says, "Never let rain touch your head, or your hair will fall out." Acid rain becomes something I have to think about more than I ever imagined.

■ ■

Andra texts to check in on me. Apparently, China's smog crisis made the news back home.

A: Can you breathe???

Em: Just barely.

A: Come home!

E: Can't. [Sad-face emoji.]

A: I'm worried about you. [Heart.]

E: Not to worry. I'm staying inside next to my air purifier. Writing.

A: About what?

E: Growing up girl.

A: Write a play and make me a star. [Star emoji.]

Then I switch to email:

E: Here's my short-term survival plan. NaNoWriMo. I'm participating in National Novel Writing Month—50,000 words in 30 days for the month of November. I'm working on a collection of essays and short stories. It gives me something to do, since I can't go outside.

A: I've been taking acting classes, since my best skill is crying at the drop of a hat. Seriously, we should do something together, like old times, a last hurrah.

E: Last hurrah seems ominous . . .

A: Send me one of your stories.

I send her "*Poubelle*," which sounds pretty but really means "trash can" in French and is about being gaslit. I tell her it's supposed to be funny, just in case she doesn't get the humor.

Here's what I don't tell her, because she'd be up all night worrying about me. Every morning I gargle with coconut oil. It's called oil pulling; they say it draws toxins from the body. I brush my teeth with bottled water and drink the sludge Dr. Love mixes up special for me, an herbal powder that I boil in filtered water. It tastes like mud. I've got a sinus infection that turned into bronchitis that I can't seem to shake, my head is stuffed, my eyes are wigging out, and I can't breathe. Dr. Love says he can help me. He's from Texas. We met at an "Eastern

Medicine for Western Women" lecture at some tagalong's apartment, and I'm not sure he's even a real doctor. The host swore by Dr. Love, said he saved her life. A month later, she was gone. People disappear abruptly in Shanghai. In Paris and Tokyo, goodbyes were an end-of-the-year ritual, tied to kids and schools, but in Shanghai people just up and leave, fast. *Take my tickets to the pirates cruise—I'm outta here.*

I sit at my desk next to an air purifier and write, comforted by the mechanical hum and the old-world smell of the desk drawers, which reminds me of my grandpa's cigars. Sometimes I practice yoga in front of the air purifier in our bedroom while listening to Wyclef Jean. "Gunpowder." In the afternoon, if the internet is working, I eat spicy Chinese peanuts alone on the couch and binge-watch television shows, even though I know in my heart that watching TV before dinner is no different than drinking before 6:00 pm.

AQI: 300–500
Code: Maroon (Hazardous)
Emergency conditions, meaning the entire population is more likely to be affected by serious health effects.

I woke coughing blood. I've been hacking like a local for a week. Next thing you know, I'll be spitting in public. Yesterday the AQI broke 270; this morning it was over 300.

"Welcome to Shanghai!" Dr. Wu jokes during my examination, adding anecdotally that he had diarrhea for six months when he first moved here.

"So I shouldn't worry?" I ask. About the cough. The itchy eyes. And digestive issues.

This is nothing, his smile seems to imply.

"Call me in a week if it doesn't get better," he says.

Charmingly unconcerned—that's the best way to describe Dr. Wu, who is Chinese-American. I sit in the chair next to his desk, fully dressed, like he's a banker and I'm asking for a loan. In a way, I am. I'm asking for three years. Three years with no lasting impact on my health.

The fact that he speaks English and was trained in the States makes me feel better. I suspect Dr. Wu's chief function at the clinic is to put expats at ease. Keep it light. As if it were all nothing more than a humorous rite of passage—pollution repositioned as something akin to Chinese sorority hazing.

"Shanghai is a fabulous city," he insists. "Don't worry about the air." And then he takes a page straight out of Kimberly's PowerPoint presentation:

Go!

Do!

Explore!

There's so much to see.

"Not today, though," he adds. "Today, maybe you should just go home and stay inside."

When I leave the health clinic, armed with cough meds and throat lozenges, traffic has slowed to a crawl because of low visibility. No tourists or expats in sight, just locals wrapped up in scarves and face masks, eyes peeking through layers of protection, wind blowing air so gritty you can almost touch it. It's like being in a desert storm, and in a way, this is war: a battle between life and unregulated, unparalleled industrial growth. Only instead of shooting guns they burn coal, lots of it, more coal than all countries in the world combined.

When the AQI blows past 400, I email Mina to ask if the company has an evacuation plan. It's more than I bargained for when I agreed to move to China. Shanghai was supposed to be the jewel of the Orient—that's what Mina (now the global mobility expert) said. When I asked if she had ever been to China, she said no. It's kind of strange, when you think about it, that she's in charge of relocating hundreds of families to a country she's never once stepped foot in. She's spouting brochure information—plausible deniability.

Me, I'm collateral damage. Which would be a great title for an essay on being a tagalong in China. Corporations are like the military: They calculate risk, run numbers, and assess whether the opportunity outweighs the threat. Back home in the States, people think China is all about cheap labor and production jobs leaving the Rust Belt, but for Gee's company, it's all about China's growing middle class. One billion–plus people is a whole lotta consumer buying power. Here's an interesting statistic: Air pollution in China causes nearly one in five deaths each year. That's the same frequency as sexual assault in the United States, but nobody puts that in the American brochure. Not to mention, but I will, that fifty percent of survivers of sexual assault will exhibit signs of PTSD. Things like anxiety.

Still, I don't understand why I'm getting sicker than Gee, despite the fact that I did not go outside for the whole month of November. I sat at my desk, writing. Could the air inside our apartment be more toxic than the air outside? Which is worse: stale, recycled air or fresh and hazardous fumes? Later, I will realize I have been pondering the wrong question. I should have wondered, Is it possible that the air is cleaner where Gee works than where we live? But that understanding won't come until after Andra sends me an article about how the Chinese government closed 150 factories to ensure that the air around Gee's job site would have blue skies and appear photo op–ready.

Not that Gee's company isn't concerned about the air. It is; that's why they decided to provide free air masks for employees and their families. Not the cute, do-nothing fashion statements the Chinese girls wear, colorful patches of rainbow cloth with dancing koalas. No, his employer passes out regulation 3M N95 industrial respirators, the kind with nose clips and foam strips, masks that provide a professional seal against toxic dust and heavy metals.

They also send someone to "handle" me. I have become a problem.

Me.

Not the air.

AQI: Off the Charts
Excuse me while I spit the sky.

"Call me Kim," she insists, like we're just two girls sitting on the couch for a gab. Kim? It seems out of character, almost disingenuous, for such a sophisticated, flawlessly coiffed, multilingual, pump-wearing, designer-wrapped package. Kimberly looks Chinese, sounds British, and thinks money. Gee's company is her cash cow, and now I am the squeaky wheel. Which is why Mina sent her to handle me. By the time she arrives, the AQI is over 500. Planes grounded, schools closed, factories shut, government cars pulled off the road, the entire megacity grinding to a halt.

She sits on our couch, nonchalantly drinking tea, willfully ignoring the soul-crushing blanket of smog that obliterates our view of Shanghai's iconic skyline. Instead, she compliments me on the decor: the fake pink Egg chair and the antique fireplace mantel propped against a blank wall.

"You must be interested in design," she remarks. This is the same woman who hosted the "Thrive vs. Survive" orientation I attended my first week in Shanghai, so I'm on to her playbook. Ignoring the obvious is her forte.

"A little," I say. But we both know she isn't here to swap decorating tips.

She zeroes in on me with laser focus, considering every possible flaw, from culture shock to underlying health conditions. "Have you made friends?" she wants to know. "What are your hobbies? Do you like the symphony? Have you joined the American Women's Club?" As if the problem is that I need a more active social life. It feels somewhere between a home invasion and a psychiatric evaluation.

"I'm not lonely," I assure her. "My chest hurts, and I'm coughing blood."

"This is temporary," Kimberly says, looking out the window at the white nothing.

Last week, in perhaps the most surreal display of Chinese indifference to reality, the window cleaners came. Hanging precariously outside our fourteenth-floor apartment, dangling from pulleys and cables, they wiped the windows so we could have a clean and pristine view of the smog that surrounds us like a cloud.

"It's an unfortunate weather pattern," Kimberly admits. "The winds will shift, and this will blow over. The government is committed to reducing pollution. And when the Chinese government puts its mind to something, it can move mountains. In a few years, air quality will not be an issue."

"That's nice," I tell her, but I don't have a long-term commitment to Shanghai. I'm thinking about going home *now*. Remembering the Chinese phrase for "don't want," I whisper, "*Bu yao*" under my breath, so as not to offend.

"Oh, good—you're learning Chinese," Kimberly says. And then, in a hushed, just-between-us-girls voice, she cautions, "The men do better when the wives are here with them." The threat of Chinese mantraps and their seductive ways comes across, thinly veiled between the lines.

I laugh out loud, thinking about how Gee rests his wire-rimmed glasses on his forehead when he reads.

"Your body just needs time to adjust," she says, switching tactics.

"I'm not sure this is something I should adjust to."

I've read that they sell bottled air in Beijing. It must cost a fortune. Like Russian caviar and Cuban cigars, Trump Tower, something only high-ranking officials can afford. What must they think, these comrades—that their luxury apartments and dark sedans with the tinted windows will protect them; that their own children don't breathe the same air on the playground as a street vendor selling pork dumplings?

"Here's my private number," Kimberly says, pressing her business card into my palm as I show her the door. "Promise you'll call me if you ever need anything. Anything. Call me first. I'm always available."

"There is something you can do," I tell her. "I want an environmental check on the air quality inside our apartment."

"That was already done before you moved in," Kimberly replies. "We would never let anyone move into an apartment without first checking for mold and other health issues."

"Can you do it again, please?" I insist.

• •

"Hi, doll," Gee says when he arrives home from work. "How was your day?"

"I had a visit from Kimberly this afternoon."

"And?"

"And she said Shanghai has a world-class symphony and that we should trust the Chinese government to fix the air."

"This is temporary, Em. It's a random weather pattern. The winds will shift, and this will blow over."

"That's what she said."

Science is his coping mechanism. I want to tell him that he doesn't need this job, but that isn't exactly true—he's contractually obligated. If he bails in the middle of a high-profile project, he won't get another such opportunity. We've still got one kid in college and a mortgage that isn't paid off. I may be following him, but he's following the company. He's a tagalong employee. I wrestle daily with what's good for him, good for us, versus what's good for me.

This day will come to be known as Airmageddon, the Airpocalypse, the smoggiest day in China's recorded history. Tomorrow the smog will start to lift and Kimberly will instruct Jake to schedule an environmental air-quality test for our apartment.

■ ■

They come wearing hazmat suits. No, just kidding—they come carrying science kits and something resembling a metal detector, like the ones people use at the beach to find sand-hidden scraps. They test every nook and cranny. The crew discovers one hot spot. My desk. My desk is a hot spot. Just the drawers—that cigar smell that reminds me of my grandfather when I open the drawer is toxic fumes. I would scream if it weren't so ironic—I just spent the entire month of November sitting at that desk, writing, to avoid the air pollution outside and instead got off-gassed inside.

When I try to return the desk, Chad tells me it's not the desk, not my desk in particular, which is fake antique, painted turquoise, with a sheet of glass on top; it's the desk in general. They're all the same. All made in China. All toxic.

Can I get a different style of desk?

"No," Chad says. It's the only desk they sell. "But you can have a different color, if you like." Instead, I empty the drawers and put them on our balcony to air out. Don't say it: how it sounds crazy to air out toxic drawers on a polluted balcony. Just do it.

WE CAME TO PLAY

I joined everything, made friends, followed everyone's advice—bought groceries online, drank bottled water, wore air masks, sat at my desk with an air purifier humming at my side, and still I got my ass kicked. Royally. Not just a little spanking, not a physical manifestation of my inner spirit dying, my arm going limp. This was no symbolic whooping.

"I can't breathe," I tell Gee. "I want to go home."

"Wait until after the holidays," he suggests. "The kids are coming. We'll have a blowout family vacation in Shanghai, and then you can go back to LA."

Rio arrives first, so I give him the high-low treatment: a foot rub at a place so skeevy they use an X-Acto knife to trim his toenails, and then traditional Chinese tea at an elegant tearoom tucked away on a side street, the kind only locals know about, where they don't speak a word of English. Tea lasts for hours and comes with seeds and nuts, fruits and wafers; it looks divine but tastes *mamahuhu*. That's Mandarin for *meh*.

"Must be an acquired taste," I say, making a sour face.

"Maybe it's like medicine," Rio responds thoughtfully, trying to tap into the mystery of Chinese customs. "Maybe it's not supposed to *taste* good; it's supposed to *be good* for you. Like a neti pot."

I'm still fighting this cough that turned into bronchitis and that Dr.

Wu will treat only with lozenges, so I'm supplementing with an herbal concoction of mothball fruit and dried lemon. I'm totally into TCM, the whole traditional Chinese medicine thing. My favorite treatment is moxibustion: a lit, cigar-size stick of mugwort held so close to your skin it almost touches. They say the heat unblocks your qi, allowing bacteria and viruses to flee the body. I've had it done a few times, proving there is no homeopathic ray-of-hope wizardry I won't try.

At first Rio made fun of me, but a week into his visit, he's not laughing anymore; he's hacking like he lives here and asks me to make him some mothball tea.

We're a pair, I think, the two of us. I'm coughing blood, and his nose is bleeding.

                                    ▪   ▪

When Ruby arrives, the family goes to this bar in Pudong with an amazing view of the Huangpu River. It takes two different elevators to get up to the eighty-seventh floor, where we're having cocktails. That's where I float the idea that I want to go home, and Ruby says flat-out no way.

The first thing that crossed my mind when she came through customs yesterday was that she looked so grown-up. It's been only six months since I last saw her, but her hair is longer, layered, and beachy. Tonight she's wearing a flowy top, skinny jeans, the boots I gave her for her birthday last year, and makeup. My daughter is dewy and sparkly. She's also prickly.

"You said I could have the house for three years," she reminds me.

"Yeah, but that was before."

"Before what?"

"Before I knew living in China might kill me."

"It's not gonna kill you, Mom. You always exaggerate."

"I just want my room back for a couple weeks, honey, just to clear my lungs, that's all."

"That wasn't the deal," she says firmly.

"When we made the deal," I say, "I didn't know how bad the air in Shanghai would be."

"It's not that bad," Ruby says, gazing out the wall of glass, at the Bund all lit up.

This is the view everyone wants when they come to Shanghai: the screaming, flashing pop art–y skyline seen from up high in the Cloud 9 bar. This is the view of the Bund from Pudong, the other side of the river from El Willy, where Gee and I ate dinner on our look-see. That first time I saw it sparkling like neon candy buildings, it left me dumbstruck. It's the view that made me say "maybe." So I know how seductive it can be.

"You promised," she says. "And besides, where would you sleep?" she asks, sipping her frozen margarita.

My daughter is quite strong. I admire this quality in her, but not when she uses it against me. Right now, I'm feeling thwarted.

I should have been clearer. That's what I'm thinking. *When we set up the house-sitting arrangement, I should have been clearer.* Rent-free in exchange for taking care of the dog, okay, but letting Ruby move into my bedroom and fill our house with her friends? Not smart. I have this crushing realization that I'm trapped. I can't go home to LA, can't go back to Detroit, can never go home to Mommy again. Nobody loves you like your mother. It used to be a whimsical observation, a joke between Andra and me. Now it feels much more piercing. Moms are the only people in the world who love you almost more than life itself. Except right now I want to strangle my own daughter. Only I don't.

Tomorrow I will take Ruby to Yuyuan Garden, visit the Buddhist temple, have dim sum in the shape of the queen's pocketbook in honor of the fact that Queen Elizabeth once dined there. We'll shop for hours in the streets surrounding the commodities market, my least favorite place in the city. Imagine a mall the size of a neighborhood;

now imagine it's filled with open stalls like a shopping bazaar, over-flowing with stuff, a clearinghouse for all things made in China: brooms, bralettes, wigs, wastebaskets, hats, and toy helicopters. *Lady, you wanna buy a watch?* I'll wait patiently while Ruby handpicks gifts for her roommates, comparing teapots and deliberating over *pu'er* versus oolong. Watch her pick out a Mao shirt for the boyfriend—the one I've never met but who I suspect is the real reason Ruby doesn't want to give up my bedroom. Afterward, I will take her to Zen Massage, a bit pricey but clean and serene. It will be a full-on mother-daughter day. I'm hoping it will buy me some points when I revisit the whole conversation about wanting to go home.

Yogaman says, "When you talk about your kids, you're just avoid-ing your own shit." I would kill to go there right now. I miss my yoga practice in LA so much I can almost smell it: the studio hot and cramped, a sweat swamp, body to body, not like in China, where they arrange the mats neatly in rows; God forbid someone gets too close or takes up too much space. Practicing yoga in Shanghai, a multina-tional community, can be challenging because poses are called out in Sanskrit through any number of foreign accents, all of which makes it difficult to follow. Half the time I'm looking around to see what the rest of the class is doing.

Once, in a twist, I turned my head to look at the guy next to me, and *snap!* An electric jolt ran from my neck down my arm and across my chest. *Shit, shit, shit!* I chastised myself, collapsing into a child's pose, cursing myself for such a rookie move. After a few minutes, I got back up, all my body parts still attached, nothing hanging limp. It seemed like I had dodged a bullet. Now my left arm is losing strength, and it hurts, but only in down dog, which is like saying "only when I laugh." I hope someday Ruby and I will laugh about this stalemate: my wanting to go home and her not letting me back into my own house.

We're still in the bar, having cocktails that last forever, stretching it out because they cost a small fortune. The mood shifts. Everyone is laughing; all talk about home leave is tabled for the time being. Gee takes out his wallet. Ruby reapplies lipstick a shade too red. I suggest hot pot at the Healthy Elixir; then everyone piles into a taxi. After dinner, the kids go bar hopping. I resist the urge to warn them off cheap liquor, to tell them it's safer to drink bottled beer at dive bars in China. On the walk home, Gee circles back to my idea of going to LA for a few weeks, saying it's too soon for me to crush Ruby's independence.

"This is an opportunity for Ruby to prove that she can be responsible, Em. Plus," he reminds me, "technically we're not entitled to home leave until we've lived here for at least a year."

That last part, the technicality, that's Gee putting his company face on. Maybe he doesn't want Mina to know I'm already considering bailing on the post. I could buy my own airline ticket—Mina would never have to know—but I don't argue the point because he's right about Ruby. I don't want to push her around. Not again. Not this time. Not after dragging her to Japan.

"The air will get better," Gee promises. "It's winter. They burn coal for heat in China. When spring comes, the sky will clear. You'll see."

I hear what he's saying. It even sounds rational. In a few months' time, the smog will lift and my chest won't feel like it's stuffed with cement. After I've been here for a year, the company will pay for my trip home and Ruby will move out of our bedroom for a few weeks. I decide not to count on that last part, on her graciously giving up my bed. Instead, I make other plans for home leave.

IN THE MITTEN

When summer comes, I go home. Heart home. Traverse City. If you're looking at the back of your hand, it's in the crease between your pinky and your ring finger. Close enough for friends and family to visit. We rent a vacation house for the whole month of August. We can walk into town, buy fudge, take yoga classes, ride bikes along the lake, canoe on the Manistee, shop at farmers' markets. Fresh corn. Cherries! And the air—the air is to breathe here! We're talking blue skies, baby—amazing azure with puffy white clouds. Pristine.

At night, the sky is pitch black, not like in China, where midnight is milky white, an unnatural sheen of streetlights reflected off the veil of pollution. Here, when I lie back on the ground, there are whole galaxies floating above me. That I can actually see! Shooting stars too. Sometimes I sit on the porch swing and do a breath meditation, inhaling and exhaling, savoring the clean, crisp air. And the water! The water is so clear, I can see my toes through it. Pebbles glisten in shades of sand and aquamarine.

Andra comes, and the two of us have a competition to see who takes the best picture. I shoot one of her on the pier near the light-house in Charlevoix, laughing. She takes one of me wading in water up to my shins, wearing a black-and-white-striped, wide-brimmed straw hat, smiling. We snap pictures of the pebbles through the water, close up, and post them as our cover photos on Facebook. There's even a local film festival. Which is why Rio decides to tag along. Ruby shows up too.

"Who's watching the pooch?" I ask her.

"My roommates," she says.

Her roommates! The girls who are living in our house, sleeping in our beds, and who Ruby said were the reason I couldn't go home to Los Angeles. I admit that I sulked about that for a few months. And then I booked this badass beach house in northern Michigan and everyone came to me. Even Ruby. Which surprised me.

"Of course I came," she says defensively. "Why wouldn't I?"

"Because you were so bitchy in Shanghai."

"You know, Mom, you shouldn't call me a bitch."

"I didn't call you a bitch. I said you were *acting* like one."

"It's the same thing."

She's sitting next to me on the swing, the one where I do breath meditation and stare at the sky, so close I can feel her hurt. It shatters my defenses. How right she is that I shouldn't call my daughter a bitch (or bitchy). Ever. Even if she is holding me hostage over my own house. I squeeze her hand, crafting a sweeping response in my head about how much I love her, but before I have time to apologize, she does.

"I'm sorry for being bitchy, Mom. I was mad. Rio's in college, and you and Dad moved to China, and all I got was the dog."

"And the house."

"And then right away you wanted to come home and ruin it."

Wow. I didn't see it from her perspective. I've been so wrapped up in being a tagalong that I didn't notice how she got left behind. Every time Gee gets a new post, I try to make it work, and it never does, not really. Someone always loses something. Tagalong math. Gee plus his job means me minus my career or me minus the kids. Or Ruby plus the house but minus her parents. Or Gee minus . . . Well, Gee never loses. That's the foundational core of tagalong math.

But right now, he's missing the Mitten. Here we are in Northern Michigan, my happy place, everything is turning out better than I could possibly imagine, and Gee is back East, visiting his parents.

"My folks were disappointed you didn't come," Gee says when he calls.

"That's because they're so old, they've forgotten how much they don't like me," I joke.

I haven't forgotten, though. *Je me souviens.* I remember it all, but I've let it go. Letting go is one thing—it's big of me; it's world-weary wise and grown-up mature—but it doesn't mean spending my home leave at Gee's parents' summer house. Even though it's lovely, rustic, an East Coast fishing village with fresh lobsters and stunning ocean views, I didn't want to go there. Not because the water is cold and you can't swim in the Atlantic, or because the mattress in the shed where we bunk is bumpy and uncomfortable, or because Milly drives me crazy and after Paris I agreed to stay with Gee on one condition: that I got to divorce his family. None of that is an issue (anymore), except the water. It's freezing. And it just isn't my home. I didn't want to fly from Shanghai to Port Clyde, from a view of the Bund to a view of the Atlantic; tag along on Gee's family vacation; be a guest in someone else's home; hide in the shed, my nose in a paperback, walking on eggshells. I wanted to connect to the stomping grounds of my own childhood. Plug in and recharge. I needed to be with my people. I needed to take care of myself.

After the kids leave, Andra and I sit on the beach and talk about this idea of hers to stage a theatrical reading of my stories.

"I'll do all the work," she says, "pull together the actors, manage rehearsals, and direct; all you have to do is edit the pieces and send them to me from China."

She's got a rock-solid vision for the show. She can already see how it flows and fits together, although I'm a little worried she might not get the tone right; she's a bit of a drama queen, always going for a hug or a cry.

"Don't make it weepy, Andra. Promise me."

"People will laugh, Em."

I start to get excited. Really excited. More excited than I've been in years. *I can do this*, I think. Go back to China. Teach yoga and edit my pieces. Shanghai is survivable as long as I have a plan. Now that I have this project with Andra, I will have something concrete to work on if the air gets too bad to go outside.

Before I return to Shanghai, though, I swing through LA for doctors' appointments and fortification. Ruby graciously vacates my bedroom. My doctor in LA assures me my lungs are perfectly healthy. "Don't worry about the AQI," he says. "It's the delta you need to be concerned with. The real question is, how much worse is the air in Shanghai than the air in LA?"

This is meant to comfort me in a shockingly cynical way. Because he's right: The air in LA is beginning to look a lot like the air in China. I order face masks online, stock up on red underwear to ward off the bad luck that is otherwise destined to befall me in the Year of the Sheep—an ancient Chinese superstition, but I'm not taking any chances. And, just to be on the safe side, I go to see this new-agey doctor in Santa Monica who talks me into an oxygen drip with a vitamin C boost. Not that I'm hard to convince, because I'm searching for Band-Aids. *Doctor, please make me invincible. My health insurance won't cover this*, I think, sitting there with the tube in my arm, mainlining oxygen.

TIC — THIS IS CHINA

Me and Ian complain a lot. It's the basis of our friendship. I always feel like I have to fake it with the tagalong crowd.

I love my life!

Gee and I are going to Bangkok!

We're so lucky!

That's the tagalong game: always be positive. Even though more than a few of my yoga students have shown up for class in the morning sad-eyed, reeking of last night's "happy" hour. They don't look joyful, but they put on a good show running frantically from a walking tour to a wine tasting. Ian and I don't play that game with each other, though. We have unofficially declared our relationship a safe space for outrage. Sometimes we share basic survival tips, like who has the best local produce (the avocado lady on Wulumuqi Lu) and where to get a great haircut.

"Em!" Ian yelled at me in a downpour when I was haphazardly slow to open my umbrella. "Your hair!"

Ian has a head of professionally streaked, fabulously tousled, dirty blondish hair. Hair is the only thing he's vain about; otherwise, his fashion sense is strictly zoo T-shirt and jeans. It may seem weird to have a best friend who's young enough to be my son, but in the expat world, sharing a common language is more important than age, and Ian speaks English, albeit with a British accent. We bonded over great apes; he studies them, and I handled marketing for the zoo in between Korea and Paris. This is how I chart my career, in stints sandwiched between Gee's overseas posts.

• •

We meet on the corner of Yueyang and Yongjia Lu and walk to dinner at a charming bistro tucked into a hidden courtyard garden. Most of the time, Ian goes on about problems he's having at work or with his partner, which seem pretty messed up and dead end–ish, but I don't tell him that. I hope that back home someone is listening to my kids sort through their lives and not making them feel worse than they already do. I've learned not to talk about my marriage. Gee and I have weathered our relationship drama. The longer we stay together, the better it feels from the inside looking out, but still I suspect that it might look totally different from the outside looking in. It might look one-sided: too much compromise and not enough caring. It might look less like dust settled and more like I settled for dust.

And speaking of dust, today I'm in a tizzy about my neighbors who are in the midst of a huge renovation project. Dust everywhere. Construction banging in my face. Just mine, not Gee's, because when the workers are pounding away, he's in a hermetically sealed, air-purified, US-regulated, corporate environment. At first it was just irritatingly noisy, but when the apartment started to smell like a vat of nail polish remover, I called Gee.

"Acetone," he said. "It's used in paint thinners. It's regulated in the States but not in China."

They'd put it in soup if it was cheaper than water. "Do I need to be worried?" I asked.

"It won't kill you, Em. Just open the windows."

Snap back to the window dilemma. To open or not to open. Never, only at night, or always when it rains? The air quality is good when it rains, but if the rain is acid rain, how can it be safe to breathe?

Acetone. Acid rain. Pesticide. Living in China is like being a contestant on a reality-TV show about your worst fears. Coping can sometimes look a lot like sleeping. A week ago, Gee came home from work early during the neighbor's construction craze and found me napping in a noxious stupor.

"Wake up! Jesus fuck, Em, can't you smell the chemicals in here?"

Gee got Jake on the phone; Jake got in touch with the building manager, who called the neighbors. They showed up with their whole family—kids, grandkids, plus an interpreter. Gee was in problem-solving mode; this is where he shines. The solution is simple, he told them: Just seal the door to the common hallway and open your own windows. The next day, the biggest basket of imported fruit arrived. Mangoes, pineapple, kiwi, and passion fruit. It must have cost a boatload of RMB. It was from the neighbors. "Sorry for the bad smell," the note said. The Chinese are big gift givers. I just wish they were better environmentalists.

A few days later, as if no one would notice, the jackhammering resumed and, once again, a toxic breeze began blowing our way. Gee says he doesn't detect the smell anymore, and most likely he doesn't. For one thing, by the time he gets home, it's dissipated somewhat. But mostly, I suspect, he sees that the hall is sealed; the problem is therefore solved. That's how his mind works. There's an underlying hint that I am being neurotic.

After dinner, I invite Ian up for a glass of wine. Secretly, I want his opinion on the smell. Odor is not like smog—you can't see it. I can't tell anymore: Does it smell in here, or is fear triggering an olfactory memory?

Ian walks in and immediately states the obvious: "It smells like a chem spill in here! This is not okay."

"'This' being all of it, right? The air, the food, the water."

"Especially split pants and kids squatting and doing their business like dogs on the street."

"Yeah." I laugh. Then we go get a drink at the bar across the street, where you have to slip your hand into a slot on the wall to open the door. Because if we have to live here, if we have to eat, breathe, and drink factory fumes, we might as well do it in a secret-handshake bar with fancy olives.

● ●

I start attending events hosted by an NGO whose mission is to minimize or reverse the environmental degradation in China brought about by economic growth. I go to a lecture with a panel of speakers, representatives from companies that sell water filtration systems, air purifiers, and face masks, and one woman who is designing a practical app for air quality, one that can compare the air quality inside a home to the air quality outside, once and for all settling the burning question of whether or not to open the windows.

At the end of the presentation, there's a Q and A.

How many air purifiers do you need?

Do you need a water filter on your showerhead if you have a reverse osmosis water system?

Where can I get one of those cool skater air masks?

Where is the resistance, the indignation, the outrage? That's what I want to know. These products are necessary tools, and I for sure couldn't live here without them, but the salesperson in me understands that this panel of experts is made up of pollution profiteers, and the rebel in me is looking for change. On the spot, I devise a resistance campaign that is so hot it could go global. I stand up and pitch my idea of a consumer boycott triggered by the AQI smog index to this room full of expats and English-speaking locals. "Let's start a social media campaign on WeChat," I suggest.

The room goes pin-drop, you-crazy-lady quiet. Afterward, during wine and cheese, a few guests come up to me and discreetly offer opinions.

I could lose my job!

I could get arrested!

I could get deported!

I realize two things: The people in this room are more afraid to speak out than breathe in. And I have tagalong privilege. I don't share their concerns about being arrested or losing a job, and I wouldn't mind being deported.

On the way home, I plug in my earbuds, cranking up Imagine Dragons: "Radioactive." And swing by happy hour to meet up with Yvette and the tagalongs. Shanghai is a cocktail party in hell. I feel it in my belly; I have weird bumps and rashes, itchy parts, hair falling out, and sties. I have this cut on my finger that won't heal. I snap a pic of it.

Meanwhile, my arm and neck are both hurting, my left arm having weakened steadily ever since that rookie move in yoga. One morning, while blow-drying my hair, I feel a thud in my chest right where my heart is.

Dr. Wu assures me it isn't a heart attack and refers me to Dr. Chong, a physical therapist at the expat health clinic. She's sort of a drill sergeant. She forces me to do sit-ups. Push, squeeze, squeeze harder, she insists. I'm crunching, I'm working up a sweat, I'm breathing deeply.

"I can taste construction dust from downstairs," I tell her.

They're renovating the lobby using no plastic protective sheets, allowing particulate debris to fly everywhere—including straight into my lungs. It was so bad when I was coming up here, I kept my mask on in the elevator.

"You should turn on the air purifier," I suggest. It's sitting next to her desk like a prop. No hum.

"Oh, okay," Dr. Chong says, as if it hasn't occurred to her and I'm being overly cautious. It's like she's in cahoots with my family. Everyone in Shanghai acts like I'm the problem, not the environment. At the end of the session, despite the full hour of therapy, I tell her my shoulder still hurts.

"Oh, okay, shoulder hurt," she says. Grabbing my head, she cracks my neck in the crook of her elbow, just like that, standing up and without asking permission. I would complain, but it feels better immediately. So good, I walk home instead of taking the metro, window shopping on Fuxing Lu, feeling euphoric, feeling like the pain is gone and it's gonna be a great day.

An hour later, I'm standing in the kitchen, making green tea. I don't even like tea, but it seems like a small step toward making peace with China. It's the least I can do. Reaching for a cup, I notice a flash of light in my right eye. *It's either an acid flashback or a stroke.* That's the first thing that crosses my mind when I start seeing light trails. Something strange always seems to be happening to my body in China, and I'm never quite sure what is real, what is in my head, what to ignore, what to be concerned about. My eye is flashing, although now that I'm studying it, it's less like a flash and more like a jagged speck of light, but I can't snap a picture of light in my eye, so it could just be my imagination. I try to call the health clinic. That's when I discover my phone is dead.

Shit like this happens in China. Sometimes email works; sometimes it doesn't. Sometimes you can see out the window; sometimes the smog is so thick, the world disappears. I email Dr. Wu a message about my eye flashing and then do exactly what my mother would have done—take half a Xanax and go to bed. A few hours later, I wake to a flurry of messages, including one from Gee: "You okay, doll? SOS is looking for you and you aren't answering your phone. Team dinner tonight. I'll be late. Xoxo G."

SOS is the international medical service Gee's company provides in case one of us has to be medevaced to Hong Kong. So it's not a good sign that the clinic called them, and now SOS is chasing down my husband. At this point I pretty much rule out an acid flashback, although there was this one time, freshman year of college, when I sat in the dorm hallway for hours, staring at a blank wall like it was a video screen, watching a stream of birthday parties and fancy cakes with dolls plunged waist-deep into the middle of the cakes, as if the icing were a princess party dress, my mom in pedal pushers and coiffed hair, in cocktail dresses and pearls, always smiling. And then I was the one holding the cakes and wearing the pearls. That freaked me out. All freshman year, I was known as that girl from third-floor Cooley who had a bad trip and stared at the wall for hours, whispering, "No, no, no, that can't be me."

It's weird how prescient that trip was, when you think about it, which for some reason I'm doing right now. Maybe because I'm seeing light trails, or maybe because Gee has taken to calling me "doll." Or maybe because tagalong life is a bit of a 1950s time warp.

I taxi back to the international clinic, where the doctor rules out stroke, but says it could be something almost as bad: retinal detachment. No time to be relieved about not dying, because now I might be going blind. I'm probably not, but if I am, I will need surgery within twenty-four hours.

"We need to rule it out," the doctor says. The test is simple, but his eye specialist is gone for the day. "It's just a precaution, but you need to go to the hospital right away."

I don't hear anything after that, not a word. All I can think is, *No way.* I am not going to the hospital, the Chinese one in Hongjiao, where the bird and flower market is. The taxi ride alone will be hours. It's out of the question, outside the bubble. I was supposed to pre-register at the hospital just in case something like this happened. Or at the very least carry with me at all times a laminated address card that said, "Take me to the hospital" in Chinese characters. Normally, I would pull up an address on my phone and hand it to the driver, but my phone is dead; now, I will have to go home and get the laminated taxi card off the fridge and grab cash from the safe, because Chinese hospitals don't accept credit cards.

And I know myself. Once I go home, I'll want to take the other half of that Xanax and pour myself a glass of wine to wash it down, and if I mix wine and Xanax, I will want to take a nap, and then I might as well get back in bed and pull the covers over my head.

"It's all handled," the doctor says, turning toward me. I'm holding on to his arm. Not holding, exactly—more like gripping. *Please don't make me go there.*

No, I tell him, I can't go to the hospital; that's not an option. It's like that Etta James song "I'd Rather Go Blind," only I don't want to go blind—I just think maybe there's a little wiggle room. I start to negotiate the time frame. We have a twenty-four-hour window to play with.

"I'll just come back in the morning to see the eye specialist," I promise.

"They're expecting you," he says, trying to pry my fingers off his shirt sleeve. They do not have an ophthalmologist on staff at night, he informs me. "Their eye specialist is on call, and they will call the doctor as soon as you arrive at the hospital."

The hospital I am never in a million years going to, especially without a phone.

I know what this must sound like: a functionally illiterate American woman who is willing to risk going blind, rather than step out of the bubble. But I'm not going to let this doctor hand me off to another clinic. I decide not to let go of his arm until he comes up with a better solution.

A part of me is thinking, *Damn Gee. I'm here as his companion, so he won't be alone in China, and he's out drinking with his team while I'm hanging on to the sleeve of some stranger in a white coat like he's a tree branch and if I let go, I'll be swallowed up by quicksand.* Another part of me is thinking, *Damn, girl, you are not going to that hospital alone.*

"If *their* specialist would have to be called in to see me at night," I ask the doctor, "why can't you call *yours?*" It's not so much a question as an observation, but it comes out sounding more like a demand. And so he calls Dr. Wang.

"It's just a vitreous tear," Dr. Wang says. "It happens to everyone sooner or later." He's trying to make me feel comfortable—*no worries, ma'am.* And it's all the sweeter considering he was probably halfway home when the clinic called him, maybe even sitting down to dinner with his family, and he had to come back to the clinic and check out the crazy expat lady who's having a total "I can't deal with this" meltdown.

"A rupture like this," the doctor notes, "is usually the result of a sports injury. Were you doing sports today?"

No, but I did go to physical therapy. "If somebody cracked your neck aggressively, could this cause such a tear?" I ask.

"Yes, I believe so."

I leave it at that. There's no point telling him it was probably one of his colleagues. I'm just relieved not to be dying or going blind. My brother the personal injury lawyer always says, "You sue for damages, Em, not bad mojo. If there are no appreciable damages, consider yourself lucky." So I put on my face mask and head home from the health clinic for the second time today. It's beginning to feel like a job, like going to work, only my job in Shanghai is to keep myself healthy. My job is not to slip too far below the baseline at which I arrived here in China. The Chinese government made us jump through hoops to get a residence card: We had to cough, cuff the arm, have X-rays, give blood, cover each eye, and read the chart. Everything but pee in a cup. A month or so later, the results came back healthy; I didn't even have a fatty liver.

●　■

"Em, where have you been? I was starting to get worried," Gee asks when I walk in the door.

"Oh, you know, TIC [this is China], and my phone is dead."

He grabs my phone and disappears out the front door.

I curl up on the couch with a book of Sufi poetry that sat on the bookshelf in Los Angeles for years, collecting dust. *Poems by Rumi*, a present from Jerry when she left Paris. I threw it in a box of books, as part of the whole spark-the-romance idea I had while packing for China, which seems so long ago, so naively quaint now. When I crack the spine, the first thing I see is the inscription: "Don't be afraid to jump off a cliff. Xo Jerry." I flip open to this page. "Like This" is the name of the poem.

Like this.
When someone asks what it means
to "die for love," point
here.

Half an hour later, Gee returns and hands me my phone, apologizing for letting it run out of money.

"Wait, what? It's a burner phone? Like drug dealers, we pay by the minute? You've been taking my phone to the corner market and putting money on it for over a year?"

"I take good care of you, doll," he says.

"Thank you, but I could have done it myself if I'd known that was the setup."

All this time, I just assumed the company paid the bills. My phone was dead, I was totally without connection to the outside world, I almost went blind, and all I had to do was go to the market on the corner where they sell spicy peanuts and put money on my phone card so I could call my husband.

I don't know who to be angrier with: him or myself.

∎ ∎

I decide to lay off yoga for a while and focus on the play instead. Andra and I are in regular communication. I send her my pieces;

she sends back comments. Meanwhile, she's meeting with actors and forwarding their headshots.

"You'll love Hazel!" she gushes. "She's going to do 'Collateral Damage.' And I found the perfect person for 'Power Cord,' the mother-daughter piece. Her name is Nita." Andra is doing "Old Dogs," the piece about Chandler, my French bulldog.

Her efforts to keep me in the loop only make me feel less connected. It all seems otherworldly. In California, there are five actors rehearsing my stories, and here I am in China, wasting time in adult daycare, wrapping yak yarn around empty wine bottles with the tagalongs. A wine-and-whine activity.

My plan is to go home for a week or two, check in on rehearsals, meet the actors, and get back to Shanghai in time for Chinese New Year in Bangkok. That's the best thing about China—its proximity to Southeast Asia. Stunning photos of rice paddies and ruins taken on exotic trips that when posted on social media make people back home envy your life. If only they knew that in between photo ops, I'm traipsing back and forth to the health clinic in a constant battle with the environment.

•   •

I switch from yoga to swimming and immediately get a "thing" on my thigh. I photograph it next to a pencil eraser head, just to track its size.

"Look!" I say to Gee a few days later, pointing to the bump, which now appears to be spreading, developing concentric red circles and pinhole sores.

"It's probably nothing," Gee says.

"But look how it's grown," I insist, handing him my phone with the photo series taken as documentation. Just in case.

"It's a pimple," Gee says, sipping his morning coffee, refusing my phone.

But what if it's flesh-eating disease? I wonder, now googling images of MRSA. The next day, my leg starts cramping as if tiny vise grips were pinching my veins. Back I go to the clinic.

"It could be a boil," Dr. Wu announces.

A boil!

I am not the kind of person who gets boils, I think indignantly. People who eat fast food and don't exercise get boils, like it's punishment for bad hygiene or poor diet. That's when I posit this theory of mine that some infection or virus is moving around my body, popping up here and there, in my lungs and belly, manifesting as an urgent need to pee, a sty in my eye, a cut that won't heal—or a boil.

"Viruses don't work that way," Dr. Wu explains without explaining. "It does look infected," he admits. "It could be any number of things, but I'd treat them all the same way: with a topical cream."

And the bump goes away, phew, but the clamping in my leg gets worse, and then my digestive system starts to act up again. I get a crushing headache, and I know I should have insisted that the doctor test the damn bump to see what it was.

• •

Ten years ago, Shanghai was a lovely city on the brink of the future. Today, it's a cautionary tale. Last month, Ava's American boyfriend, who is under thirty and scoots around town on a longboard, had an environmentally related heart attack. My physical therapist, the one who didn't use her air purifier, recently had "chest surgery." That's what the receptionist said when she canceled my appointments indefinitely. Chest surgery. In a few weeks, Ian will be in the hospital with pneumonia. A few months from now, I'll be sitting in a dental chair, listening to Dr. Bob, the dentist from Croatia, explain how my tooth appears to have disintegrated from the inside out, either from a bacterial infection or because of some sort of systemic issue.

Inhale, hold for two, exhale . . . That'll be me, trying to practice yoga breathing so as not to scream.

"Do you have an autoimmune disease?" he'll ask, while showing me the X-ray of my tooth, which is now more like an empty peanut shell.

He's very handsome, Dr. Bob. He's reminiscent of the actor who played a werewolf on my favorite vampire series, and I'll kinda like him, even though we'll have only just met and he'll be delivering bad news. I'll feel Bangkok slipping away as he explains how a trip to Thailand might be risky in terms of infection, unless I let him pull the tooth first. "The surgery is simple," he'll say. He could have me on a plane to Bangkok in a few days, with a hole in my smile. A minor inconvenience. It will take six months for the implant process. And then, that bad-boy smile, those werewolf teeth, he'll say, "You'll be good as new."

I don't need to be good as new, I'll think. I just want to be as good as I was when I arrived in China and the intake exam mandated by the bureaucracy here proclaimed me to be in perfect health.

I'll be taking it all in: Dr. Bob, the Croatian dentist in Shanghai, who looks like he's straight outta Hollywood casting; the tube that rinses your mouth with water attached to the bowl where you spit. I'll be wondering if that water is filtered. This is something the old me, the LA girl, would never think to question. Until Flint, Michigan, and toxic water was discovered in the Mitten. Now, water quality is always a question. Everywhere.

Before they bring back coal mining, everyone should be required to visit China for a reality check.

"Can you send me a digital copy of the X-ray?" I'll ask. "I'd like to email my dentist back home for a second opinion."

"We don't have digital equipment," he'll apologize, "but you can keep this." And he'll hand me a slide. A slide! Shanghai has one foot in the skyscraping future and one foot stuck in the backwoods muck of a country peasant's thatch-roof hut. They can build a 128-floor super-high-rise with the world's fastest elevators and indoor gardens, and an entirely enclosed, LEED-certified green community with restaurants, shopping malls, hotels, offices, and apartments, but they don't have proper dental equipment. Or clean air, electric cars, reliable internet access, or drinkable water. Of course, if they had those things, they wouldn't need to construct an environmentally controlled bubble for rich people.

I'll be thinking about that AQI disclaimer: Air quality is acceptable; however, there may be a small number of people who are unusually sensitive to certain pollutants. Gee says living in China for three years won't kill you. As if three years weren't a huge chunk of our lives, as if there were some mathematical curve, a point at which one might be overexposed, and three years is on the safe side of that curve. And I'll be thinking that I was right about accelerated decay, that it's not just a built-world term.

I'm right about a lot of things. If only I listened to myself. Yogaman has this rap he gives on "knowing"—or, rather, the many ways in which we avoid the inconvenient truth, the deals we make with ourselves, the rationalizations. Like how Gee says living in China for three years won't kill us. Yogaman says it's simple: "When you know, you *know*. You know that fire will burn your hand, so you don't put your hand in the flame." But let's say you've read the Surgeon General's warning that cigarettes can kill, and still you sneak an occasional smoke on the balcony, just one after dinner on Sunday nights, or maybe you bum them off a friend, but only when you're drinking . . . or living in Paris. In that case, so says my yogi master, "You don't *really* know; you just think you know."

"How do you know when to call it quits?" I once asked my therapist. When your partner cheats on you? When you cheat on your partner? When the kids are grown—that's the usual answer. When the kissing is gone—that's what Andra says. When your Chinese girlfriend bites

you? Or maybe you wait till she smashes your laptop. Definitely beat-
ing your partner with the shower hose is a love kill. That happens, the
cops told a colleague of Gee's. Don't mess with Chinese girls. How
'bout when your husband asks you to sacrifice your career for his?
Or maybe when he puts you in a situation that risks *your* health for
his job? At some point, you have to stop shopping for answers and
start listening to yourself. When the cognitive dissonance gets loud
enough, you'll know.

THIS IS NOT OKAY

The boys expect me to shriek, but I don't say anything when the fat cockroach saunters sluggishly across the table. Gee drains his glass, flips it over, and with one fell swoop traps the bug and leaves it sitting there in the middle of the table. Like a centerpiece. The dystopian future.

This is not okay, I think but don't say. The phrase has become worn. It covers a wide range of things that happen in China, like unreliable internet access, unbreathable air, acid rain—things that don't work or don't make any sense, like drivers who don't stop for pedestrians. And cockroaches that act like they own the place.

We're eating peanut butter noodles in a hole in the wall on a street I call Rodeo Drive because it is lined with palm trees. That's about as far as the comparison goes. This is not Gee's favorite noodle place; there is a smaller, even dirtier dive in a back alley off Huaihai, inside a rickety building. You go upstairs, like you're eating on the second floor of someone's home, which you probably are.

"This is the real deal," Gee announced with immense satisfaction when he took me there.

But the real deal is pork and who knows what else, and so today he humors me and Ian, who is also vegetarian, and settles for peanut butter noodles.

It's not easy being vegetarian in China. And I'm beginning to think it wasn't smart, either. I came here so yoga-teacher, my-body-is-a-temple sure of myself. Now, two years into this relo, my health seesawing, I'm beginning to wonder about all the salads I ate, all that raw food, especially after we went on the outing to the organic farm and discovered that it was sandwiched in between two factories. Sure, they don't spray the zucchini with pesticides, they've got butterflies fluttering about, but toxic smoke billows all around that farm. It took some of the shine out of our home-delivered, overpriced, locally sourced, organic tomatoes, that's for sure. We'd have been better off buying groceries from a veggie stand down the street, boiling the carrots beyond recognition, dousing them with vinegar and oil and sugar, like the Chinese do. That's why they say, "Eat like the locals."

Sometimes I feel like a sports announcer giving a detached commentary on the stuff that has gone wrong with me here. First it's a blow to the head: eyes wiggy, throat scratchy, bloody cough (not British "bloody"—red blood). Then it's digestive problems, weight loss (okay, that was kinda cool), hair loss (not so cool) . . . No, wait, it's a full-body press, an infection that seems to have taken up permanent residence inside me, just casually making the rounds, popping up as a mysterious rash or a boil on my thigh that spreads into something that looks a lot like flesh-eating disease. And then the final indignity, the tooth that disintegrated from the inside out, leaving just a shell of enamel.

I wish my mom were still alive; she would counsel me to get the hell out of Dodge, but Gee can't acknowledge what's happening, can't let my health get in the way of the job he came here to do. He has a hard time juggling conflicting thoughts. *Shanghai is super cool,* and *it's toxic. I have a great job,* but *it's killing my wife.* His head might just explode.

I had this dream recently. The three of us were in the car—Gee was in the driver's seat, I was in the passenger seat, and Mom was in back, and then Gee turned around and started talking to my mother.

"Gee!" I screamed. "Pay attention to the road!"

Next thing you know, his butt was in the windshield and he was sandwiched between two bucket seats, trying to climb into the back with my mom. No one was driving the car. And my mom said, "Emma, take the wheel."

Nobody loves you like your mother.

Three giant bowls of noodles arrive, so big the three of us could easily have shared one dish. It's more food than I usually eat in one sitting. Ian and Gee are laughing about the cockroach, trying to get a reaction out of me. They think I live in a bubble, spending my days with the tagalong ladies, eating at trendy, sanitized expat restaurants. Restaurants with powder rooms and toilet paper. And I do, mostly, but also I spend time in the real world.

"They have this latrine," I say, "in the school where I teach English to the children of migrant workers." I've never seen a latrine in a women's john before. It's like a trough. "One end is elevated; then it slopes down until it gets to the other end, where there's a hole in the ground. That's for number two. So the pee flows south across a bank of individual stalls and naturally flushes the poo. It's an elegant solution, don't you think? And energy-efficient. Not to mention a bit of a workout, great for the glutes. Nowhere to hang your bag, though. That's the gross part, putting your purse on the ground, and you have to, because it takes both hands, in a squatting position, to keep your clothes from touching the concrete or getting wet. One hand to hold up your dress and the other to pull your panties forward, in front of your pee. It requires balance; you gotta lean into it, but not too far, or you could tip over. You don't want to have to put your hand on the ground, not even to steady yourself, because the latrine is narrow, you're supposed to straddle it, and, well, sometimes a girl misses the target." I pause to slurp some noodles, then continue, "I took a picture of it. Wanna see?"

Gee's mom has this rule about "the things you can't talk about *at table*, dear, the three Ds: death, dirt, and disease." Pretty much that cockroach under glass covers all bases, but if Gee's breaking the rules, so can I. I'm still eating, the whole time I'm recounting this scatological story. My peanut noodles are yummy, by the way, on a lazy Saturday afternoon in Shanghai when we have nothing better to do.

Only now I have something to do, something I really want to do, back in Los Angeles. This morning, Andra emailed to say she's starting to rehearse actors for our show. It feels like I should be there. Not that she needs me, but it feels like I'm missing out on something kind of important. *To me.*

"How are the noodles?" Gee asks.

"Pas mal," I say. "A blend of oily and creamy. Is there a word for that?"

"Creamoily?"

"Oily with a hint of peanut."

"Nah, it's more than a hint."

"Slippery, with a legume base and a hint of roach," Ian chimes in with the definitive description.

I'm looking at that cockroach trapped under the glass. He's fucked. He can't dig a hole in the table, can't slip under the glass. He's just gotta hope he can hold on 'till they clean the table, and then, if he's lucky, they'll swipe him off the top, as opposed to smashing him, and he'll live to see another day. Cockroach like that, big and fat—that bug's been around awhile. He's a survivor. Me? I'm turning out to be not so hardy.

As a tagalong wife, I have weathered loneliness and infidelity, marginalized my career, and traded community roots for life experience, all with ballsy, can-do, must-keep-it-together aplomb. But underneath that steely persona is flesh and blood, an immune system that can be taxed beyond its limits. I am apparently a sensitive being.

"You can go home, Em," Gee says. But he doesn't say it like he means it. He says it like it's an insurance policy against a future argument, so I can't throw it back in his face someday that he made me move to Paris or made me stay in China. He says it while we're in bed and he's holding me so tight that I know I'm as much his life preserver as he is mine.

"What odds do you give him?" Ian asks.

Gee goes into his cockroaches-will-survive-a-nuclear-holocaust thing.

Because they are adaptable?

No, because they are a simple organism.

Like Gee. Not that Gee's a cockroach, but he is a man of simple needs. He's sort of an unconscious Buddhist, meaning he wants exactly what he has. Most of us spend years in down dog, trying to get to that place of peace, the feeling that we have everything we want. I've been following Gee all over the world in a mad attempt to have it all. In the process, I've lost the very thing I really need: my own life.

Thick Dodger-blue eyeglass frames perch on Gee's nose. He bought them in Tianzifang for one hundred quai, which is about ten US dollars. I tell him how cool they look, but in truth they're borderline-midlife-crisis sports-car glasses. Still, I love that he's embraced color, that he's beginning to loosen up and be more like the guy I married, the punk rocker with the Mohawk. It occurs to me that it's Gee who's trapped: by a career he set in motion years ago, a résumé that says, *Have passport, will travel.*

"I'm just about done with my noodles," I announce.

"Wow," Gee says, "I'm impressed. You ate the whole bowl."

"That," I say, "is because I am never, and I mean *not ever*, coming back here again." I wipe my mouth on my sleeve; a place like this has no napkins.

The boys decide to go to Boxing Cat Brewery, Gee's favorite watering hole, for a beer. "Wanna come?" they ask.

"No, thanks. I don't feel like tagging along. I've got stuff to do."

After they leave, I compose an email to Mina, notifying her that I want to repatriate as soon as possible. I hesitate for a moment before pressing SEND. Part of me still feels like it's not fair to leave Gee here alone. And it's chickenshit of me not to tell him first. But any discussion with him would just end up with me compromising more. So I cc Gee and send the message. My days of being a human petri dish are over.

On my way out of the restaurant, I free the cockroach.

Maybe Gee will get a Chinese girlfriend. Maybe he'll go to Bar Rouge or M1NT, the club with the shark tank, and pick up some easy, pretty Chinese dream girl for a night. Perhaps he'll get a deep massage with a happy ending at the down-and-dirty spa on Wulumuqi. I like to think he's wised up some and will choose a superior foot rub with Ian. Whatever. *BU YAO*. All caps. Using my big-girl voice. Don't want to buy another fake market purse or spend another day tagging along on this post. I'm going home.

GET LOUD

Andra and I launch our show in the North Hollywood Arts District: ten monologues written by me. This is my version of jumping off a cliff, about as far out of my comfort zone as it gets. Yogaman would be proud.

The show is sold out, and the theater is filled with a smattering of friends and a whole lot of strangers. In a little bit, they'll all know way more about me than they do now. More about me than my own family knows, perhaps. If I could slink down low in the back row, wearing sunglasses and a wig, I would.

"Welcome to *Growing Up Girl*," I announce, standing center stage, wearing black skinny jeans and a white muscle T-shirt that reads GET LOUD in big block type across the outline of a guitar. I can't see a thing because of the spotlight in my eyes, which doesn't make sense because we didn't hire a lighting designer.

Andra didn't want to pay for stage lights. Not surprisingly, that didn't go over well with the talent, who are performing for dough-nuts and coffee. The lights (or lack thereof) caused a mini-mutiny behind Andra's back among her actors and put me smack in the middle, not wanting to choose sides. Andra and I have been through a lot together—my marriage, her divorce, a few jobs—but this is our first solo endeavor, and we've had some creative differences. For one thing, she encouraged the actors to weep all over my words.

"I want my voice to sound fierce."

"People need to feel your pain, Em," she insisted.

That was bullshit; she was using my writing to showcase her the-atrical chops. Being the writer is like being a tagalong all over again: The director has all the power. You hand your stories, which in this case amounted to my life, over to the director and hope that they have your best interests at heart. That they will not treat your work opportunistically. I might have stayed quiet if it hadn't been for her take on "Rape Me." Andra wanted the actress to sit on a stool and tearfully deliver a piece about sexual assault that was meant to be slam poetry, not a sob story.

"She needs to stand up," I said during rehearsal. "And she can't cry."

You could hear all five actors suck in air. The writer is not supposed to challenge the director—it's totally taboo—but I'd had enough of going along with other people's vision of how my life should play out. I let Andra run the whole production side of the show—casting, blocking, lights—even though I suspected the actors were right about the lights.

"We don't need stage lights," Andra insisted.

"You need lights, Em," my husband contradicted over the phone.

He's a global show producer with a bazillion-dollar budget, so he expects a different level of professionalism on set; this is just a theat-rical reading, very loving hands at home. We're not even in the same league. Or on the same continent.

"Andra says house lights will be fine," I told him.

"How's it going otherwise?"

"I'm nervous. I wish you could be here."

"I'll try to make it," he promised.

That's what people say when they know they can't do something. You mean well, but you can't commit, and most likely you won't make it, but by not saying no outright, you avoid a fight. And hus-band number three and I don't fight. We're partners. We just do our best and hope it's good enough.

"You should tape it, Em," he suggested.

Now I knew for sure he wasn't coming. He wanted me to tape the performance so he could watch it later. That way, at least he'd be able to see it. But it meant he wouldn't be there to support me if it was a disaster. And having Ruby and Rio there wasn't the same thing; they'd sit next to me, but they wouldn't hug me if it was bad. Maybe that was okay; maybe I wouldn't want anyone to touch me if it bombed. Maybe I'd slink off into the woods alone.

"Please try to come. I'm in a bit of a head spin," I told him. "I'm worried no one will show up, or, worse, they'll come but they won't laugh. And it will be awkward. And—"

"I'll try, Em."

"Love you," I said, before hanging up. He might not be able to make it to my opening night, but I wasn't about to let his absence ruin the experience for me or strain our marriage. I've learned a few things along the way.

My first husband was a roadie. We were madly in love. We were that couple at a party who are always glued to each other, smiling. He was my lover, my best friend, and my personal tech support. He hooked up our stereo, backed up my computer, checked my oil and brake fluid, even put air in my tires.

"I take good care of you," he'd say.

And he did. He filled in the blanks where my own skill set was weak; he knew stuff I didn't, about sound systems and cars and earthquakes. The first time I felt the apartment shake (me, a girl from the D!), I ran around in circles—*The sky is falling!*—before crawling underneath the bed . . . only to discover I might be claustrophobic.

"I can't stay down here!" I screamed. It was like someone had hit the panic button and cranked it up to eleven.

"Em, it's an earthquake," he said calmly, still tangled in sheets, holding the energy of a sleeping baby. He was just a boy, really. Ripped T-shirts and a ponytail. El Niño.

"Stand in the doorway," he suggested.

I half suspected he was pulling my leg, that he just wanted to stare at me totally naked, standing there like an idiot in the doorjamb, but then he explained about reinforced framing and load-bearing walls, and I believed him. It's not true—you're not safer in a doorway. You're better off under a desk next to a wall. But that's not the point. The point is that he made me feel safe. And I made him happy. Whenever one of us got a raise or a promotion or a new job, I'd throw a celebratory bed picnic, with finger foods—olives, cheese, chocolate-covered pretzels—and champagne. We were just kids staring into the future, and it looked pretty perfect. Then his career took off and he left me waiting for the phone to ring. Packed his bag. Turned off the light. Closed the door behind him.

My second husband was a bit of a shit, but he was the father of my children, so I stayed with him, followed him all over the world, tagging along, me and the kids—make way for ducklings. It was all about his job, his project, his career, his bonus, his next gig. Him telling me to put my eggs in his basket and me saying I wanted my own damn basket, thank you very much.

"We're a team, Em," he said.

Only one of us was actually on that team; the other was sidelined, watching the game from the bleachers. This is a metaphor, but it could so easily wind up being a literal description of a person's life. When we lived in Paris, he signed up for a twenty-four-hour rollerblading relay somewhere in the middle of France that took place on my birthday.

"You can come," he suggested.

"Lemme get this straight. For my birthday, you want me to tag along on your boy-bonding, blade-running weekend?" It was a rhetorical question, but he answered it anyway; he was that obtuse.

"All the wives will be there," he said. "It'll be fun; you and the kids can cheer me on."

We were so French by then, politely extending invitations intended to be declined. My birthday is in June, during *les soldes*, the Paris sales, and I wasn't about to miss that for a seat in the bleachers. Instead, I treated myself and a dear friend to lunch at Tour d'Argent, the oldest restaurant in Paris, deliciously musty, ridiculously expensive, known for its extensive wine cellar and breathtaking view of the Seine, and then we went shoe shopping on Rue des Francs-Bourgeois.

Husband number two treated me like his assistant, so I treated him like my own personal ATM, making him pay for all of it: the traveling, the jobs I quit, the promotions I'd never get. Sometimes you get stuck in a dysfunctional relationship out of fear, imagining that it might be worse on your own, but what happens is that you rob yourself of the possibility that it could actually be better. I guess that's what Yogaman meant by "playing it safe."

I'm standing center stage, shielding my eyes from the glare, about to give the "power down your cell phones" speech, wondering, *How come there are lights if we didn't hire anyone to run them?* In the wings, stage left, Andra is holding up her ring finger, mouthing something I can't quite make out, pointing at the control booth. That's when I realize that he's here, that it's Gee shining the light in my eyes. Husband number three (and two and one). The way I look at it, I've been married three times to the same guy. A boy, a jerk, and a life partner.

"You came," I say, covering my heart with both hands. Then I take a breath and step into the moment.

ACKNOWLEDGMENTS

This book owes a huge debt to the support of the Thursdays with Al writers group: Mary Birdsong, Paul Hughes, Terry Maratos, and Courtney Rackley. There would be no book without you guys, it's that simple. Thanks also to those who generously offered to read early drafts: Louise Davis, Claire Doble, Corine Gantz, Marilyn Mandel, Joseph Simas, and Edee Simon-Israel. I continue to be appreciative of my amazing writing teachers, Anya Achtenberg, Laurie Wagner, and Al Watt. Shout-out to my overseas lifeline, Writers.com, an online English-speaking writers' community.

Big love to all the women who are reflected in the composite character Andra: Terrie Fishman Birndorf, Patty Blumberg, Jone Bouman, Louise Davis, Julie Finkel, Cynthia Lapporte, Janet Lombardi-Perwerton, Patti Weston Vandersteel, and Penny Wolf. I am so fortunate to have such great female friends.

I am grateful for the team of experts who helped bring this mess of a book together: Samantha Strom and my publisher Brooke Warner, She Writes Press; copyeditor Annie Tucker; and especially my proofreader Anne Durette, who not only understood my voice, but she cleaned up my French, as well! Thank you also to Pam Cangioli, my developmental editor for her enthusiasm, encouragement and guidance. Special thanks to Leah Lerner, my friend, whose opinion I trust.

Inspiration for the final chapter, "Get Loud," came from Esther Perel's TED talk "Rethinking Infidelity: A Talk for Anyone Who Has Ever Loved."

ABOUT THE AUTHOR

© Daniel Reichert

Marcie Maxfield's voice is fierce, authentic, and personal. Her debut novel, *Em's Awful Good Fortune,* is based on her experiences living overseas as a tagalong wife. Her play *Girls Together Always*—a collection of coming-of-age stories about "growing up girl"—won the ENCORE! Producer's Award at the Hollywood Fringe Festival. Maxfield lives in Los Angeles. She is married with two kids, a French bulldog, and two rescue cats named Hunky and Dory.

Marcie Maxfield is available for readings and book clubs. For more information or to join her mailing list, please visit her website: www.marciemaxfield.com

SELECTED TITLES FROM SHE WRITES PRESS

She Writes Press is an independent publishing company founded to serve women writers everywhere. Visit us at www.shewritespress.com.

A Wife in Bangkok by Iris Mitlin Lav. $16.95, 978-1-63152-707-4
After moving with her husband and children from a small Oklahoma town to 1975 Thailand, Crystal is confronted with a strange culture and a frightening series of events. She finds beauty in Thailand but also struggles to fight loneliness, depression, and, ultimately, betrayal, even as she tries to be the good wife she thinks she ought to be.

The Trumpet Lesson by Dianne Romain. $16.95, 978-1-63152-598-8
Fascinated by a young woman's performance of "The Lost Child" in Guanajuato's central plaza, painfully shy expat Callie Quinn asks the woman for a trumpet lesson—and ends up confronting her longing to know her own lost child, the biracial daughter she gave up for adoption more than thirty years ago.

The Moon Always Rising by Alice C. Early. $16.95, 978-1-63152-683-1
When Eleanor "Els" Gordon's life cracks apart, she exiles herself to a derelict plantation house on the Caribbean island of Nevis—and discovers, with the help of her resident ghost, that only through love and forgiveness can she untangle years-old family secrets and set herself free to love again.

As Long As It's Perfect by Lisa Tognola. $16.95, 978-1-63152-624-4
What happens when you ignore the signs that you're living beyond your means? When married mother of three Janie Margolis's house lust gets the best of her, she is catapulted into a years-long quest for domicile perfection—one that nearly ruins her marriage.

Center Ring by Nicole Waggoner. $17.95, 978-1-63152-034-1
When a startling confession rattles a group of tightly knit women to its core, the friends are left analyzing their own roads not taken and the vastly different choices they've made in life and love.